Restored

Restored

Sheryl Brown-Norman

RESTORED

iUniverse books may be ordered through booksellers or by contacting:

iUniverse
1663 Liberty Drive
Bloomington, IN 47403
www.iuniverse.com
1-800-Authors (1-800-288-4677)

ISBN: 978-1-4917-7081-8 (sc)
ISBN: 978-1-4917-7080-1 (e)

Library of Congress Control Number: 2015910352

Print information available on the last page.

iUniverse rev. date: 03/02/2016

Chapter One

Sometime in the Near Future

A wine bottle ... really! Savannah Hartford looked out from under the bench where she'd just dove for cover and saw her best friend, Cara Williams, laughing. "I thought ... it was a gunshot," Savannah added, now staring at the bartender with a towel draped over his shoulder, pouring wine from the bottle he had just uncorked.

"Figures. It's 'cause you overthink things," Cara said, arching her well-groomed brows. "This trip's gonna be an adventure. Nothin' bad is gonna happen."

Humiliated, Savannah crawled out of the confined space. Admittedly, she was socially awkward, but diving under a bench in a crowded airport was a bit much, even for her. It also didn't help that Cara couldn't stop laughing, which was drawing attention from all the men. Cara was a light-skinned black woman with short, curly hair and a curvaceous body. And although short in stature, she packed a lot of confidence. In comparison, Savannah was tall and slender, with long black hair falling to her waist, complementing her caramel-colored skin. Her hair was naturally curly, but she preferred it straightened. She might have looked like a black supermodel if she possessed even a modicum of confidence. But she was confident about nothing, including this trip.

"C'mon, Savannah, it's gonna be fun. I can feel it."

"All I feel is sick," Savannah grumbled, grabbing her luggage off the baggage carousel. Three months before, she'd been contacted, first by letter and then by phone, about an inheritance of property in Jamaica. The minute she'd heard the news, her distrustful nature kicked in. And

1

when the lawyer offered a free trip to complete the paperwork, she again presumed the worst. Cara had called her a paranoid pessimist, and then she'd invited herself along. Surprisingly, the lawyer agreed and provided two all-paid plane fares to Jamaica, with complimentary lodging.

But speeding over the narrow, winding roads in a Jamaican cab had Savannah's feelings changing. The lush landscape was erasing her feeling of doom and replacing it with a sense of home. Since her grandmother's death six months ago, Savannah had felt so out of place. Yet, somehow, this foreign place was comforting, like one of Grandma Nene's stories.

Grandma Nene had been the best storyteller ever, and her last story had been a doozy. She'd told it in the hospital right before she died. Savannah remembered like it was yesterday.

"You can't take your sweet time comin' when death's approachin'," Grandma Nene had fussed. "There's one more story that you need to hear to pass on to your children. You remember the African princess?"

"Yeah, it's my favorite of all the folklore stories."

"Folklore! It's our history!" Grandma Nene had scolded. "Sometimes things are not what they seem. I'll admit that over the years things have probably been embellished, but the essence of the story is still true. And the African princess's lover set aside something for her children—your family. I don't know what it is, but I know it'll be worth millions and accompanied by a letter." Even though Grandma Nene was on a morphine drip, she still managed to add a bit of mystery to the story. "The letter's important, maybe worth more than the money. Don't be sharin' the part 'bout the money till it happens. The rest—definitely share. The stories keep the family alive."

At the time, Savannah had wanted to laugh. Millions of dollars somehow winding its way through time seemed absurd. And even though the story hadn't been told with Grandma Nene's usual flair, still there was no denying the sincerity in her eyes. Maybe it was time to start believing in folktales. After all, here she was sitting in a cab, racing over narrow Jamaican streets, about to inherit property from a relative that she never knew existed.

The cab stopped in front of a one-story, ranch-style villa surrounded by palm trees and low-lying bushes. The roof was triangular shaped and made from bamboo. And although there were villas on either side, the dense foliage provided an illusion of isolation. On cue, a dark-brown, heavyset woman dressed in a gray uniform and white nursing shoes exited the house.

"Welcome to Velocity Villas. My name's Alice Green. I'll be your maid during your stay," she said to them, speaking perfect English with only a hint of an accent. Then the car door opened, and they were greeted by the most distinguished-looking man, dressed in a white cotton tunic, white pants, and tan sandals. The outfit showcased his ripped body and it popped against his flawless, coffee-colored skin.

"Afternoon, ladies, I'm Marcus Dyson. I'll be your butler."

"A maid and a butler. I think I done died and gone to heaven," Cara whispered. "And our butler is *so* cute. Makes you appreciate the phrase bein' nice to the help."

"Just remember heaven is temporary—a week to be exact," Savannah cautioned. Although there was no denying that the villa, the maid, and the butler had caught her off guard as well.

When they walked in, the villa was completely open, allowing a warm tropical breeze to blow through. Standing in the living room, one could see straight through to the crystal-blue waters of the ocean. The walls and floors of the villa were white—the color coming from the furniture, which had a bright pink, red, green, and orange floral-patterned fabric. In the living room there were three large couches that encircled a large flat-screen TV and entertainment system. Behind the living room was the dining room with a long white table that sat eight.

Bedrooms were on either side of the dining room. The doors were kept closed to keep them cool. Once opened, the rooms resembled those of any high-priced hotel in New York—from the marble countertops in the bathroom to the king-size beds decoratively made up. One wall of the bedrooms was made completely of glass and opened to a tiny Garden of Eden. Palm trees, ferns, and sandalwood bramble outlined the house. The green foliage was complemented by bright, vivid colors from hibiscus, orchids, and calla lilies in full bloom.

"I'm never leavin'. I don't care what you say. I've never seen anythin' this beautiful," Cara said, lounging on the couch after their tour. "And if I'm dreamin', don't wake me." Then, sitting up in a panic, she asked, "What if this isn't real? What if in an hour the alarm goes off and I wake up alone in my dingy bedroom, wondering what to wear to work?"

"It's real," Savannah said reassuringly, even though her feelings of anxiety still rumbled beneath the surface.

"These annoying bugs certainly seem real," Cara admitted, swatting at a bug.

"Don't worry, ma'am, I can fix that," Marcus replied, crossing the room to plug in a Vape Mat heater designed to drive the bugs away. When the doorbell rang, he again sprang into action, answering the door.

"Package for Ms. Hartford," a nondescript deliveryman announced.

"That's me." Savannah jumped up, elated. After signing, she was handed a gorgeous fruit basket wrapped in beautiful multicolored ribbons and plastic. Finding money in her pockets, she tipped the uniformed man. Apparently a decent tip, based upon his smile.

"Ooh, that looks expensive. Who's it from?" Cara asked, coming closer to inspect.

Searching through the enormous ribbons, Savannah finally located a card. "It just says, 'Glad to be doing business with you.' I'm sure it's from that lawyer guy that I'll be meeting with tomorrow," Savannah answered, continuing to remove the packaging.

"Still, it's weird that there's no name. Wasn't that the downfall of Snow White—an anonymous basket of apples?"

"Would you stop?" Now Savannah was wondering whether there was something wrong with the anonymous fruit.

Just then, Alice returned. "Dinner will be in an hour. What would you like?"

"Surprise us," Savannah answered. "Haven't you been saying that this trip should be an adventure?" she asked, seeing Cara's concerned look. "Then why not start with dinner?"

"Touché!" Cara said, smiling.

Chapter Two

"Sir, your eight o'clock is here," Mary announced. Mary was pencil thin and hid her beady eyes behind wire-framed glasses. She'd been around the law firm of Jenkins and Anderson a long time and had no patience for the young upstart lawyer for whom she now worked. But she had known his father, Jack Anderson. He was a good man who died before his time. And that was the only thing that kept her from going to the partners and requesting reassignment. "They're in the green conference room," she said in a louder voice when there was no answer.

After a lingering pause, Brandon Anderson acknowledged her. "Tell Ms. Hartford I'll be with her shortly." Then he waved Mary out with the back of his hand.

"Young squirt," Mary mumbled before slamming the door behind her.

Unfazed, Brandon continued to sit. Mary was paid to put up with his moods, and Savannah Hartford was just a minor business detail. His mind was on another woman—Trinity Hall. Picking up her photograph, he traced her face with his finger. They'd met four years earlier in a coffee shop. He'd been running late for court and forgotten his wallet. Turning, he saw the most angelic face. Without thinking, he'd asked her to pay. Later that day, they talked for hours when she came to the firm on the premise of collecting her eight hundred Jamaican dollars, and they'd been together ever since. They'd had plenty of rocky times but now were at the precipice of marriage.

Although Trinity was a pretty woman, last night she pushed past pretty and went straight to spectacular in a short, flirty coral dress. He remembered enjoying all five feet nine inches of her descending the stairs. Planning to be a gentleman, his hand had been on the car door handle ready to release it, but before he could open it, she'd bolted out of her apartment complex like a gazelle on the run, although she took her time coming down the winding steps. He didn't know if that was to ensure he received the full impact of the outfit or to maneuver the six-inch, muted buff heels (which is the way Trinity always described the color of those shoes). Whatever the reason, she left an impression—her voluptuous shape, her short hair immaculately styled, and her flawless, cashew-colored skin. Without hesitation, she accepted his marriage proposal, and later that night, she revealed more than gratitude. Brandon smiled remembering. Finally all of his plans were falling into place.

When the conference room door opened, in stepped the most incredible-looking black man—tan and tall, perhaps six foot five. Even though he had a slim build, his muscles were quite apparent in his custom-made, blue pinstripe suit. His hair was cut short and he sported a five o'clock shadow. Gorgeous was the word that came to Savannah's mind. "I'm Savannah Hartford," she said, extending her hand.

"Brandon Anderson, counsel for Carapone Industries."

"Nice to finally meet you." After a kick under the table, she added, "And this is my representative, Cara Williams."

"A pleasure, Ms. Williams," Brandon replied, smiling dismissively.

"When does she get her money?" Cara asked, visually sizing up the handsome attorney.

"Soon, Ms. Williams." Then he turned back toward Savannah. "Carapone Industries is interested in buying your property, but first you have to inherit it. To do that, we'll need Mr. Abernathy. He represents Haggerty's estate. One moment," he said, pushing a button. Suddenly, an image of the thin, beady-eyed secretary appeared in midair. "Mary, can you send in Mr. Abernathy?" After releasing the button, the image disappeared. "Once Abernathy gets here, then everything can begin."

"That's fine … and … oh … I almost forgot … the fruit. Thanks," Savannah added, only now remembering the generous basket.

"Fruit?"

"Yeah, the basket that was delivered to the villa yesterday."

"Must've been the Carapones." Fredrick Haggerty, the prior owner, had also received fruit when negotiations started. Now he was dead. The fruit was a strong reminder that Ms. Hartford wasn't just a pretty woman. She was the biggest deal of his career, and if he messed it up, it could be the end of both of them.

"Oh, one more thing. Are you sure that I'm the right person to inherit this property? I'm not aware of any relatives from Jamaica."

"Our researchers are quite thorough. If they say that you're a descendent of Ruby Lee, then you are."

"Ruby Lee? Who's that?" Savannah asked, scrunching her brow.

"The great-great-great-great-great-great-grandmother of Savannah Hartford," Abernathy answered, entering the room. "Carlos Abernathy at your service," he said, extending his hand. "I represent Fredrick Haggerty's estate. Fred was a good friend of mine, which makes me happy to be the one to fulfill his final wishes. I still can't get over the fact that he died of a massive heart attack, given that he was such a health nut. But he elected to fulfill the wishes of a distant relative, Charles Haggerty. He requested that the property go to a descendant of Ruby Lee's. Ms. Hartford, you are apparently the only heir of Ms. Lee," he said, looking at Savannah. "It seems that Fred's misfortune has become your good fortune."

"How is Ruby Lee related to Charles Haggerty?"

"Ruby Lee was Charles Haggerty's slave and mistress. Before he died, he tried to leave property to her descendants. Unfortunately, the laws at that time didn't allow for it. After a succession of wills, Charles has finally managed to leave property to a descendant—you. Each of the last five wills associated with this property has included the same provision—if the bloodline of Haggerty ends, then the property is to be given to a descendant of Ruby Lee's or to charity to be used as a museum for ten years. It's a house located on a beautiful piece of land in Saint Catherine's parish."

"And once I inherit the property, I'm free to sell it?"

"Absolutely. The only requirement is to view the property and own it for twenty-four hours."

"Why?" Savannah asked with an odd look on her face.

"I don't know," Abernathy answered honestly. "My job is to execute the will, not to understand it. Although Haggerty was a friend, he was a very private man. I do, however, have the documents that you'll need to transfer the title, which I can file today. Your twenty-four-hour clock starts once it's filed." Spreading several documents before her, he began explaining each one. "Any questions?"

"No, you've explained everything perfectly. I just need a pen," she said, finally accepting that this was real.

"Then let me." Brandon pulled a silver pen out of his inside coat pocket.

"Thanks, and please ... call me Savannah." She couldn't help but stare at the handsome young attorney. There was something intriguing about him, but there was also something she distrusted.

"All right, Savannah ... you're welcome." He watched her sign the deed. The first step to closing this deal. The final step would be signing the property over to the Carapones. After the papers were signed, Abernathy placed a key ring with four copper keys of varying shapes and sizes on the table.

"Check out your property. I'll get this recorded."

"Thank you," Savannah replied, unable to stop smiling.

"You're very welcome, my dear, and, Anderson, always a pleasure," Abernathy said, extending his hand again.

"Likewise," Brandon replied, shaking again. "And please file the papers ASAP. If you go right now, we can meet tomorrow around ten in the morning. Then I can make Ms. Hartford ... I mean Savannah ... a rich woman."

After Abernathy left, Brandon turned back to Savannah. "I'm guessin' that you can't wait until tomorrow, huh? You must be itchin' to get back to the States to invest your new funds."

"Actually, I'm just anxious to see the property," Savannah confessed, still staring at the keys.

"Why? You should be out celebratin'. Have you guys heard of Orion?"

"No."

"I have," Cara chimed in excitedly. "It's an exclusive restaurant where celebrities usually go. It's almost impossible to get a reservation. Why?"

"Because I can get you in ... if you're interested."

"Interested! Oh yeah!" Cara cooed. "Orion is a playground for the rich and famous. Who wouldn't want to go? How can you get us in?"

"My firm represents the restaurant. Normally, they can accommodate our clients if we don't make reservations during their busy times—8:00

to 10:00 p.m. Why don't I make reservations for say … six thirty? That should give you plenty of time to get ready. Perhaps you'd like to visit a salon and a boutique. The firm would be happy to pick up the tab."

"Are you serious?" Cara asked.

"I am. Should I make the reservations?"

"Wait," Savannah interrupted. "Is there a reason why you're being so generous?"

"No. The firm does this kind of thing all the time for its clients. Somethin' wrong with that?"

"No … I guess not," she replied, still thinking there was something unnerving about him and this whole transaction.

"Do the reservations have to be for two?" Cara chimed in again. "If we get dressed up, we'll need dates. Could it be for four?" Brandon's shocked expression had her immediately backpedaling. "Am I out of line?"

"No, I just thought that this was your first trip to Jamaica," he said, standing up.

"It is, but how long does it take to meet someone?"

"For you, I'm guessin' not too long." He then smiled condescendingly before moving toward the door. "I'll make the reservations for four. Give me a moment." Leaving the room, he stopped to talk to their driver. "Derrick, whatever you do, I need you to keep Ms. Hartford away from that property that she just inherited. I'm plannin' to keep them busy, but just in case that doesn't work, I need you to be my backup. This deal needs to go through. I want no hiccups."

"You got it, boss."

Chapter Three

The women's pampering journey began at the House of Hair, where Savannah got highlights and a trim, and Cara got a weave of long, reddish-brown hair. Then it was off to Petals—a boutique that carried gorgeous evening gowns. By the time they finished, Derrick, their driver, insisted on going straight to the villa, which wasn't surprising since he'd been coming up with lame excuses all day.

Back at the villa, Savannah was intent on regaining control. She'd been to fancy restaurants before but had never owned property. She was going to see her inheritance if it was the last thing she did. Changing into a yellow halter top and a pair of hip-hugger jeans, she barged into Cara's room. "Cara," Savannah said cautiously, "there's something I gotta do."

"Please don't tell me that we can't go to Orion because you need to see some stupid ole house," Cara moaned. "You've been talkin' bout that place since we left the lawyer."

"Because it's my history. And I want to know why Brandon Anderson has gone out of his way to ensure that we don't see it. I just have a feeling that I was meant to see it. You remember Grandma Nene's story about the African princess? There's more to the story. Apparently, something valuable was left for my family, and whatever it is —is now worth millions. This promise of wealth has been passed down through the generations. And before Grandma Nene died, she made me promise to pass it on to my children. Then a month later, I received a letter telling me about this property."

"Seriously, Savannah, you believe your grandmother's folklore is related to your inheritance?"

"It sounds ridiculous, I know. But when you get a house out of the blue, and it comes just like Grandma Nene described … well … it sort of makes you wonder."

"Don't you see what your grandmother was doin'? You were lookin' at her death as yours too. By promisin' to tell this story to your kids, it gives you a reason to go on with life. It's psychology 101."

"Psychology or not, at least now you know why I have to see this house, and Derrick can't or won't take us. You were saying that you hit it off with our butler, Marcus. Do you think you could get him to do it?"

"Puh-lease," Cara said, rolling her eyes. "I can get a man to do anythin' if I choose to." Then seeing Savannah's pleading look, she finally caved. "Fine. I'll call him."

Chapter Four

Driving onto the property, the view was spectacular—on one side peaceful waves, on the other a field of hibiscus, blooming in red, yellow, and pink, along with a peppering of purple orchids and Peruvian lilies. "Where's the little dilapidated house?" Savannah asked, amazed by the dense foliage they were now passing. "I know it's from the 1800s. But it must still be here if they wanted to turn it into a museum."

"It's still here, but it's not a dilapidated, little house. It's a mansion," Marcus corrected. "And it's straight ahead," he said, keeping his tone casual. He was still upset about his trip to Orion being cancelled, especially since he'd spent the last hour getting ready. Although he wasn't surprised when Cara asked him to go, since they'd hit it off that first night. Her interest in him had risen once he told her that the butler gig was just a side job and that he was actually an architect. He knew her type and figured it would take only one date to get her into bed. And going to Orion would have made his job that much easier. But what's done is done. Parking the car, he focused on salvaging the evening.

Once out of the car, all Savannah could do was stare. Mansion was clearly the right description. The house, located on a peninsula, was a massive, four-story, freshly painted, yellow brick and stone house with white shutters. And it was far from dilapidated with a walkout balcony that stretched across the entire second level. Sitting on a hill, the house provided a tremendous view and was bordered by sandalwood bramble. A stone fence surrounded the property, separating it from the white, sandy beach, and a large Jamaican dogwood dominated the yard. Compared to the buildings, hotels, and villas that she'd seen on the rest of the island, the house seemed completely out of place, resembling a castle out of Ireland.

Jacob Spencer watched as they fell under the spell of the seductive house. He'd arrived moments earlier, but no one noticed him. But with architecture like that, who could blame them? "She's a beauty, right?" he whispered, coming up behind Savannah.

Startled, she turned and stared. At six foot four, this man had hazel eyes and pecan-colored skin, which he kept clean-shaven. His curly, black hair suggested that he was a product of multiple races. His six-pack abs immediately drew her eyes, and the muscles in his arms and shoulders were works of art. And all of this was all in plain sight, since he was holding his shirt instead of wearing it.

"Air's out in my truck." He smiled, seeing the disappointment on the women's faces as he put his shirt back on. "Name's Jacob, Jacob Spencer," he said, extending his hand to Savannah. It'd been a while since a woman had him staring, but this one certainly did. She was wearing a yellow halter top that showed just enough skin to ignite the imagination and perfect fitting jeans that had him yearning for his wilder days. "Marcus called me ... to show the house," he explained, when she gave him a confused look.

"Jay, whad gwaan, mon," Marcus jumped in, revealing more of his Jamaican accent. "Thanks for comin'."

"I should be thankin' you, man," Jacob said, slapping him on the back. "Where's the new owner?" Instantly, his gaze returned to the beautiful woman in front of him. "Are you scoutin' the place out for your boss?" Marcus had called and invited Jacob to give a tour to the new owner. Loving the house as he did, he'd agreed.

"Careful, bro. You're lookin' at the new owner, Savannah Hartford."

"You're kiddin', right?" Jacob asked, looking directly into light brown eyes that peered out from a face that had a light dusting of blush.

"Sorry to disappoint you, but I am the owner," Savannah curtly replied.

"My bad. I just assumed the property was being willed to family." Normally, women flirted openly, but not her, and that had him wondering who she was. "You're not related to Haggerty, are you?" he asked, thinking back on the ultra-thin, very pale, deeply weathered-worn man.

"I came to see the house, not to share my life story," Savannah snapped. "Can we go inside?"

"You got a problem?" he said, veiling his temper. Normally, he wasn't so direct, but there was something about this woman that irked him—or was it intrigue? It was hard to tell.

"Jay, go easy on her, man," Marcus jumped in. "She's been dealin' with Brandon. She's entitled to be a little grumpy."

"Brandon! Well, why didn't you say so? Then it's all good," Jacob said, reigning in his anger. Having had his share of troubles with Brandon, he understood. "But why Brandon? He's not Haggerty's attorney."

"Brandon represents the people she's sellin' the place to."

"Sellin'? You're kiddin', right?"

"Is all this necessary to show the house? Maybe I should find a less nosey tour guide."

"Maybe you should!" Turning, Jacob headed back toward his truck, his pace matching his fury. He'd rearranged his schedule to help this woman, and this was how she thanked him. It was enough to settle the matter for him. He was definitely going to say "No thanks" to her. Why was he tripping with this woman when he had salt fish, provision, and a chilled malt waiting for him at home?

"Wait," she called out. Although Jacob stopped, he didn't turn around. "I'm trying to apologize. The least you can do is look at me."

Everything in him wanted to keep walking, but after all, he was a gentleman and supposedly a man of God. But even that wasn't enough to diffuse his anger. Yet, he did stop and he did turn around, although his temper remained. "You're apologizin'? Cuz you don't sound all that sorry."

"I didn't mean it the way it came out. I really would like to see the house. That is, if you're still willing to show it to me."

Jacob was still having difficulty sizing her up, but he complied. "You got the keys?"

While Savannah dug for the keys, Cara pulled Jacob aside. "I'm Cara, Savannah's best friend. You'll have to forgive her dismissive attitude. It's this house. It has her on edge."

"Nice meeting you, Cara, but it's hard to be sold on a woman who needs to be constantly explained." His impression of Cara was that she was loyal. She was wearing a bikini top with tiny shorts—which was impressive, just not impressing him. He preferred a woman who was more reserved—a woman that required him to use his imagination and hunting skills—a woman like Savannah Hartford. Why was he always attracted to the difficult ones?

"Play hard to get," Cara said, smiling. "But I can see that you're blown away by her. In fact, every guy in Jamaica seems to be fallin' for her, and it's irritatin' me to no end."

"Now you, I definitely like," he said, loving her spunk. "But the jury's still out on Miss Savannah." Again, he looked over at the irritable, young woman. She was definitely intriguing, but he decided to pass.

—⟩⟨⟨⟨—

Entering the house, Savannah was in awe. Just after the foyer were wooden steps, leading up to a stained-glass window with a picture of Jesus and his disciples. The surrounding rooms were large and open—made of solid oak, making the house appear sturdy but dark. Furnished with antiques, it came across as something out of an old movie.

"According to Haggerty, this house has been in his family for six generations," Jacob told her, making conversation. "Some of this furniture dates back to the 1700s."

"Wow! I feel like I've stumbled upon some kind of archaeological design find." Moving to a chair, she ran her hand over the wood. "Which explains why the furniture's so gorgeous, although it needs reupholstering." She was thinking rich, luxurious textiles. "Is there a lot more?"

"Oh yeah!"

It took an hour to complete the tour, for no one wanted to interrupt the love affair that Savannah was having with the house. Her dream was to be a designer, and this house was a designer's dream. Finally, Cara spoke up. "Savannah, you were right. You needed to see this house. It's like you're connected to it."

"Yeah, but tomorrow, it'll belong to someone else."

"Why?" Jacob pushed. "I don't know your story or how you ended up with this property, but I know that Haggerty loved it. It had been in his family for six generations. You get it and hold it for six minutes."

She saw the emotion in his eyes. He cared about this place. But so did she. Even though she'd only just seen it, she was in love. So how dare he treat her like she didn't care. "That's not fair!" she said, chastising him. "I don't have the funds to fix this place up. And I live in the US. Besides, Brandon's clients are fixing it up as a tourist attraction."

"Says who?" Jacob grunted.

She could just imagine that with the kind of money that Brandon's clients must have, they easily could restore the house to its former glory. "They're building a resort."

"Which to Brandon means tearin' this place down and puttin' up some modern piece of junk."

"No," she said, shuddering at the thought. "They can't! Isn't it a historical landmark?"

"No, and demolishin' and rebuildin' will be cheaper. You're the only one who can save it."

Frustrated, she lashed out again. "How? I've got no money. I don't live in Jamaica, and I don't want to live in Jamaica!"

"Why not?"

"Because …" Then she stopped. She had no family, no rewarding job, and no ties. Still, the idea of living outside of the United States terrified her. "Because that's where I belong," she finally stated, unwilling to admit her fears to a total stranger.

"I hate to break up this little argument," Cara intervened, "but I'm starvin'. It's too late for Orion, but can't we go somewhere?"

"I bet you can still go to Orion," Marcus piped up. "Six thirty was probably a bogus time to keep you away from this house. My guess is that good ole Brandon, who's courtin' you for your property, could push the reservation back to seven thirty or maybe even eight if he thought you hadn't seen the house and had just lost track of time."

"Do you really think so?" Cara asked eagerly. "Please try," she pleaded, staying close as he stepped outside to get a stronger signal.

Jacob stayed with Savannah. "Look, sorry I pressured you. I get it. It's not worth the risk."

Something about this man always had her on the defensive. Thanks to him, she was now feeling guilty about selling the house, almost like she was abandoning it. Her feelings had her challenging him. "You're saying I'm scared!"

"No," he corrected. "I'm sayin' it's a huge investment, and one day's not enough time to consider somethin' like this."

Once again, she walked around the room. "I can't get over the connection that I feel to this place. I wonder if Ruby Lee would want me to sell."

"Who's Ruby Lee?"

"She's my great-great …" Pausing, she laughed. "I really don't know how many greats it was, but she was a distant grandmother on my father's side. For some unknown reason, Fredrick Haggerty left this property to her descendants. I'm apparently her last living relative."

"No kiddin'. Well, Haggerty was a talkative old man. He shared a lot of stories. I bet you'd love to hear some."

"Really? His attorney said that Haggerty was a private man."

"Well, I got the impression he wasn't keen on attorneys. He'd told me that some lawyers were trying to take his land. Now that Brandon's involved, it's all starting to make sense. Wouldn't hearing the stories be helpful to learn more about the house?"

"Then how 'bout tellin' her at Orion?" Cara barged in smiling. "Marcus did it! He convinced our driver that we lost track of time lookin' at art, which wasn't a complete lie because no one would argue that this house isn't art. Then Brandon was somehow able to switch the reservation from six thirty to eight. So Orion is back on!"

"Join us," Savannah said, turning to Jacob. "Then you can tell us about the house."

"Sorry, but no one crashes Orion. It's that exclusive. If you had reservations for three, you better show up with three. I'm not interested in ending up on the evening news."

"But we have reservations for four," Cara stated, smiling. "It just seemed wrong to go to Orion without dates. So I told Brandon to make it for four, anticipatin' that we'd find some. And even though he looked at me like I was a hooker, I stood my ground. Obviously, it was fate. So you have to go."

"I guess I can't argue with fate. And Orion sounds a lot better than what I had at home."

"Good!" Savannah squealed. Then seeing a smile from Jacob, she quickly added, "I mean … it's good that we can continue talking about the house."

"Right, *the house*," Cara said, winking at Savannah.

"Okay, kids, we need a plan," Marcus interjected. "Since I'm dressed, I'll take the ladies back to the villa. Jacob, you get dressed and join us. And everyone should hurry because I'm not askin' Brandon to change the reservation again."

"Works for me," Savannah replied. "I just want to take one more look at—"

"Oh no, you don't," Cara replied. "You've already made us miss one reservation. You're not gonna mess up another one. Let's lock this baby up."

"But—"

"The only butt I want to see is yours gettin' in the car."

Chapter Five

"Welcome to Orion." Their waitress greeted them with a slight Jamaican accent. "My name's Vanessa Green." Vanessa was tall and the color of midnight, and her short haircut emphasized her black, back-plunging, sequined gown.

"You're friends of Brandon Anderson. Would you care to share your names?" Once introductions were completed, she continued. "My job is to ensure that you enjoy the evening. I'll leave you with our menu. If you see nothing of interest, our world-renowned chefs would be happy to customize a dish for you. Our powder rooms are located behind the large golden lion. I'll be back shortly to take your order," she said, using her most professional tone.

"This place is off the chain," Cara exclaimed after Vanessa left. "Whoever designed it has your style, Savannah. That waterfall in the center of the restaurant is just majestic."

"It definitely leaves an impression. But I prefer the ceiling-to-floor, S-shaped fish tank. I think I saw more fish in there than I saw in the ocean. And this view. Wow! Unbelievable! I can see all of Jamaica from here. I'd love to see this place in the daytime."

"Possible but not probable," Marcus replied. "Given their clientele and their prices, they only need to be open for dinner. Occasionally, they will do a Sunday brunch, but you never know when. An announcement comes out on social media, and two hours later, it's booked."

"I've never heard of a restaurant working that way," Savannah admitted. "We're not even restricted to a menu!"

"I know!" Cara squealed. "And the icin' on the cake—it's all free. We gotta order some wine ... no ... wait ... champagne."

"I certainly don't feel bad eatin' like a king off ole Brandon," Marcus replied, leaning back in his chair. "But he'd probably have a cow if he knew I was here."

"You?" Jacob interjected. "Imagine what he'd say if he saw me."

"What happened between you three?" Savannah asked.

"We had a fallin' out," Marcus explained. "We were boys before that—went to college together."

"Really? Where? Jammin' University?" Cara asked in jest.

"Jammin' University—good one. No, UCLA. We're not actually from Jamaica. We're from the other J—Jersey."

"And here I thought we were hangin' with real Jamaicans, although I did notice that you didn't have much of an accent."

"Whad ya talkin' 'bout, mon? Mi as real a Jamaican as dey com," Jacob responded, in an overly exaggerated accent that sounded more Trinidadian than Jamaican.

"Nice try. Then how did y'all end up here?" Cara asked, taking a bite of a roll.

Savannah resisted the rolls, but Jacob eagerly grabbed one before answering. "Brandon. When we graduated, Brandon's father got us jobs. I was a construction site manager. Marcus apprenticed at a top architectural firm."

"Sounds incredible. So what went wrong?" Savannah asked, just as Vanessa returned.

"Are you ready to order?" Vanessa asked, again using her sweetest voice even though her feet were killing her, and the seams of her dress were screaming from the extra ten pounds she'd gained. But being one complaint away from unemployment, she had no choice but to grin and bear it. The only consolation was that Brandon Anderson was always generous with his gratuities. "It's going to get busy. I'd recommend putting your order in as soon as you can. Any questions about our menu?"

"Not for me," Cara jumped in. "I'd like the roasted chicken with apple stuffin', with the buttered asparagus and a side of lobster mashed potatoes with fried dumplin's."

"Absolutely," Vanessa stated, instantly hating the woman but loving her red Marilyn Monroe gown. Despite Ms. Williams's taste in gowns, she seemed classless, uncultured, and completely out of her element. "And you, Ms. Hartford?"

"I'll have the lemon blackened grouper with pomegranate relish … well done … with garlic spinach and corn compote."

"Thank you." Now, Ms. Hartford had class, Vanessa thought. The yellow venetian-styled, one-shoulder dress was not as eye catching, but it suited Ms. Hartford. Vanessa then turned to Mr. Spencer, who was a true looker—perhaps an actor. "Mr. Spencer, what would you like?"

"The lady's got great taste. I'll have what she's having."

"Nice," Vanessa acknowledged. "And last but not least, Mr. Dyson?"

"I'll have the fillet mignon in jerk sauce, rare, with the orange liquor yams and the garlic spinach."

"Bro, that red meat's gonna kill you," Jacob chastised. "I thought you were off that stuff."

"Sorry, Mom. I didn't know I needed to discuss my dietary changes with you."

"You're off red meat?" Savannah asked, turning to Jacob.

"Yep, pork and chicken too. I'm close to my goal of being vegan."

"Vegan!" Cara shrieked. "Shoot, the foods vegans give up are my only reason for livin'!"

"I used to think that way before I saw the difference it made," he stated, rubbing his flat stomach. "But it's more than just feelin' better. My religious beliefs actually drive my health reform."

Impressed, Vanessa added, "We actually have some great vegan dishes, Mr. Spencer." Pulling out a vegan menu, she handed it to him. "Lots of celebrities have turned vegan," she said out loud, but inwardly she was thinking that she'd never met a religious actor. That was new.

"You're right," Jacob said, skimming the menu. "They look good, but tonight I'm sticking with the grouper."

"Would you like any appetizers or wine?"

"Oh yeah," Cara jumped in. "We'd like some champagne, the sesame-crusted calamari, and the curried spinach dip with goat cheese."

Right, Vanessa thought, rolling her eyes. Poor people. Why couldn't they understand that when you're hanging with the rich and famous, you should eat like them? She'd certainly sampled Orion's delicacies, despite the fact that it was against the rules. "Would you like the house champagne? It's the best."

"The best sounds perfect."

"Ms. Harford, Mr. Spencer, Mr. Dyson, can I get you something else?"

"Ms. Williams seems to have ordered for everybody, so I guess not," Savannah answered.

"Not everyone," Jacob said. "I'll have a lemonade. No alcohol—religious reasons again."

"One glass of lemonade coming right up." Mr. Spencer was definitely different from most men, Vanessa thought. "I'll put your orders in right away. If you need anything else, just push the crystal button on your table."

"It's a call button—like on planes?" Cara asked excitedly.

"Yes, Ms. Williams," Vanessa said mockingly. "Your enthusiasm suggests that you should get out more!" After her statement, everyone went silent. "I'll be back shortly with your appetizers and champagne," she said, ignoring the awkward silence. Turning to Jacob, she flirted, "And your lemonade."

"You may want to check your customer service skills," Cara said, calling Vanessa out.

"My skills? I think the issue is that you're just not used to this kind of luxury," Vanessa said without thinking.

"Excuse you! I don't have to take this. I'd like to discuss your customer service skills with your manager!"

Immediately, fear crept onto Vanessa's face. "Is that really necessary?"

Seeing her fear, Cara relented. "Perhaps, we just got off on the wrong foot. I was a waitress once, and I've no desire to get a fellow waitress in trouble. But I'd definitely check the attitude."

"Yes, Ms. Williams," Vanessa said in a more demure tone. "If there's nothing else, then I'll put in your orders."

After Vanessa left, Marcus let out a robust laugh. "That was gracious of you. I thought for sure that Babylon was gonna have to be called up in here."

"We've all been young and dumb." Switching topics, she turned to Jacob. "You don't drink?"

"Nope, gave it up. Back in the day, I drank a lot. Then I joined a church that frowned upon it, so I cut down but still had a drink every so often. But after my wife, Kimberly, was killed by a drunk driver, I've not touched the stuff."

"Your wife!" Cara gasped. "How long were you married? And what happened?"

"We were married for five years. She's been dead for three. I don't know anythin' else, except that it was a silver car that hit her. They never caught the person."

"Are you like a grieving widower now?" Cara asked. That would definitely explain why a man of his caliber was free tonight and didn't have some sexy date waiting for him. Poor Savannah. He'd seemed like a good catch for her. For although Jacob was good looking, it was Marcus who had caught Cara's eye. "So you're done with the dating scene?" she asked, even before he answered the first question.

"I loved my wife, but she's gone now. She obviously fulfilled her purpose. Now, I gotta figure out what mine is. I'm definitely hopin' that includes another try at love." Then looking over at Cara, he revealed a sexy smile. "Besides, I don't think any man is ever truly complete without a woman," he said cleverly. "Didn't God say it's not good for man to be alone?" This time he stared straight at Savannah.

"Good answer," Cara said, smiling, noticing the look he gave Savannah.

When Vanessa returned, the mood changed to a more festive one as she served the champagne, calamari, spinach dip, and Jacob's lemonade. Marcus poured the champagne, but Cara was the first to taste it.

"That's good," she said, licking her lips. "Jacob, you're missin' out. I just don't understand how you can deal with all your restrictions."

"My restrictions, as you call them, have actually freed me."

"How so?" Cara asked, raising her glass of champagne.

"I used to get so drunk that I'd end up waking up next to some woman who I never would've slept with if I'd been sober. Now, that never happens."

"I guess that makes sense," Cara noted, even though she continued guzzling down champagne.

"I'm not the only one who believes this way. Marcus also gave up drinkin'."

"Marcus? So how is it that you're still drinkin' champagne?" Cara asked.

Marcus gave Jacob a dirty look before replying, "I'm not deep into church stuff like Jacob, and tonight seems like a good night to backslide, don't you think?"

"I do. Here's a toast to my little rebel," she said, clinking glasses. Pushing the hors d'oeuvres toward Jacob, she added, "You can at least have some calamari. It's good."

"Don't do sea scavengers—another religious thing."

"And I don't backslide on that one," Marcus concurred. "I hate calamari."

"Then why didn't you say something when I was orderin' it?"

"Cause you wanted it, baby, and this is your night."

"It's not just my night. It's everybody's night. Now, back to Brandon. Y'all were tellin' us what went down between you."

"Jacob stole Brandon's girl," Marcus blurted out.

"Uh, that's not what I remember. I remember Marcus goin' black pride on everybody and embarrassin' Brandon's late father," Jacob countered while buttering more bread.

"Okay, stop it with the teasers," Savannah scolded. "Tell us the story from the beginning."

"Kimberly had been dead for about a month," Jacob began. "And Trinity, Brandon's girl, thought it was time for me to join the datin' scene again. And I guess she'd had a fight with Brandon and was thinking she should be the one to get me back into the dating scene. She was attractive. You know, the kind of woman to bring you to your knees, the icin' on the—"

"We get the point!" Savannah and Cara snapped simultaneously.

"I see," he said, releasing a grin. "But Brandon was my boy, and you don't stab friends in the back. Durin' this same time, Marcus had run into some petty racism on the job. I told him to just blow it off. Instead, he blew me off and confronted the racism head on."

"Dude, we don't need the extra commentary," Marcus complained.

"Because of Marcus, there was backlash on Brandon's father, which naturally spilled over to Brandon. Brandon and Marcus got into it, and Marcus made a point of sayin' that Brandon was always losin' his women to me. Brandon had also been interested in my wife, Kimberly, but had lost that battle too, which I thought he was cool with. But I guess the remark rubbed him the wrong way, and that was the end of the friendship and my job. I've reached out to Brandon, but he's not interested in mendin' any fences."

"Then how come Marcus works as a butler for Brandon?" Savannah pressed.

"Once I left the architectural firm, I went out on my own," Marcus said, picking up the story. "Brandon got into a jam and needed an architect. He came to me. His client was happy. Because of that, Brandon and I basically began a business relationship. He offered me the butler gig, and I took it. Livin' on the property gave me an opportunity to build my business while keepin' my expenses low. When I first took the job, it was a lot busier. But the past year or two, it's slowed down considerably. It's been real nice havin' an empty villa at my disposal."

"Which explains how our butler is also an architect," Savannah laughed. Turning to Jacob, she asked, "But you and Brandon never even built a business relationship again?"

"Nah. In fact, I had to start a company under a different name just to get jobs. I guess the lesson learned is you can mess with a man's father but not his girl."

"Given your religiosity, the break must be killing you, huh?"

"Well, it's more embarrassin' than anythin' else. Since we're fightin' like women over a woman," Jacob joked, hiding the pain that he really felt.

"Whatever." She laughed, hitting him with her napkin. And then, for the first time, their eyes met, and they had a moment, which was quickly interrupted by Cara announcing, "Food's here!" Then they all eagerly watched as the food servers placed their respective plates before them— each one a work of art.

"If I weren't so hungry, I'd just stare at my food," Cara said. "It's beautiful. Who knew chicken could be art. I don't even know how to eat it without messin' it up."

"Just take a picture," Savannah suggested.

"Good idea," Cara agreed, grabbing her phone. "I definitely want to tweet this out."

Once they started eating, all conversation stopped until Savannah admitted, "I don't think that I've ever eaten this much food. Grandma Nene used to always say to leave something on your plate. That way you don't look greedy, but everything was so good. I ate every crumb."

"Who's Grandma Nene?" Jacob asked.

"She's my dad's mom. After my parents died, I ..."

"Your parents died?"

"In a car accident, when I was twelve. Grandma Nene took me in, which was asking a lot of a seventy-eight-year-old woman. She died six months ago at ninety-eight. I didn't know my mom's family because she left home at eighteen and never returned. My dad's family was small—his brother and Grandma Nene. My grandfather died when my father was a boy. My uncle died in the war. When Grandma Nene died several months ago, I was literally all alone."

"Too bad you're not keepin' that house. Imagine the family history you might find in there."

"I wish, but how can I walk away from $250,000?"

"Two hundred and fifty thousand?" Jacob said, spewing out lemonade. "What's that—the first installment?"

"Installment … no … that's the whole amount," Savannah answered, confused.

"Brandon! I swear, he can't be trusted. They offered Haggerty 1.6 million. They're definitely lowballin' you," Jacob said, shaking his head. "Marcus, does your friend still work in real estate? Can you find out how much that property's worth?"

"Sure. What's the address? I'll text her now. She's always workin'. So she'll probably be able to get back to us quickly."

"The dislike for this Brandon fellow just keeps growin'," Cara noted, sucking on a chicken bone.

"For me too," Savannah added. "All day I've had the feeling that he's been playing me. I wish I could keep the house just to spite him."

"Then do it," Jacob said.

"There you go again," Savannah said, sighing. "What in the world would I do with a forty-room house, and it's just me? Besides, I couldn't even afford the taxes on that place."

"Haggerty made some bad investments, and from what I could tell, he didn't have a lot of money either," Jacob stated. "He was plannin' on makin' a comeback by turnin' the house into a bed-and-breakfast. Why couldn't you do that?"

"I've never run a business," Savannah said, panicking. "The whole idea was to get funding to develop my talent of interior design, not to run a bed-and-breakfast."

"I didn't know you were a designer," Jacob said, impressed. "So use your design talent to create the best bed-and-breakfast ever, and then hire people to run the place."

"And exactly where's all this money coming from?"

"Well, lovely lady, it looks like you're rich," Marcus announced, looking up from his phone. "My friend just sent me a text. Your property's worth 4.6 million."

"Whoa, you're like a millionaire four times over!" Cara gasped, finally dropping her chicken bone.

"Which removes your money excuse," Jacob stated.

"Not really. It's property, not liquid money, which makes me the poorest rich person ever. Like I said, I couldn't even afford the taxes on that place—let alone renovations."

"Do what Haggerty was going to do. Obtain a line of credit usin' the property as collateral."

"Savannah, that's brilliant," Cara seconded. "You could make that house look spectacular, just like Orion. Cater to the rich. Make it so exclusive that only celebrities stay there. And I can help. I took some business management courses, and I could have my dream boutique right in your B and B." Holding Savannah's hand, Cara added, "We came here for a week, but it looks like we're bein' handed a whole new life. You know there's nothin' tyin' us to the US."

"Cara, stop!" Savannah said, pulling her hand away. "This is crazy. Starting a business in the US is hard—let alone in a foreign country."

"True," Jacob agreed, "but it's not impossible, and it doesn't have to be done in a day."

"But I promised that I'd sign the papers tomorrow."

"Oh puh-lease!" Cara blurted out. "You were actin' in good faith when you agreed. Brandon wasn't. Why do you feel obligated to meet his timetable?"

"I don't, but c'mon … me … starting a business. I can't!"

"You're not givin' Brandon a decision until tomorrow. So sleep on it," Jacob suggested.

"Guys, is that who I think it is?" Cara asked, spotting Mark O'Leary, an A-list celebrity.

"I think it is." Marcus smiled and waved, and then they all followed suit.

"He's so down to earth. Did you see that! He waved at us," Cara squealed.

"Any normal person's going to return a wave," Jacob stated, unimpressed.

"Yeah, but celebrities aren't normal." Then pausing, Cara's eyes went big. "You know what this means, don't you? It's a sign. Just as you're makin' a life-changin' decision, someone walks by who took a similar gamble and won. He was your sign!"

Jacob smiled. "God does work in mysterious ways."

"Stop it, you guys! I don't believe in fate or God. It's about taking calculated, rational risks. Keeping that house is irrational. So can we drop it? Let me sleep on it, like Jacob suggested."

Just then, a well-dressed man approached. "Excuse me. I'm Michael Spean, the floor manager. It's come to my attention that your dining experience may have been less than stellar. Your interaction with your waitress was overheard and reported to me. On behalf of Orion, please accept my apologies. We will be offering a discount toward your bill for your troubles. And you should know that your waitress has been let go."

"Let go! Was that necessary?" Cara asked, alarmed.

"It was, and it's done. Yours was not the only complaint we received tonight. Please enjoy the rest of your evening," he stated before excusing himself.

"I feel terrible," Cara moaned. "I mean … I feel deliciously full with a nice buzz from the champagne, but still, I feel bad for Vanessa."

"You heard the manager. We weren't her only complaint," Savannah reminded Cara. "Besides, how can you be in the hospitality business when you're not hospitable?"

"Good point!"

They spent the next hour enjoying dessert before tipping their new waitress, who was phenomenally nicer than Vanessa. As they left, they all took one last look at Orion, but when they turned around, Vanessa was standing behind them.

"I hope you're satisfied!" she screamed at them. "You've ruined my life! I'll get you for this. I'd watch my back if I were you!" Then she turned and stomped off.

"Did she just threaten us?" Cara asked.

"She's bluffing. Don't let her ruin a perfectly good night," Marcus said, keeping them on track. "Let's continue this party back at the villa. I still have more plans for the night," he said, smiling down at Cara.

Chapter Six

"No Woman, No Cry" came to mind as Jacob drove back to the villa. It was a song by the old reggae artist Bob Marley. The song basically reminded men that life is a whole lot easier without women. But who wants an easy life? Women made life worth living. And he knew that better than anyone, for it had taken three years to calm his emotions after losing Kimberly, and now, after just a couple of hours with Savannah, they were raging again. He'd give anything to know what she was thinking slumped over in her seat. And who doesn't believe in God? While most people live like there is no God, still most believe. Why was she different?

Pulling up to the villa, Savannah surprisingly asked him in. "What do you offer a man who doesn't drink as a night cap? Hot chocolate?"

"Sounds perfect," he answered. Once inside, Jacob headed back toward the pool. Ordinarily, he would have offered to help. But Savannah seemed the type to do things on her own. And so, he waited—alone—since Marcus and Cara had disappeared into her bedroom.

Sitting there alone, Jacob was reminded of his bad boy days. There wasn't a woman he had dated that hadn't fallen effortlessly in bed with him after just one date. Then he'd gotten religion and respect for women, in that order. Marriage had made him faithful, but then Kimberly died. And then it was back to the struggle, although grief had calmed his sexual desires some. But now, Savannah had unleashed those feelings again. Sitting in one of the pool chairs, he tried not to think about what he truly wanted to be doing with Savannah at this moment.

Fifteen minutes later, Savannah joined him. She'd replaced the gown with shorts and a T-shirt. "I wondered where you'd disappeared to." Handing him a cup, she sat down next to him. "Hopefully you don't think it's weird drinking hot chocolate when it's eighty-five degrees." She laughed.

"Hot chocolate always works," he said, enjoying her laugh. Setting his hot chocolate down to cool, he smiled at the wardrobe change. He'd loved the gown but preferred this look. Having gotten past her armor, he was now seeing her in a different light. Staring, he noticed a scar above her left eye. But it didn't take away from her; instead, it added to her mystery. In fact, everything about her excited him—the eyebrows that came together when she was thinking; the mouth that pouted when she was defensive; and the tongue that lashed out with little provocation. His heart seemed to be requesting him to reconsider and give Miss Savannah another chance.

"I haven't exactly been the greatest date tonight, but …"

"Oh, we were on a date?" Jacob interrupted, remembering her numerous objections to the contrary.

"Don't start," she said, giving him a dirty look. "I'm apologizing about the house."

"No need," he said, rubbing her arm ever so lightly with the tip of his finger. He expected her to move away, but she didn't. "I understand that you're bein' asked to do somethin' that seems completely out of the ordinary, but isn't inheritin' property worth 4.6 million unusual too?"

"Which is why I keep thinking that someone's going to say, 'I'm sorry, you're the wrong Savannah. Give everything back and pay for the stuff that you've used.' Good things just don't happen to me."

"That's surprisin'," he replied, still staring at her. "I thought good things always happened to beautiful people."

"You love this whole complimenting thing, don't you?" Sipping her hot chocolate, she refused to look at him. "You're a gorgeous guy. Do only good things happen to you? No. You told me that when you shared your story about Kimberly."

"You think I'm gorgeous?"

"Is that all you heard?"

"Pretty much." He laughed. Then seeing her irritation, he quickly added, "That rule doesn't apply to men. We were meant to have it hard— our legacy from Adam—although good things have happened to me. What makes life good is your perspective. I've come to find joy in everything, even in the death of my wife. You know the famous saying, 'Count it all joy.'"

"Sure. Socrates said that … right?"

"No," he said, laughing again, realizing that there was absolutely nothing religious about her. "James, from the Bible," he corrected. "'Consider it all joy, my brethren, when you encounter various trials,'" he replied, quoting James 2:1.

"You're serious about your religion, aren't you? But how does your wife's death bring you joy? Are you some kind of homicidal maniac?"

"No." This woman sure knew how to press his buttons. Sipping his hot chocolate, he searched for a civil way to respond. "I just meant her struggles are now over. The next sound that she'll hear will be God sayin', 'Wake up! Time to go home.'" He could feel a lump forming just from talking about Kimberly. "Truth is that I'm a better Christian havin' gone through this experience," he said, forcing himself to continue. "I used to rely very heavily on Kimberly for my relationship with God. Now I've come to rely on God for myself." It was the first time he'd admitted that to anyone, including himself.

Now it was Savannah's turn to laugh. "A grown man talking about God? Really? Religion is a fairy tale for the poor, the young, and the uninformed."

"Only a fool says there is no God," he told her, again holding his temper at bay.

"You're calling me a fool?"

"Not me," he replied with a gentle smile, shrugging his shoulders. And just like that, her hurt feelings calmed him. "Your argument's with King David, not me, since he's the one who wrote Psalm 14:1, which I was quotin'. But hey, if the shoe fits …"

"I'm not a fool," she said crossly. "Unlike you, I'm a realist. You honestly believe that there's some deity out there that allows children to starve, women to get raped, and psychopaths to roam free?"

"I do," he said, nodding his head. "Sin has to run its course. But God's comin' back to get those who believe in Him, and then, they'll live in a world where those kinds of things never happen."

"So, you believe in fairy tales," she said in jest. "What's he going to do? Wave his magic wand? Show up in some superhero suit and save the world? Seriously, you believe that? If we need saving, then we have to do it ourselves. Relying on some unseen deity is as ridiculous as kissing a toad and hoping that it'll turn into a prince."

"You're a real piece of work," he said, shaking his head. "Humor me and look up." When she did it, he said, "Now, tell me what you see."

"Sky, stars, moon," she rattled off. "What am I supposed to see?"

"That's it. Where'd they come from?"

"I don't know." Frustrated, she stood up. "They've always been there," she finally answered, still moving away from him. "It's the whole big bang theory. I don't know the particulars. I'm not really into science."

"That's good, since that's not science. What started the big bang?"

"Don't know. I've never really thought about it."

"Really? 'Cause I think about it all the time," he said, finally rising and going over to her. Standing behind her, he whispered in her ear. "'The heavens declare the glory of God, and the firmament shows his handiwork.'" Feeling the uneasiness in her body, he backed up. "Whenever I look up, I know that the stars and moon just didn't appear. They were put there by someone."

Turning her around to face him, he added, "I can't imagine what it must be like for you. To be alone in everything you do." This time when he rubbed her arm lightly, she moved away. But the more she pulled away, the more he was drawn to her.

"You've made some valid points, but I'm too tired to launch a defense tonight. Perhaps we could continue this discussion some other time."

"You got it," he said, winking at her. "But I also get that you're throwin' me out." Taking the back of her hand, he kissed it. "It's been a pleasure, Ms. Hartford. I haven't been on a date … we are sayin' it's a date, right?" Before she could complain, he continued. "I haven't been on a date like this … ever," he realized. "I'm not sure whether to thank you or hit you." Being this close to her, he could smell her jasmine perfume. Without thinking, he pulled her in closer. Her body stiffened against his.

"I'm sorry, but I'm not that type of girl," she said, trying to pull away.

"What type of girl is that?" he whispered, refusing to let her go.

"I don't have sex … casually, that is. I mean … you're attractive and all, but I'm not Cara."

"I did notice that," he said, slowly releasing her. "And just so you know, I'm not Marcus."

"Please! Men are all the same."

"I disagree," he replied with a smirk as the muscles tightened in his jaw. "But I'll say goodnight. I'll see you tomorrow."

"Tomorrow?" she asked, perplexed.

"Yeah, I want to know what happens between you and Brandon."

"You really shouldn't get your hopes up," she said, still backing away.

"Too late," he said, winking. "Get some rest." He kissed her forehead before opening the door. "I hope that wasn't too inappropriate for a first date."

Closing the door behind him, she leaned against it and smiled.

Chapter Seven

After leaving Brandon's office, Savannah's first thought was to call Cara, but her fingers dialed Jacob's number instead. "I did it!" Savannah exploded when he answered.

"You sold the property?"

"Nope. I said I wouldn't sell for less than two million!" she announced, putting on lipstick. It was weird how just thinking of Jacob made her focus on her appearance.

"Two million—impressive! And what did Brandon say?"

"It's what he didn't say. He didn't say no. Instead, he started talking about new agreements, suggesting he had the power to offer that much all along."

"Knowin' Brandon, I'd say you're right. But look at you, actin' like a shrewd businesswoman. I think you'd make a great B and B owner."

"Don't start," she whined.

"I'm not. I'm just excited for you. How 'bout lunch?"

"Lunch? I'm still full from breakfast," she said, patting her stomach. "And while we're on the subject, I'd like to apologize for this morning." Earlier he had surprised her with breakfast in bed, which would have been romantic if she hadn't been wearing a granny gown with acne medication smeared across her forehead. Humiliated, she had ducked under the covers, and instead of thanking him, she'd hollered at him. After he left, she felt terrible, especially when she spotted a single red rose lying next to her toast. "It was very sweet," she now admitted. "Particularly the rose. I just didn't want to be seen in that ugly state."

"Woman, please, you have no ugly state. Where are you headed?"

"Back to the villa," she answered, still primping.

"Great. I'll pick you up in an hour. That should be sufficient time for your breakfast to digest."

Clicking off her cell phone, she realized that she'd been completely out-maneuvered. And what perturbed her even more was how much she was looking forward to seeing him again.

On the second visit, her property seemed even more alluring. Jacob had suggested picnicking under the dogwood tree for lunch, and Savannah had loved the idea. The food was good, and the conversation came easily. Surprisingly, she even felt comfortable lying beside him, staring out at the ocean. It was so peaceful, and that had her wondering if Charles and Ruby had found it peaceful too.

"Somethin' on your mind?" Jacob asked, noticing her serious expression.

"Charles Haggerty and Ruby Lee. I wondered if they were in love, given that they were owner and slave."

"I'd go with lovers, if a $4.6 million dollar house is any indication." He laughed. Placing a stray hair behind her ear, he watched her squirm.

"If Grandma Nene were here, she'd have created a whole storyline for Charles and Ruby," she said, pulling away from him.

"Really? So tell me one of your grandma's stories."

"Seriously?" she said, looking at him suspiciously. "You want to hear a story?"

"I do," he replied, taking off his shirt to relax.

"Okay." Clearing her throat, she started, "Once upon a time, there was a beautiful African princess. She was the color of fresh-cut wood, with long, thick hair like silken cords. She was magnificent, like a tree—sturdy and larger than life. Everyone adored her."

"Sounds like the storyteller can relate," he said, teasing her.

"You wanna hear this story or not?" When he nodded contritely, she added, "Then stop interrupting. Now, where was I? Oh yeah … her beauty. Unfortunately, her beauty became her obsession and eventually her downfall. She started thinking of herself as being above the men in her village, seeing none of them as potential mates. She became so enamored with herself that she began belittling the village leaders, the customs of her people, and the practices of the village gods. She wanted to explore the world and hated being tied down by tradition. The gods, however, were not pleased, believing she was misusing her beauty. So, one fateful night, they took her beauty away, and for the first time in her life, she was ordinary. And that very night, the slave traders raided her tiny African village. With her beauty no longer as a protection, she was taken from her homeland and placed into the bonds of slavery. No one noticed her in the bottom of the slave ship. No one worshipped her in the new land called America." Savannah stopped to let that sink in.

"In fact," she started again in almost a whisper, "The African princess was treated less than human. She became a field slave working long hours, feeling the lash of the whip and the sting of the sun. One night, she cried out to the gods to return her beauty. The gods acquiesced. In that instant, she was restored to her former glory. And just as her transformation was complete, the slave owner spotted her and fell deeply in love. But love between a slave and a master was forbidden in America. So, he hid his love, which was hard to do, since he continually kept improving her station in life. She moved from field slave to privately held slave with her own room. And when the private room was insufficient, he built her a house—a house that was hidden from the rest of the world—a house where she'd be safe. It worked," Savannah said, once again pausing for effect, "for a while, until the people found out. Then her true love was savagely torn from her arms. Unable to bear losing him and going back to the cruel world of slavery, she cried herself to sleep—the kind of sleep from which you never wake. And according to Grandma Nene, her spirit is now trapped in the walls of a North Carolina plantation house. You can hear her crying over her lost love. And that's the story of the African princess," she said, taking a bow.

"Well done," he said, clapping loudly. "Had me on the edge of my blanket."

"You should've heard Grandma Nene's version. I tell the story, but Grandma Nene, she became the story. She'd take a purple afghan and wrap it all around her." Savannah picked up his shirt to demonstrate. "Then she'd lower her voice to a silky alto tone, and she'd become the African princess." Mimicking her grandmother, Savannah said in a snotty tone, "Little man, you can't be the best this village has to offer.'" Stopping, she laughed at her own impersonation. "And the part where the gods took away the African princess's beauty, Grandma Nene would act that out by flinging herself to the ground, and she'd heave with such emotion, you'd be crying too." That brief memory had Savannah tearing up.

"You really miss your grandmother, don't you? You know you can talk to me. Unfortunately, I know a lot about loss."

"I'm fine," she lied. "But putting my storytelling aside, what did you think of the actual story?"

"It was a great folktale."

"You didn't believe it was true?"

"Uh-uh. First of all, I believe there's only one God, and He's more interested in what your heart looks like than your outside packagin'. I also don't believe in ghosts. You're probably tired of me quotin' the Bible, but Ecclesiastes 9:5 says, 'For the living know that they shall die: but the dead know not anything,' If dead people don't know anythin', how can they haunt houses? Besides, if people died and went to heaven, what would be the point in God returnin' like it says He will in Thessalonians 4:16?"

"For the record, I think its folklore too, although for different reasons. The idea of a slave falling for the very one who took her liberty seems ridiculous." But if the first part of the story was folklore, then so was the part about the money, she realized. "My relatives weren't religious or logical. They believed the story, especially Grandma Nene. Cara thought it was romantic."

"I can see Cara feelin' that way."

"Cara but not me?"

"I didn't say that."

"But it's what you meant. And you didn't really want to hear any of Grandma Nene's stories. You just wanted me to focus on the past so I wouldn't sell this place," she said, unloading on him.

"Okay, hold up. I wanted to hear a story because I saw it was important to you. That's all that's happenin' here. I'm not used to havin' my motives questioned."

"Sorry," she said, now realizing that her attack had been unfair. "But just because I'm selling and going back to the US doesn't stop us from being friends, right?"

"I don't do long distance."

Jacob wasn't making this any easier. "More pressure to make me stay?" she said, irritated with him, although she had no reason to be.

"Just me being honest," he said, keeping his tone steady.

Frustrated by his honesty, she turned once again to stare at the house. "I've only been here twice, but I've fallen in love. The thought of this place being torn down just kills me."

"Then do somethin', owner," he said, nudging her.

"What? Like run a bed-and-breakfast?" she said, sarcastically. The truth was that the idea both frightened and excited her. "Do you really think I could? If only I could have some guarantee," she said, wavering. "Because all I see is turning down the money and then losing the house because I can't even afford the taxes."

"One guarantee you could probably get is findin' out whether you can use the property as collateral for a line of credit."

"By Friday?"

"Still don't know why you're puttin' yourself on Brandon's timetable. But my bankin' guy could probably pull some strings. They do that for the rich."

"But I'm not rich."

"Oh yeah, tell that to the mansion behind you that's sittin' on one of the choicest pieces of land in Jamaica." Just moments ago he'd wanted to strangle her, and now all he could think of was holding her. "Why don't you check with Haggerty's attorney. See what plans he had. It might avoid startin' from scratch."

"I guess ... I'm scared," she finally admitted.

"Welcome to life, love. It's about takin' risks. But I'm tellin' you there's nothin' better than bein' your own boss. At least check out the possibilities."

"Well played, Mr. Spencer," she said, smiling at him approvingly.

"Does that mean I'm a keeper?"

"I don't know about all of that. I've had way better dates," she teased.

"Is that right?" His eyebrows rose at the challenge. "Then I guess we need to spice things up." Standing, he scooped her up in his arms and headed toward the water.

"What're you doing? Jacob!" Struggling to get down, she added, "Jacob, don't do anything stupid. Where are you going?" Without replying, he simply stepped into the ocean. "No! Not the water! My hair!" Seeing the hours in the salon about to be erased, she cried out, "You can't throw a black woman in the—" But the rest of the sentence was lost as she plunged headfirst into the ocean. When she finally found her footing and stood up, she found him lying in the water laughing hysterically. "Oh, it's on!"

"Why, Ms. Hartford, who knew you were such a wild woman," he said, easily dodging her wild swings.

"I can't believe you did that! Look at my hair—it's ruined!

"Actually, it's beautiful. Now, you look like that African princess you just told me about. Believe me—water can't wash away your appeal. And since I'm already in the dog house, I might as well go all the way." Being perfectly positioned, he kissed her.

At first, Savannah resisted, but then she thought, *Why?* It was perfect timing. And so, she returned his kiss before dunking him in the water.

Chapter Eight

"What did the bank say?" Jacob asked as Marcus and Cara stood by.

"Bank's offering a $1.5 million dollar line of credit," Savannah announced. "If additional funds are needed, they'll extend, if I provide additional plans." Earlier that morning, she had playfully challenged God to prove He existed by working things out at the bank. Was it possible that her prayer had just been answered?

"What're you thinkin'?" Jacob asked.

"That I should stay and make the best bed-and-breakfast ever!"

"Yea!" Cara shouted, jumping up excitedly. "I'll get some wine to toast."

"What changed your mind?" Jacob asked, visibly pleased by the news.

"Just seemed like the right thing to do." For now, she thought it best not to get his evangelistic hopes up by suggesting that God had answered her prayer, and now, she was staying to find out if He was real.

Within seconds, Cara returned carrying wine and glasses. Jacob politely refused. "Don't worry, religious man. You can toast with soda. I just ran out of hands." After handing out the glasses, she began pouring the wine.

"I'm with Jacob," Savannah admitted, covering her glass. "I've never been much of a drinker, and the idea of staying in control makes a lot of sense. Especially now that I'm going to be a business owner." Looking at Jacob, she added, "Don't get too excited. I'm not giving up alcohol for you or for religious reasons. It just makes sense to me."

"Right," Jacob said, smiling, even though he wasn't buying her explanation.

"You guys are sickenin'," Cara interjected. "Just means more for me and Marcus."

"You plannin' on gettin' drunk again?" Marcus asked. "You know, you're a lot of fun when you're tipsy," he taunted her, attempting to pour more wine into her glass.

"Whoa, sinner man," Cara said, now covering her glass. "It's still mornin', and this is a celebration, not a chance for you to score. You lucked out the other night with me bein' drunk, but you better watch yourself. You're gettin' the wrong impression of me," she snapped before heading back to the kitchen.

"Just teasin' you, babe," Marcus called after her. "I'm thrilled with you being sober."

"Well, Brandon certainly won't be thrilled," Savannah added.

"Brandon isn't gonna take this lyin' down," Jacob admitted. "But I'd love to see him bully you while I'm around."

"You're planning on being my knight in shining armor?"

"My armor's not all that shiny, but I accept the job," he replied, winking at her.

"Ain't y'all sweet," Marcus said, mocking them. "Well I hope the armor's ready, 'cause you're 'bout to be on, bro," he said, pointing through the open door at an approaching car.

"Brandon. He must be here for the papers," Savannah said nervously.

"I'd better go," Jacob stated.

"Go?" Grabbing his arm, she stopped him. "What happened to my knight?"

"I'm still here, but Brandon hates my guts. If he sees me, it will only make things worse. Don't worry. I'll come out if needed. Trust me," he whispered before ducking in the bedroom.

"Ladies," Brandon stated, strolling in without an invitation. "Have you had fun? Are you packed and ready to go?"

"Yes, it's been a great week," Savannah answered, thinking of the house and Jacob. "And we're not packed yet, but we will be."

"I'm about to make it a better week," he smiled, waving the white envelope in his hand like a flag. "I've got your check. Shall we do a little tradin'?"

Picking up the wine, he grinned. "Looks like you've already been celebratin'."

"Would you like some?" Savannah asked.

40

"Wine's not my thing." Growing up with a Bible-quoting-and-toting mama, he'd been given lots of reasons for not pursuing life's vices. He'd had twelve years of Christian schools and camps, a lifetime of sermons, and endless prayers of his mother and her continually quoting Proverbs 22:6, "Train up a child in the way he should go and when he is old he will not depart from it." Unfortunately, he'd been the exception. Because once he grew up, he'd departed rather quickly. Sobriety was the only part of the training that had stuck. "I'll have some soda. I'll just grab a glass from Alice."

"Alice ran to the store," Marcus lied, coming out of the kitchen with a glass. Alice's child had been sick. So they'd all agreed to cook and clean for themselves for the day. That way, Alice wouldn't have to ask for a replacement and could still get paid. After handing Brandon the glass, Marcus again retreated to the kitchen.

"Yeah, I was just dyin' to have some fried chicken, and you know Alice, always tryin' to please," Cara said, continuing the lie.

"It's always nice to hear good things about the staff," he said, although he was sensing that something was wrong. "You ready to do business?" he asked, pouring coconut soda.

"Yeah, I've got the papers. And I had my attorney review them," Savannah responded as she went to retrieve them. "They seem fine."

Releasing a sigh of relief, he gulped down the soda. "Then let's do this," he said, still holding his glass.

"Here you go," Savannah said, placing the papers in his free hand. "But you'll find that they're not signed."

"Why? No pen?" he asked, nervously.

"I've decided not to sell."

"What!" he thundered, slamming the glass down on the table and shattering it in his hand. Blood dripped from tiny cuts in his palm.

"Is there a problem?" Marcus asked, coming out of the kitchen again.

"You tell me, Ms. Hartford. Because … I thought … you said the paperwork was fine," he said grimacing, trying to control his temper.

"It is fine," Savannah said, feeling stronger with Marcus being there. "I just couldn't sell knowing that you plan to tear down that architectural masterpiece. If Haggerty wasn't willing to sell, then I don't think I should either."

"You got any idea what kind of people you're dealin' with here? They mean business!"

"Are you threatening me, Mr. Anderson? Because if you are, you should know that I've taken out my own will. Something happens to me, the property goes to charity and can't be sold for ten years. Sound familiar?"

"Ms. Hartford, you're making a big mistake," he said in a nicer tone. "Two million is a lot of money. That house is brick and mortar, nothin' more. If you sold it, it could be your future."

"It is my future, and that's why I can't let you reduce it to rubble."

Brandon's anger was now visible on his face. "Did you ever intend to sell, you lying piece of—"

"Yo, bro, keep it professional," Marcus jumped in. "If you need some space, maybe you should leave and settle down."

"Leave! This is my villa! They should leave! In fact, I want you both out of here in the next hour," he said, changing gears.

"The next hour?" Cara whined. "But our flight isn't until 8:00 p.m."

"Not my problem." Scowling, he looked down at the unsigned papers in his hand. "And call a cab, because my driver, maid, and butler are no longer at your disposal. You picked the wrong person to double cross!" he snapped, throwing the papers down on the table.

"I didn't double cross you. I simply decided not to sell."

"Yeah ... well ... good luck with that, and you can expect my bill shortly!"

"Bill?" Cara asked, confused.

"Your flight, lodgin', House of Hair, Petals, Orion—ring a bell?"

"Those things were complimentary," Savannah reminded him.

"When you were sellin', they were complimentary. Now, you've got one hour to get out with your bill paid, or you can sign those papers. The choice is yours!" Although Brandon left, his effect didn't as they continued to stare at his car fumes as he drove away.

"You guys okay?" Jacob asked, coming out of the bedroom.

"I should've just signed the papers!" Savannah cried, collapsing into his arms.

"No, you shouldn't have. Brandon's a bully. He needs to be put in his place."

"His place!" she said, rising off Jacob's chest. "This is his place! I'm the one with nowhere to go. See! I knew this would happen. This shows that you all should listen to my warnings."

"Actually, it shows that you should stop puttin' negative vibes out there," Cara stated. "If you have the power to make things happen, then you should start sayin' stuff like Cara should win the lottery."

"Not funny! How are we going to pay for all this stuff?"

"You don't how much it costs yet," Jacob pointed out.

Just then a buzzing sound came from the kitchen. "I bet that's your bill comin' over the fax," Marcus said. "I'll check."

"Jacob, I can't do this," Savannah said, now completely panic-stricken. "Whatever possessed me to go up against Brandon?"

"You worry too much. I think the worst is behind you."

"Uh, maybe not," Marcus said, coming back in. "You owe $14,000."

"Fourteen thousand dollars!" Savannah and Cara both gasped.

Grabbing the bill, Savannah stared at it. "I don't have $14,000. Game over."

"You want that house?" Jacob asked her.

"Yeah, but how—" Her sentence was interrupted as he kissed her firmly.

After the kiss, Jacob took charge. "Marcus, call Alice. She'll have to bring the sick kid. Tell her to take a cab. I'll pay for it. Brandon's on the warpath. We don't want her becoming a casualty of war."

"Makes sense. I'm on it," Marcus said, heading off to make the call.

"You two go pack. You can stay at my place until your flight."

"We're leavin'? I thought we were stayin'," Cara said, still confused.

"We have to go home," Savannah explained. "We can't start a new life without closing out the old one. But what about the $14,000, Mr. Fix It?"

"I've got a business credit card that I use for small supplies. It has a $25,000 limit, which I just paid off." Reaching into his wallet, he pulled out the card. "You can use it. It's in my uncle's name, so Brandon still won't know that I'm involved."

"I can't let you do that!"

"Why not? It's an investment. I have a construction company, and you'll need one. Choose me, and I'll include all this in your bill. You can pay me back using your line of credit."

"You've thought of everything, huh?"

"That's what knights in shiny armor do," he said, smiling at her.

Chapter Nine

Six weeks had passed since Savannah's refusal to sell. The Carapones hadn't take the news well. Their first attempt to change her mind had been holding her up in immigration. When that failed, they moved to more sinister plans. Plans that Brandon was now trying to stop. Driving up in his gray jaguar, his mind was spinning as to how to convince Savannah to leave.

"Stay in the car," he said to Trinity, who had ridden over with him. "This is business, not a social call." He hadn't planned to bring her, but she'd shown up, insisting he take her to lunch. When he mentioned this meeting as his excuse, she'd invited herself along.

"Okay, but don't take too long. I'm starvin'," Trinity acquiesced.

Grabbing a bag of mango chips from the glove compartment, he tossed them to her. "This should hold you for fifteen minutes or so. I'll make it faster if I can. It all depends on Ms. Hartford." Leaning over, he kissed her on the forehead. "I'll be back in a few."

Finding the door open, Brandon walked in. Immediately, he spotted Savannah. With all of the activity, she didn't notice him. Thanks to Haggerty's attorney, Brandon had learned that she was creating a bed-and-breakfast. Based on his assessment, things were going well. She'd torn down some of the interior walls, creating more space, possibly to build a lobby, and she'd replaced the wooden floors with a white marble-like tile. The place looked good, and so did she, with her hair pulled back in a ponytail and wearing a light blue, striped, fitted sundress. She seemed more bronze and much more relaxed than the last time he'd seen her. "Is this a good time to talk, Ms. Hartford?"

Looking up, Savannah grimaced. "Mr. Anderson, I don't see that we have anything to discuss."

"Give me five minutes." The Carapones had advised him to lay low so she'd drop her guard. Then they were hoping to hit her with a tragedy that would force her to sell—classic Carapone behavior. "There's got to be some quiet place we can talk."

"You've got two minutes," she said, leading him to a back alcove. Once resituated, she wasted no time. "What do you want?"

"To save your life. You're familiar with the Carapones' reputation, aren't you?"

"No."

"Then let me tell you," he said, agitated. "They'll destroy you. You're not a stupid woman," he said, playing on her sensibilities. "Didn't it seem a little odd that the prior owner who was perfectly healthy suddenly gets a heart attack when he refuses to play ball?"

"You're saying Fredrick Haggerty was murdered?"

"I ain't sayin' nothin', but I had to warn you because I don't think you've a clue about the monsters that you're dealin' with," he said, watching her. He could tell that she was shaken by this news. "You don't have to end up like Haggerty. I can still get you some money out of this. Then you can build a new life in the US or even here. If you're not a threat to the Carapones, they won't bother you. C'mon, Ms. Hartford. Is this property worth your life?" Hopefully, he was getting through to her. He'd wrapped up a lot of deals, but this one was so elusive, and this woman didn't seem to be falling for any of his charms.

"Yes, and your time's up."

Frustrated by her response, he snapped, "Did you hear what I said?" Grabbing her arm, he said in a sterner voice, "You're willin' to risk your life?"

"I already told you yes." Pulling hard, she tried to break free, but Brandon's grip was too strong. When he didn't ease up, she yelled, "I mean it. Let go of me!"

Instead of being angry, he found himself aroused. The scent of jasmine filled his nostrils, and her skin pressed against his felt like butter. Without thinking, just feeling, he kissed her, his mouth hungrily exploring. She struggled, but he barely noticed as he satisfied his need to consume her. She tasted sweet, and the fact that she was forbidden made his passions stronger. Although she scratched and clawed, he didn't stop. The kiss lasted only seconds, but it felt like forever—until the unthinkable happened.

"Brandon!"

The familiar voice of Trinity brought reality rushing back, which was followed by a hard right from Jacob. The blow knocked Brandon to the floor. From the floor, he looked first at Trinity's stunned expression and then over at Jacob's angry one, which had Brandon wondering why Jacob was there.

"You devil," Savannah screamed. "Get out and take your threats with you! Come back again, I'm going to the police!" Still recovering, it took Brandon a while to get off the floor, but that didn't stop Savannah from kicking him. She was about to kick him again when Jacob grabbed her.

"You want him to leave, then let him get up," Jacob advised.

Trinity watched in silence. Clearly, Brandon had fallen for this girl, and apparently, so had Jacob. "We're through!" she finally managed to get out.

"Trinity, I'll explain in the car," Brandon said, making it to his feet.

"You lyin', rude, natty boy!" she said in a heavy Jamaican accent. "You outta order, you know. Mi not goin' nowhere wid you!" Schooled in the states, Trinity had learned to control her accent—giving her the ability to use it when she chose to do so. But there were times when her anger erased that training and her heritage came shining through. "Afta what you did, mi tinkin' you dun gone crazy!"

"Trinity, would you just c'mon?" he said, now noticing the workmen staring.

"Mi not care what you say! Take your rude self on! Mi not goin' nowhere!"

"Fine! Stay if you want." Embarrassed, he limped out the door.

"Must've been hard seein' that," Jacob sympathized. "Want a ride home?"

"Mi dun want nothin' from you," Trinity snapped.

"Why you doggin' me? Your boyfriend's the one you should be mad at—not me."

"He's not mi boyfriend. He's mi fiancé … or at least he was," she said in a softer tone. Holding up her ring finger, she showed off the sparkling rock on her finger. "And mi dun't need your pity!" she screamed but not with much force. "Mi just need a …" but she couldn't finish the sentence.

Feeling dizzy, she collapsed into Jacob's arms. Looking up, she saw his concerned face, and then everything went black.

—⟋⟍⟍⟍—

Heading to the kitchen to get a wet cloth, Savannah was consumed with jealously. Trinity had curves in all the right places with a fair complexion that usually turned a black man's head. When she returned, Trinity was awake and lying on Jacob's chest. "Oh, you're up. Perhaps you could take a little lemonade," Savannah suggested, not really caring if Trinity drank the lemonade, just wanting her off Jacob.

Trinity took a sip. "Thanks. I hadn't eaten," she explained. "Brandon and I were supposed to be goin' to lunch. I'm guessin' not eatin', mixed with all the emotions, must've been too much. The lemonade is helpin' though. If you could just call me a cab, then I'll be out of your hair."

And just like that, Savannah's jealously vanished. "We were about to get lunch. Why don't you join us? I know circumstances haven't really set us up to be friends, but I know how I get when I haven't eaten."

"Well … seeing how I'm too weak to argue … I'm game."

"Why don't I bring something back?" Jacob suggested.

Once Jacob was out the door, Trinity asked, "You and Jacob are an item?"

"No. Jacob's construction company is renovating the house. Because of that, we spend a lot of time together, but he doesn't consider me his girlfriend.

"Baby cakes, you may not see yourselves as an item, but he definitely does."

"And that bothers you?" Savannah asked, sitting down in a nearby chair.

"No. I'm happy for you … and Jacob. Is my pride hurt because a gorgeous man was not interested in me but is interested in you? Yeah. Am I vexed that my fiancé kissed you? Oh yeah. Mi hatin' that bandulu right now, but people are free agents. I should probably thank you for pointin' out Brandon's weaknesses before I married him," she said, easily sliding in and out of accents.

"Brandon's back?" Cara asked, entering the alcove.

"Unfortunately … and this is Trinity," Savannah said, making the introduction.

"I'm Cara," she said, extending her hand. "Now, where've I heard your name?"

"Trinity's Brandon Anderson's fiancée," Savannah explained.

"Ex-fiancée," Trinity said, crossing her arms defiantly.

"I'm sensin' I missed somethin' good," Cara said, dropping her purse and sitting next to Trinity on the couch.

"Not really," Savannah said, downplaying the last few minutes. "Just that Brandon came by and threatened me. When I refused to sell, he kissed me. Jacob punched him. I kicked him. And Trinity refused to go with him. Then Trinity fainted. And now Jacob's gone for take-out."

"You've gotta be kiddin' me! And y'all are cool with this?"

"Yeah," Savannah stated.

"Yep, me too," Trinity threw in.

"Unbelievable."

"Why's it so unbelievable?" Trinity asked, downing the rest of her lemonade like vodka. "Why should we let triflin' men come between us?"

"I like you," Cara said, smiling at Trinity's spunk.

"Thanks, and, Savannah, please tell me why all the men are fallin' for you."

"Yeah, I want to know that too," Cara added.

"That's not what's happening," Savannah replied, putting her feet up on the coffee table. "But when I came here, I didn't have men on the brain. I was worried about this property and whether it was a scam. And of course guys don't really appeal to me."

"Why?" Trinity asked. "Are you gay?"

"No."

"What then?"

Savannah paused, having never told her story to anyone, not even Grandma Nene or Cara. But now, a total stranger was inquiring.

"Oh, honey, what is it? If somethin's got you so messed up that you can't talk, then it's probably dominatin' every part of your life. You're amongst friends here."

Standing up, Savannah walked toward the window. Even though it had been a while since "the incident," which was how she referred to what had happened, her emotions were still fresh. "I can't, it's silly," she finally said, convinced that they wouldn't understand.

"Talkin' helps," Trinity said, not giving up. "You ever considered counselin'?" Reaching into her pocket, she pulled out a card. "I want you to call my doctor. Just this mornin' I ran into her and got some cards."

"You have a shrink?" Savannah asked, skimming the card.

"Yeah, although I haven't actually seen her professionally for eight years. Still, we've remained friends. I went to her because …" Lowering her eyes, Trinity paused. "I can't believe that I still feel weird talking about this." After a couple of seconds, she spat out, "I was … afraid of the dark." Seeing their disappointment, she explained. "It's a real problem, especially when you're not four," she said defensively. "I wouldn't go to movies. I was scared to go out at night. I even missed my prom. Turned out, I'd seen some horror movie, which I'd internalized, and that's what drove my fear. I suffered needlessly for years because I was too ashamed to talk about it."

"I can relate," Cara jumped in. "I've had this unnatural fear of flyin' birds since I saw that really old Hitchcock movie about killer birds in a history class."

"Really, Cara," Savannah said, giggling. "That's your big fear."

"Stop laughin'. I didn't laugh at you guys. The point is that things happen in our lives that may not be that monumental to others but could be life changin' to us.

"I'll think about it," Savannah said, still laughing.

When Jacob returned, he took his food and left the women alone to eat theirs. After they ate, Trinity resumed their conversation. "Earlier, you were about to tell us why you're gettin' all the men."

"Right," Savannah said, remembering the awkward conversation. "Maybe men are attracted to me because I offer a bit of a challenge. When a woman gives in too quickly, I think the man gets bored."

"So, we're sluts, and that's why we can't find a good man," Cara summarized.

"Maybe," Trinity admitted. "I did try too hard with Jacob. It was right after his wife died. And I slept with Brandon on the first date."

"And I slept with Marcus on our first date, but it was only because I was drunk," Cara confessed. "I don't normally do that. I usually wait ninety days, like my grandmother told me. But with the champagne, Marcus was irresistible, like black gold." She smiled, wide-eyed.

"You're with Marcus?" Trinity said, surprised. "You know that Marcus, Brandon, and Jacob used to be friends. They used to belong to the same church."

"Yeah we know, but why is it that Jacob is the only one who acts religious?"

"Don't know. Although it's too bad because I think all three of them are hot, but Jacob's religious convictions make him a little sexier," Trinity noted.

"How does religion make you sexy?" Savannah asked. "I would think it would be the opposite."

"If a man is willin' to go against social norms based on his belief in God, then eventually that kind of conviction will trickle down, making him faithful to you. And a good-lookin' faithful man is just … sexy."

"I guess I can see that." Savannah laughed.

"That's the problem with Brandon." Seeing their faces, Trinity stopped. "Okay, I get it. You see Brandon as some demon, and right now, he's looking like a big ole devil to me too. But you didn't see him when we first started datin'. He looked at me as a partner. After Brandon left the church, he changed. Now, he's all about the money. That's why he's so obsessed with this property. Because he didn't close the deal, he's lost his office, his secretary, and his chance at partnership."

"I had no idea," Savannah said, shaking her head. For the first time, she felt something for Brandon besides hatred. "But I won't give up my property," Savannah said defiantly.

"I'm not askin' you to. In fact, I gave my business contract to Brandon, but did he look at it? No! That's my point. We don't need this deal. We could start our own businesses."

"Really? What business are you in?"

"I'm a chef. Graduated at the top of my class but can't find a job. Crazy, huh?"

"Why don't you come and work with us?" Savannah asked.

"You're offerin' me a job?"

"More of an opportunity—the goal is to have a B and B. I'm designing it, and then I'll run it while doing some design work on the side. Cara's going to run a small boutique. And so, I'm offering you the chance to run a small restaurant."

"Is this for real? Don't you want to taste my food or conduct an interview?"

"Yeah, it's for real, and we don't need all that," Savannah assured Trinity, hoping the offer wasn't a mistake. But for someone reason, she felt it would be fine. That God had somehow orchestrated their meeting. And Jacob would be happy to know that she was finally beginning to believe.

Chapter Ten

Last time Trinity entered this incredible house, she'd lost her man, her balance, and her dignity, but she'd found a job—a job that was officially starting today. "Hey, guys," Trinity said, barging into the kitchen. "I thought I'd seal our new partnership with my famous cinnamon rolls," she announced, placing the rolls in the center of the table.

"Oh, they smell yummy," Cara stated, leaning over to inhale the aroma. Picking one up, she squealed, "They're still warm."

"You didn't have to do that," Savannah said, helping herself to a roll as well. "Wow," she said, licking the dripping icing. "This is good, but you don't have to earn the right to be here."

"Speak for yourself," Cara jumped in. "If your cookin's this good, you can bring all the food you want."

"Thanks," Trinity said, dropping her purse and taking a seat. "I'm always tryin' out new recipes. I used to try them out on Brandon, but since he's history, I guess I'll need new tasters."

"I'm game," Cara piped up.

"Cara!" Savannah said harshly. "Have you no heart?" Turning back to Trinity, Savannah asked, "You think it's over?"

"I don't know," Trinity stated guardedly, reminding herself that this was business not friendship, which meant talking about Brandon should be avoided. But they had asked. "My problem is that I'm engaged to a silver-tongued devil." Grabbing a cinnamon roll herself, she added, "and I have no doubt that he's gonna wiggle his way back into my life. I just wish for once that I could be strong enough to actually kick him to the curb. It might be nice to try some other flavors. Like a nice Asian man or maybe some blond, blue-eyed daredevil."

"I hear ya, my sistah," Cara said before noticing Savannah's disapproving look. "What? You don't believe in interracial dating?"

"Huh … oh yeah … of course, I do. I'm a firm believer that a woman should have all options available to her. The reference just reminded me of my grandmother's story about the blue-eyed devil."

"Yeah, I love that one," Cara joined in. "It's about a gorgeous, honey-colored slave that got into all kinds of trouble. But he had these dazzling blue eyes that hypnotized the slave masters, allowing him to get away with murder. You should've heard Grandma Nene describing that man."

"I just miss her so much." Savannah burst out crying, grabbing a napkin off the table. These days, it took only the smallest of things to trigger a memory, bringing her grief rushing back. "I wish you could've met her," she said, turning toward Trinity. "Grandma Nene would've loved you, and she would've had all kinds of advice about Brandon."

"She sounds nice. Maybe you could tell me some of her stories sometime."

"You're on. Grandma Nene used to always say to share the stories. Remind me to tell you the one about the African princess. They're just folktales, but I still love them."

"Are we interruptin'?" Marcus asked, coming in with Jacob right behind him.

"Nope, you're right on time," Savannah answered, quickly drying her eyes. "Trinity, this is why I wanted you to come by. We're designing the kitchen. I wanted to make sure that I included all of your ideas."

"For real?" Trinity shrieked, although she was still swallowing hard from seeing Marcus. It was starting to seem like old times, and she couldn't believe that they were now asking her opinions on the kitchen. "I actually do have some ideas," she said, not feeling the least bit shy.

"Good," Savannah said, smiling. "We obviously have a limited budget, but I'd get all of your wish list items out on the table."

"Great," Trinity stated, raring to go, but then she paused. "Y'all hear that?"

"Isn't it pipes?" Savannah asked. "I've heard that sound a couple of times in here. I always chalked it up to old pipes."

"I don't think that's the pipes," Jacob said, going in the direction of the sound. "It's comin' from over by the cabinets. There shouldn't be any pipes over here," he said, investigating.

"The first order of business has to be tearing down all of those ugly cabinets. It should be set up like a restaurant kitchen. Right, Trinity?" Savannah asked.

"Absolutely," Trinity said.

"Since the cabinets are comin' down, let's take a look behind them," Jacob stated, grabbing a crow bar from another room. It didn't take long before he'd removed two cabinets and found a small door. "A weird place for a door. I wonder what it leads to." Pulling on the handle, he found it stuck. "Marcus, wanna give me a hand?"

With the two men working together, they eventually opened it. Once opened, a big, black, bat-like bird flew out. With his wings outstretched, the bird looked enormous and made a terrifying noise, making the guys jump and the girls scream.

"At least now we know what the knocking was," Marcus said, still spooked.

"Get him out!" Cara screamed, waving her hands wildly in front of her face. "I'm scared of birds!" Then looking over at Trinity and Savannah, Cara added angrily, "And stop laughin' at me."

Grabbing a broom, Jacob tried to steer the bird outside. But the bird was frightened, so it took several minutes between Jacob, Marcus, and a couple of construction workers before they were able to get the bird to fly outside.

"This place is certainly excitin', isn't it?" Trinity asked once everyone had settled back down. "But where'd that bird come from? It didn't look like it was a hundred years old, and clearly that door hasn't been opened in ages," she said, kneeling down examining it.

"There must be an opening to the outside," Jacob concluded. "I'm gonna take a look," he said, taking out a flashlight that was hanging on his belt.

"By yourself?" Savannah asked, alarmed. "You're not scared?"

Winking at her, he smiled. "That's the beauty of believing in God; you're never alone."

"Whatever," Savannah said, rolling her eyes. "Just be careful. I don't have liability insurance yet."

"Good thing I do!" he replied. "I have insurance and assurance," he joked, as he shined his flashlight through the door. "Definitely looks like it was used at some time. There are steps," he noted before squeezing through the cabinet-sized door. "The steps aren't that great, but they're holding," he hollered back up.

Once down, he shined his flashlight around and watched the rodents scramble. Looking around, he could tell that it was some sort of tunnel.

"Jacob, you okay?" Savannah yelled down.

"Yeah, I'm good. I'm just gonna see what's down here."

"I still think that you should've gone with him," Savannah said, turning back to Marcus. "It's always good to have someone to fall back on in case something goes wrong."

"Jacob can handle himself. Besides, if somethin's down there, then there's no point in both of us gettin' messed up."

"Oh, that's real Christian of you," Trinity teased, surprised at how comfortable she still felt around him. "Back in the day, you would've followed Jacob everywhere. You, Jacob, and Brandon used to be inseparable. Remember?"

"See," Marcus said, shaking his head, "that's the problem with bringin' in people from your past. They're always bringin' up stuff you're tryin to forget."

Although he'd spoken in jest, his words disturbed her. She'd always thought that one day they'd be reunited. "You're tryin' to forget those times when the three of you hung out?"

"Nah. Those were definitely good times." He smiled. "But they're gone now, probably for good—too much water under the bridge now." Seeing the cinnamon rolls, he reached for one and took a bite. "Your doin'. Right, Trinity?" he said, looking up at her. "Now, your cookin'," he said, smiling again, "that I've definitely missed."

"I appreciate you reminiscing, but Jacob may need help," Savannah butted in. "I don't hear him anymore." Moving back to the opening, she called down, "Jacob!" But there was no answer. "You may have to go down there. He should've been back up here by now or at least answering me."

Marcus took the last bite of his roll before walking toward the door. "I really don't wanna go down there. Jacob!"

"Yeah," Jacob answered, walking back into the kitchen.

"How'd you do that?" Cara asked.

"It's a tunnel that leads outside," Jacob explained, sitting back down at the table. "Closin' that up will be the first order of business. That's how that bird got in. There are a bunch of other little critters down there too."

"I knew I didn't want to go down there," Marcus said, sitting back down at the table.

"Oh, Marcus, man up," Cara teased him.

"Right, and this from a woman scared of a little bird."

"It was a huge bird, and it was flyin' in the house!"

"Can you two stay focused?" Savannah interjected. "Getting back to Jacob's suggestion, do we have to close off the tunnel? It's part of the house's history."

"I agree," Trinity stated. "Destroyin' the tunnel would be like losin' part of the house."

"How big is the space?" Marcus asked, pulling out his sketchbook.

"There's a nice size cellar space that could be used for storage before it turns into a tunnel, but you'd need a better way to get down there."

"Let's give the tunnel a makeover," Savannah suggested. "Put in real steps, get some light down there, and close it off so that birds and rodents don't get in. Can we do that?"

"I don't see why not," Marcus confirmed. "We'll probably need to reinforce the tunnel to make sure its sturdy. I'm guessin' that you'd want the space finished off like a real room in a house, huh?"

"Yeah. I also don't want to tell anyone about this tunnel, at least not yet. I definitely don't want the Carapones to know about it. Looking over at Trinity, Savannah asked, "Is it going to be a problem keeping things from Brandon?"

"No. What happens here stays here. You have my word on that."

After the kitchen designs were completed, Savannah continued to work with Marcus on the back gardens. She wanted a place where guests could read and have a shaded spot to eat. A large water fountain and sunbathing areas would be nice too. She was putting most of the money toward the inside of the house because Mother Nature had already outdone herself. Still, Savannah had just a few ideas to assist. After an hour, Marcus left, but she stayed outside dreaming up more designs. Around sundown, Jacob joined her.

"Hungry?" he asked, sitting beside her.

"I am," she said, now hearing her stomach growling. "Sometimes I get so wrapped up in my work that I forget about everything, even eating."

"I've noticed that. But when you work in beauty, it's easy to get lost. I know I have," he said, playing with her hair.

"There you go with your compliments again," she said, noticing him hiding something. "What's in your hand?"

"Your surprise, or should I say the blindfold I'm usin' to take you to your surprise," he said, revealing a scarf. "While you were workin', I was workin' on a little somethin' of my own."

As he guided her, she was amazed at how much she'd come to trust him, at least with the house—although not yet with her heart. Hearing the gurgling water, she immediately guessed her surprise. Instantly, her heart raced in anticipation.

When the blindfold was finally removed, it took her a moment to catch her breath. Before her stood a floor-to-ceiling pebbled water fountain. The inspiration was from the waterfall at Orion. While Orion's was more ostentatious, meant to impress, her's was meant to soothe like a babbling brook, and the yellow and red lights running through it were perfect. He had turned off all other lights. Only the fountain and a couple of well-placed candles illuminated the room. He had also spread out a blanket and had sparkling pomegranate juice chilling with sandwiches and fruit.

"You okay?" he asked when she went silent. "You're awfully quiet."

"Speechless would be the proper term," she stated, staring up at him. But when the moment became too intense, she looked away. "So, where's everyone else?" she inquired, moving away from him. "Why aren't they enjoying this moment?"

"Trinity left, and Cara and Marcus went out for dinner. That just leaves us."

"Just us," she said shakily. "We're all alone," she said nervously.

"You okay with that? Because all I want to do is talk," he said, easing her mind. "Maybe hear more of Grandma Nene's stories."

Instantly, her blood pressure lowered. "Sounds fun, besides, it's time you heard the rest of the African princess story, and you're going to love the one about the blue-eyed devil." Falling down on the blanket, she was completely at ease again. "What kind of sandwiches are these?"

"Tuna," he answered. And just like that, his chameleon woman changed from timid woman to dramatic storyteller. Grandma Nene obviously was the key to unlocking her past, and he tucked that thought away. "You holdin' out on me, huh? You're tellin' me there's a princess sequel."

"You just never know what to expect from me," she said, smiling.

"Yeah, I'm learnin' that."

Chapter Eleven

Flooded with thoughts of vanities, tiles and fixtures, Savannah drove with complete contentment. Today, she was focusing on one of the bathrooms—funny how one of the smallest rooms can be one of the most challenging to decorate. For the bathroom was the one room where everyone found some sort of solace. Mothers could escape children, employees could escape bosses, and lovers could find a moment to regroup. It was a huge responsibility to create a personal space for a person to read, think, and dream.

Grabbing her supplies, she balanced her uncovered glass of orange juice in one hand while closing the car door with her foot. With her arms laden and her mind focused, it was only when she got to the front steps that she gasped, as the items in her arms fell haphazardly to the ground. Panic seized her as she took in the scene. Before her was a life-sized doll with long, black hair. The doll hung from one of the pillars on the back porch in a noose, and "payback" had been spray-painted on the backdoor.

Overwhelmed, she collapsed to the ground. Once again, she was reminded of the doom she felt when she'd first arrived. Who could have done such an awful thing? Brandon! Was he nearby laughing at this devilish prank? But from where she sat, she saw no one, and she didn't have the energy or courage to investigate further. Instead, she just sat and stared at the swinging doll as she remembered Brandon's allegation that the Carapones had killed Fredrick Haggerty. She must have sat for at least an hour before Jacob and his crew arrived.

Jacob's jaw muscles tightened when he saw the doll. "Who did this? Did you call the police?"

"No," she said, feeling silly that it hadn't even occurred to her. Sitting by numbly, she watched as he took out his phone and made the call.

After several minutes of repeating the same information, he informed her that the police were on their way. "You been inside yet?" When she shook her head no, he said, "I'm goin' in. I wanna make sure there's no damage inside." He motioned to one of his men to wait with her while he took another inside. Still numb, she watched Jacob until he disappeared.

Minutes later, Cara came running up. "Jacob called me and told me to come over qui—" Seeing the doll, she couldn't finish her sentence. She finally managed to get out, "Oh my goodness!"

"They didn't get inside," Jacob said, reappearing. "I'll have my men enter through the front so as not to disturb the evidence." Then he set off to give his men instructions.

"What are you gonna do about this?" Cara asked once they were alone again.

"What can I do? I won't give up my property," Savannah said with defiance. "Even though I know they can kill me."

"I'll admit that the Carapones went too far this time. But they're business people. The only death they'll inflict is a financial one. And honestly, you've been dead financially for years."

"The Carapones killed Frederick Haggerty."

"That's crazy! Haggerty died of a heart attack."

"I'm just repeating what Brandon said. He asked me why I wasn't concerned about Haggerty conveniently getting a heart attack right at the time he was refusing to sell his land. Then this happens," she said, pointing to the swinging doll.

"Does he have proof?"

"No, but he's convinced that the Carapones did it. He'll never admit it, though. He told me so." Just then a police car drove up, and the conversation stopped.

It took thirty minutes for the police to collect the evidence, but nothing was found that would help identify the culprit. For now, it was just an anonymous prank, and the police considered the evidence against the Carapones to be pure conjecture, especially once the waitress from Orion was mentioned.

"What am I supposed to do now?" Savannah asked.

"Take some precautions," Lieutenant Black replied. "Never be alone on the property and install a security system."

"Already on that," Jacob replied, having contacted a friend moments before for an estimate. "I hope you don't mind."

"Mind? I'm glad you had the foresight to do that because I clearly haven't been thinking straight."

"And understandably so," Cara said with concern. "I can't believe that's all you're gonna do," she replied, looking at the lieutenant with disgust. "These people have already killed once. Is it your plan to wait around until they kill Savannah?"

"What are you talkin' 'bout?" Jacob demanded before the police could respond.

"Cara's upset because I told her that Brandon believes that the Carapones murdered Haggerty. Brandon thought the timing was suspicious. He apparently feared for my safety, and that's why he's been so insistent on me selling this property."

"Why didn't you say somethin'?" Jacob asked, his brow furrowed with worry.

"Honestly, so much has happened. I really didn't focus on it until today."

"Any proof that the former owner was murdered?" Lieutenant Black asked.

"No," Savannah said, shaking her head sadly.

"Why should that matter? Why can't you get proof?" Cara erupted. "Get the body exhumed. Look for poisons that produce heart attacks."

"This isn't a TV show. I can't start an investigation on a whim. I need evidence to go after more evidence. I know there are officers who won't go after the Carapones, but I'm not one of them. But I'm also not going to go spouting off without some evidence, and neither should you. I'll keep my eyes and ears open, but I need you to keep me informed of anything that you hear," he said in a polished Jamaican accent.

"Maybe, you should sell," Jacob suggested, not even waiting for Savannah. "You were all set to do that until I stepped in."

"I made the decision to stay, not you," she said, reassuring him. "For now, I'm keeping the house," she replied with resolve. "If you need me, I'll be in the bathroom completing my vision!" Then she walked past the swinging doll and into the house.

"She's a tough one," Lieutenant Black stated, admiring her strength.

"She's a good actor," Jacob countered.

Chapter Twelve

After weeks of nonstop work, Savannah finally finished a room—the lobby. Collapsing into one of her newly reupholstered chairs, she relaxed her tired muscles against the rich fabrics, still not believing how nicely everything had come together.

In the center of the ceiling was a lovely chandelier, comprised of hundreds of upside-down champagne glasses with ice cube light bulbs. The glasses hung from cords of varying lengths, creating a spectacular display. Under the chandelier sat a large ottoman, resembling eight high-back, cushioned chairs, joined together in a circular fashion. Each chair had been reupholstered in a different coordinating fabric, accented with gold nail-head trim. Then those same fabrics were used in the eight different sitting areas in the lobby.

At first glance, the red, blue, and gold colors made the lobby look cohesive, but upon closer inspection, each sitting area had its own eclectic look with unique conversation pieces—like the large circle lamps, the rhinoceros coffee table, and the blue antique heart-shaped desk. And the custom-designed, floor-to-ceiling illuminated waterfall was the crowning touch, which, thanks to Jacob, would always remind her of tuna sandwiches, pomegranate juice, and Grandma Nene's stories. For her, the lobby represented history, hard work, and love, but to everyone else, it would be a spectacular lobby that you'd find in any boutique hotel.

Although tired, she was filled with contentment. Snuggling further into the chair, she happened to look over at the reception area, and then she smiled even bigger. On the marble desk were three-dozen red and yellow hibiscuses in a large, triangular crystal vase. They were the perfect finishing detail. Who'd bought them? With renewed energy, she hopped up to investigate.

Spotting the card, she read, "Just wanted to say thanks for the beauty. Lobby looks great. Congrats. Jacob." Laughing, she buried her face in the flowers.

Jacob entered the lobby in his standard fare—white, cotton T-shirt, jeans, and work boots. His eyes instinctively zeroed in on Savannah. Dressed simply in a blue smock top and jean shorts, her legs looked like they went on forever, and her arms were strong and defined. The island had deepened her color, and the red in her cheeks was now natural and not from makeup. The stressful look that she typically wore was gone. She now fit right in with the opulence that she had created. Unlike him and his men, she didn't have that worn-out, haggardly look, even though she should have, given the way she'd worked. Instead, she looked as refreshed as the wealthy tourists who would soon inhabit this place.

"You're smiling. Does that mean that you like the flowers?"

"Like? Try love!" she said, turning to face him. "Now I'm going to have to keep flowers in here forever because I can't imagine coming in and not seeing them. Thank you," she said, running over and kissing him lightly on the lips.

"You're welcome, but where's all this energy comin' from?"

"Don't be fooled by the flower effect," she said, dropping back down into a chair. "Every muscle I own hurts."

"Well, we're almost done, but suggestin' you goin' home would be useless, huh?"

"Pretty much. You know I'm addicted," she said, feeling like a child, refusing to go to bed because she might miss something. "Which reminds me," she said, facing him again. "Did you figure out why you couldn't break through the wall?"

"We found a room that wasn't on the floor plan."

"A secret room?" she asked, sitting up excitedly. "And you wanted me to go home. Why didn't you tell me about this before?"

"I hate to burst your bubble," he said, smiling at her enthusiasm, "but in houses this old, it's common to have rooms that aren't on the blueprints … though they're not usually sealed."

"So, it's unusual to have a sealed secret room?"

"I'm just sayin' I've never seen it before," he said, laughing at her. "Anyway, we're close to breakin' through, and then I'm sendin' the guys home," he said, now yawing. "You wanna get somethin' to eat?"

"Can't." Rubbing her neck, she admitted, "Too tired. Besides, there's a plate in the mini-fridge for you, compliments of Trinity."

"You gotta love the food perks that come with this job," he said, exiting the room. Moments later, he reemerged, carrying a plate and a glass of lemonade. After twenty minutes, one of his guys came in.

"Hey, boss, we've broken through."

"Did you check out the room?" Jacob asked, finishing off his lemonade.

"We thought you might want to do the honors."

"No, let me," Savannah interjected. "After all, it's my first big find. Second if you count the tunnel."

"Well, don't let me stop you—go excavate," Jacob said, laughing again.

Stepping inside the dark room, a rush of adrenaline filled Savannah. Pointing her flashlight at the papered walls, she could see they were faded, yellowed, and missing in patches. Despite the decay, she was able to make out the imprint of rose buds, suggesting that it might've once belonged to a woman, and that raised her hopes of finding jewels. But then, moving the light toward the center of the room, her heart stopped. Instinctively, her hand covered her mouth to stifle the scream she knew was coming. Everything in her was telling her to run, but there was something that held her in place, that had her marveling at the mystery of it all—the wide-brim hat, the long, tattered dress, and the antique shoes—all remnants of a life gone by. She stared until the images became too much, and she screamed and ran out.

Jacob jumped up just in time to catch her. "What happened?" When she failed to answer, he motioned to one of his men to go investigate. But when the worker stepped back out, he looked just as shook up.

"Uh, boss, you better come take a look at this."

Passing Savannah off to a nearby worker, Jacob slowly walked through the door, where he stared at a skeleton dressed in eighteenth-century clothes, lying on a bed. At least now he knew why the room had been sealed. It was a tomb.

Savannah sat on the couch, sipping the tea that Jacob had made, which was warming her but not removing the chill. They were alone now. Jacob had sent his men home, and they now waited for the police to arrive. "Who do you think she was?"

"Don't know," Jacob responded, still visibly shaken by the whole incident.

"Maybe it was Haggerty's wife. He probably killed her and then hid her in that room. And that's why he went to such lengths to keep the property in the family. Ruby Lee was probably a trusted slave, and Haggerty figured that her descendants would be too."

"There you go again." Jacob smiled, seeing her color returning. "Why are you always so pessimistic? What if he loved his wife and couldn't bear to be separated from her even in death?"

"And how does finding a skeleton make you think of a love story?" she asked with sarcasm. "Come to think of it, she might not even be that old. Someone could have dressed her up to throw us off," she said, thinking of the Carapones.

"Nah, I'm guessin' in a sealed room with that much decay, she was pretty old."

"Maybe … but it's still spooky having a skeleton in the house."

"It's not spooky. We talked about this. Remember? The dead are dead. They don't haunt houses."

"Yeah, I remember your biblical explanation, and for me, it works. But most people don't believe that. If the public finds out about this, they might think the place is haunted."

Hunching his shoulders, Jacob thought before adding, "Then tell the police to keep it under wraps. If it's an old case, then what would be the point of advertisin' it?" Just then the doorbell rang. "That's gotta be the police," he said, going to the door.

After forty-five minutes of watching the police, Savannah collapsed on the couch and watched Jacob escort them out. Grateful for his strength, she wondered if she even had enough energy to drive to Brandon's villa, where she and Cara were secretly staying. Marcus had been covering for them because there was no extra money for a hotel. The air-conditioning units and furniture would be arriving soon, and then they could stay on the property. Yet, even with Jacob's explanation, it still felt weird staying in a house where a skeleton had been found.

"I think that's enough excitement for one day," Jacob stated, after closing the door behind the last officer. "Why don't I take you home?" he offered. "Your car should be fine stayin' here overnight. I can give you a lift in the mornin'." When she started to protest, he insisted. "I'm not takin' no for an answer."

"Then I won't say no." She sighed, relieved that he'd offered.

Driving to the villa, both Savannah and Jacob were unusually quiet. For some reason, she found herself staring at him as they drove. Jacob was quite the catch—a gorgeous, sensitive man who actually cared. So why keep pushing him away? But she knew the answer—her inescapable past. Perhaps it was time to stop pushing. And of all nights, this was probably a good one not to be alone.

When they pulled up, the villa was dark, which to Savannah was a good sign. It meant no unwanted interruptions. Jacob had said his good-byes and was merely waiting for her to get out of his truck. Stalling, she tried to think of an excuse to invite him in.

"I still feel a little shaky," she said, turning her head so he wouldn't see she was lying. "I know it's late, but could you stay until we sleep … I mean until I fall asleep," she said, recovering from the slip.

"Sure," he said quickly, and then got out of the car and opened her door.

She felt bad knowing that he was completely unaware of her deceptions as she continued to plot as they walked inside. "I'll get changed," she said, grabbing her nightclothes and disappearing into the adjoining bathroom.

Dropping his keys on the nightstand, Jacob sat on the side of the bed, impressed by Savannah's modesty. He'd certainly known women who would have stripped right in front of him and thought nothing of it, but Savannah was different.

Feeling hot himself, he pulled off his own shirt, folded it, placed it on the nightstand, and lay on the bed. He hoped his need to relax wouldn't give her the wrong impression. It was strange that he had to think about such things with her. Normally, he had to fight the women off, but with Savannah, he hadn't even made it to first base.

But maybe her shyness was a blessing. For she was the first woman since his wife who had tempted him to toss out the no-sex-before-marriage rule. Those long, thin legs, that silky hair, that tiny waist that emphasized her hips, these were the things that drove him wild. In fact, lately, a kiss on the forehead was all he trusted himself to do. His biggest fear was that if the right moment presented itself, he wouldn't be able to resist her, although tonight, he figured she was safe. Finding a skeleton and being tired enough to sleep for a week made staying away from her not only possible but probable. In fact, the only thing that might happen is that he'd fall asleep in her room, and then she'd have to endure a lot of innuendos from Cara. But he could remedy that. Setting his phone to alarm in thirty minutes, he relaxed. Should he fall asleep, it would wake him. He'd leave the room, and Savannah's reputation would remain intact, although he wasn't sure that he'd be headed home.

Studying her reflection in the mirror, Savannah imagined Jacob's reaction. Hopefully, the sheer blue robe would erase the memory of the granny gown, stocking cap, and acne medication that had been smeared across her forehead when he'd surprised her with breakfast in bed several months ago. But what if Jacob didn't like it? What if she'd misread him? What if … then she stopped. This man had done everything but stalk her. He was definitely attracted, and he would definitely be pleased. The only question was: could she put "the incident" behind her?

Stepping out in all of her glory, she prepared to please her man, but instead of wowing him, she found him softly snoring. Not the reception she'd hoped for, but still she appreciated the moment. He looked so handsome sleeping on her bed—like he belonged there—his steady breathing, his relaxed body—all of which seemed to be waiting for her. Then as quickly as she had warmed to him, she froze. She saw the keys on the nightstand. That one item brought the memories flooding back. There had been keys that night too. She could feel her breathing change and her heart quicken. Just as she was about to retreat, she noticed his folded shirt.

That hadn't happened in the incident. A folded shirt now had her standing before Jacob completely vulnerable. He'd been so patient, looking at her with eyes of desire but respecting that she wasn't ready. Very few men would've put up with that, especially without an explanation. There'd been so many times when she'd been tempted to tell him. Explain why her first thought was always to withdraw. But each time, she'd lost her nerve. Perhaps she should lose her nerve tonight too. Leave him sleeping and simply slide in next to him. But then how would she ever get past her insecurities? That thought had her shaking him. "Jacob."

—w—

Startled and disoriented, Jacob opened his eyes. Although he had imagined Savannah without clothes, he'd obviously done her an injustice. Surveying the view, he felt his sexual desires rising. Before he could respond, she upped the ante by taking off the invisible blue layer between them. "You're naked," he said in a shaky voice.

"You're observant," she said, laughing.

But Jacob could tell it was a nervous laugh. His instincts told him something was wrong. That she didn't come to him freely. Yet Jacob ignored his thoughts and his body instinctively responded to the woman in front of him. Feelings safely buried for three years now savagely surfaced. Eagerly he found her mouth. His arms wrapped around soft flesh as he became engulfed in her scent, his hands freely exploring.

But while his body sped ahead, his mind continued to catch up. Flooded by thoughts of God and protecting her, he realized his weakness as an ordinary man. How could he compete against such strong feelings of desire? The story of Joseph flashed through his mind along with 1 Corinthians 6:18, *Flee fornication. Every sin that a man does is without the body, but he that commits fornication sins against his own body.* "I can't do this!" Grabbing his keys and shirt, he headed for the door.

"Jacob!" Savannah called out. "What's wrong?"

Turning around, he saw her beautiful body framed by the doorpost. Although tempted, with the whisper of a prayer, he walked out, leaving her stunned.

"You guys fightin'?" Cara asked, peeping out of her bedroom door. "I'm tryin' to sl—" But then she stopped, seeing a naked Savannah. "Clearly, you need some space. I'll talk to ya later."

Embarrassed, Savannah ducked back inside, slamming her bedroom door. Luckily, it had only been Cara and not Marcus. But now she was kicking herself for being so stupid. She'd forced herself to become vulnerable, but Jacob had made her feel like some cheap prostitute. Drifting off to sleep, her last thoughts were of how she'd get even with Jacob.

Chapter Thirteen

The next morning, Savannah was up early. Dressed modestly in a long-sleeve, white blouse and an ankle-length, denim skirt, she was determined not to lead another man on. Content with her appearance, she grabbed a cab and headed to the property. She wanted a moment alone, without workmen, without Cara, without Trinity, without Marcus, and especially without Jacob.

She came to the property seeking comfort, like a hurt child runs to her mother. And as ridiculous as it sounded, it worked. Walking along the beach, a calmness steadied her, making her realize that it was no longer Jacob who was delaying her going back inside the house. It was the fear of going back to where the skeleton had been found. And who was the skeleton woman? Was it even legit?

Although the police had advised her never to be alone in the house, her curiosity had her opening the house and disengaging the alarm. Before long, she was standing in the doorway of the room that she had run out of the night before. Sunlight lit the room up some but not enough. Grabbing a flashlight, she shined the light around the room, staying close to the door.

It was a decent-sized room. Given its placement, it might be the better place for Cara's boutique. Growing braver, she moved from studying the furniture from the doorway to rubbing her hands along the large, ancient bed. Shining her light under the bed, she found more than just good workmanship. A large framed picture was lodged underneath the bed. Carefully, she slid it out. The frame looked expensive, but the picture was badly faded. Leaning it up against the bed, her interest turned to the chest of drawers. The picture had her hoping to find more treasures—old clothing, jewelry, letters, something. Finally, she was rewarded. In the last drawer, she found three large bound books.

Ledgers, she thought. A ledger could tell her a lot about the day-to-day activities of the house's prior residents. Opening one, she discovered neat penmanship and dates in the corner. To her surprise, it wasn't a ledger but a diary. Skimming the first line, her mouth fell open as she read, *"These are the thoughts and memories of Ruby Lee."* Hadn't Haggerty's attorney said that Ruby Lee was a slave? Then how could she have memoirs? Without thinking, Savannah plopped down onto the ancient bed, even though less than twenty-four hours earlier, the remains of an unidentified woman had lain there. But Savannah wasn't focused on that now.

Just as she began to read, Jacob's men arrived. Panicking, her first thought was to hide everything. She'd finish her work early and then head to the villa to read them privately. After hiding her discoveries, she came out to the lobby, where she found Jacob's men already hard at work. And that had her wondering where Jacob was. Intent on avoiding him, she developed a plan, which failed miserably, since an hour later he cornered her getting rug samples out of her car.

"We need to talk," he said, pinning her against the car, his mind searching for the right words to explain. Why had he been so weak last night? Why didn't he just tell her that he'd made a vow to save sex for marriage? After Kimberly's death, celibacy had seemed so simple, but now, with Savannah, it seemed impossible. Didn't God understand that he was a hot-blooded man who hadn't slept with a woman in three years, and now, being with Savannah these last few months had intensified those needs? "I want to explain about last night," he began.

"Explain what? Your leaving did all the talking," she said in a disinterested fashion.

"No, it didn't," he replied, gently pushing her back up against the car. He couldn't let his temper get the best of him. He needed to remain calm. "That's why I'm here. I want to explain."

"You're probably going to offer some lame excuse. But unless you're gay, you can save it!" she snapped, folding her arms across her chest.

She looked like a young schoolgirl playing with him. It made him smile. Then he remembered how her body had captivated him. "Nah, baby, I'm definitely not gay." He laughed.

"You think this is funny? I don't! It took a lot to be that vulnerable, and then, to be rejected." She stopped when her emotions started to seep through and turned away from him.

"I didn't reject you," he answered softly, now understanding how she must have felt. "But you gotta understand that walkin' away from you was one of the hardest things I've ever done. You were incredibly beautiful. My bad. I should've just told you that I'd made a commitment to God ..."

"Don't tell me this is your religion thing again!" she snapped, turning to face him once more.

"It's not a thing. It's a way of life. Last night, you were shocked, tired, and probably just showin' your appreciation for me bein' there ..."

"Oh, now you're a mind reader?" she said, dropping her hands to her hips. "I wasn't doing it out of appreciation. I did it out of love."

"Love?" he said with a smirk, his irritation showing as well. "You love me, do ya?" he asked. "Then let's go to the courthouse," he said, pulling her off the car.

"All right, fine." She sighed, pushing him away. "I'll admit that I'm not at the I-love-you-enough-to-get-married stage, but I thought we were ready to take things up a notch."

"But why last night?" he asked her, backing away and sticking his hands in his pockets.

"I don't know ... the skeleton, the house, your constant support."

"Exactly, but that's not love." It hurt him that she didn't love him, not like he loved her. "To me, love is you lookin' at me and seein' a future. Right now, I'm not feelin' that from you, not even a little bit. To sleep with you now would have just been sex."

Thinking back to his past, he laughed again. "Of course, there was a time when sex would've been enough, but not anymore. I've learned it's worth the wait. I waited for Kimberly, not because of my commitment but because of hers," he said, recalling their courtship. "I tried everything to get Kimberly to sleep with me, but she never did. And because we waited, our weddin' night was phenomenal. I was no virgin, but I sure felt like one after bein' celibate for a year and a half. Puttin' sex on hold gives you a chance to see if you're right for each other. Your judgment's not clouded by the person being a good lover. That's what I want for us," he said, finally looking at her. "Besides, if I gave in to every beautiful woman, I'd end up with a lot of baby mama drama. Is that the kind of man you're lookin' for?"

"Well, no, but ..."

"There are no buts; either I hold onto the things I value or I don't. And for the record, I didn't reject you. I respected you."

"Respected me!" she exploded. "Who asked you to? I'm not Aretha Franklin. I wanted intimacy not respect."

"But I needed more. That's why I did a Joseph."

"A Joseph?" she asked, giving him a confused look.

"Yeah, you know, Joseph from the Bible. He was sold into slavery and then seduced by his master's wife. To avoid temptation, he ran." When Savannah rolled her eyes, he added, "Oh c'mon, you know the only reason you've been interested in studyin' the Bible at all is because of my commitment. Admit it. You've been wonderin' what makes a grown man voluntarily give up smokin', drinkin', and violatin' women. But if I'd given in to you last night, then I would've been like every other guy. I get that for you last night showed trust, but for us, as a couple, it would've been a mistake." He could tell by the change in her body language that he was getting through.

"I hear you." She sighed. "From day one, you've been living your religion. I just ..." She stopped again.

"You just thought that you had a rockin' body, and once I saw it I'd forget all about God," he said, finishing her sentence. "You were right about one thing. I did want you last night, but then I realized that I was in love with you, and that's why I couldn't make love to you ... especially knowing that you weren't ready." At that moment, he wanted nothing more than to hold her in his arms, but given that she'd already put a good bit of distance between them, he knew that wasn't happening. And that thought had him wondering how this one woman could wreak such havoc on his emotions.

As a boy, he'd been taught to hide his emotions. It was what males did. He never understood why that was the rule; he'd just accepted it. Given that training, he couldn't understand why his body was now flooded with a whirlwind of uncontrollable emotions. Hatred. Love. Aggravation. Compassion. Annoyance. Tenderness. Fear. It was the same feelings that had consumed him at Kimberly's death. But he'd been intimately involved with Kimberly for years. So how was it that this woman, whom he'd just met, was able to unleash such strong emotions in him when he'd practiced for years not to feel at all? And the dominating feeling was fear—the fear of giving himself completely to another human being again—and this time to a woman who wasn't all that stable. He watched her continuing to inch away from him. And that small act shifted his emotions from fear to anger.

"Next time, be careful who you seduce." Ignoring her body language, he walked over and pulled her to him. "Because, Ms. Hartford, like it or not, I'm in love with you," he said in a husky tone, close enough to kiss her. And although he could tell that she wanted him to, he refrained. Bypassing her lips, he whispered in her ear, "Ever ask yourself how you can share your body but not your past?" Although she squirmed uncomfortably, he continued. "A real man waits for his woman to be ready. Last night, I may not have been the man you wanted, but I was definitely the one you needed. Next time," he said, looking directly into her eyes, "before you seduce me, woman up and be honest about what it is you really want."

———※———

No fair, Savannah thought angrily, watching him walk away. Now embarrassed and upset, she headed toward the house. Only the diaries could salvage this day. But for that to happen, she needed to stop obsessing, put everything behind her, and get her work done.

"Still fightin' with Jacob?' Cara asked when Savannah entered the kitchen. "Oh and by the way, congrats on moving your relationship to a more intimate level," Cara said, opening the muffin container for Savannah to get one out. "It's not often that you see a naked Savannah callin' after a man." Cara laughed while pouring herself some juice. Then she motioned to Savannah to see if she wanted some. When she shook her head no, Cara put the juice away.

"I'm even more surprised that Jacob did it," she continued talking, while closing the mini-fridge. "Most religious people save sex for marriage, don't they?" Then sitting back down at the table, she sighed. "I guess a man's a man. Even a religious man can't withstand the powers of a beautiful woman."

"Oh, he withstood just fine," Savannah snapped, peeling the paper off her muffin.

"What do you mean?"

But before Savannah could answer, Trinity entered. "Hey, guys, whad gwaan?"

"Trinity, do you ever go to work? Now don't go and get yourself fired because I'm not ready to put another person on the payroll," Savannah teased.

"Mi goin' to work." Grabbing a muffin, Trinity added, "Mi not officially late till ten o'clock."

"Then come and hear the latest chapter in Savannah's love life," Cara said, luring Trinity in. "Savannah and Jacob did the horizontal mambo last night."

"Cara!" Savannah shrieked.

"Jacob slept with you?" Trinity said with surprise.

"No, and haven't you two heard of a little thing called privacy?"

"Oh c'mon," Trinity stated, "there's no privacy amongst friends." Because now she had completely given up the idea of them just being business partners.

"Well, there should be," Savannah said, unable to face them.

"Oh my goodness. Jacob couldn't perform," Cara began guessing.

"Now, don't be shy," Trinity encouraged. "We tell each other everythin'. I even shared how Brandon wiggled himself back in to my good graces," she admitted. "And Cara and Marcus are livin' poster children for sexual dysfunction."

"Not anymore," Cara announced. "It's the truth," she added, seeing their skeptical looks. "For the last two weeks, I haven't given Marcus anything. Now, I don't know if he's cheated with other women, but that's on him. I've been readin' the Bible, and God does not approve of fornication." Seeing Savannah's face, Cara added, "Don't act all surprised. I've seen you studyin' with Jacob, and I didn't want to be left behind. I was even thinkin' 'bout maybe goin' to church."

"I had no idea," Savannah said, taken aback. "I've recently started going to church myself, so you can go with me and Jacob. You can study with us too … that is, if I ever speak to him again."

"Okay, spill it. What happened?" Trinity pressed. "We're not gonna let this go. You might as well tell us."

"Fine," Savannah said, caving. "Last night, I thought I'd show Jacob my gratitude." She stopped, remembering Jacob's words—gratitude is not love. "And so, when we got to the villa, we …"

"Villa? You guys stay in a villa?" Trinity interrupted. "Isn't that pricey?"

"Well … uh … I mean …"

"Oh my goodness, you're staying at the firm's villa, aren't you?"

"Are you gonna tell on us?" Cara asked concerned.

"Please, you two rate much higher than Brandon. I'm not gonna say a word, so back to your story. He dropped you off at the villa and …"

"And I invited him in, slipped into a sheer robe, and then I came out in all my glory, thinking that he'd be mesmerized, but he wasn't."

"How embarrassin'," slipped out of Cara's mouth. "Jacob must've said somethin'."

"He said, 'I can't,' and then ran out."

"He did a Joseph," Trinity noted.

"What's a Joseph?" Cara asked, looking at the two of them bewildered.

"You know the Bible story of Joseph," Trinity explained. "His master's wife seduced him, but to keep his vows to the Lord, he took off running. Now, whenever a man runs from sexual temptation, it's called 'doing the Joseph.' But I can't believe that's all Jacob did."

"This morning, he talked about wanting to wait for marriage and that even though it took everything in him to leave, it was the right thing to do, blah, blah, blah," Savannah said, annoyed.

"Kudos to Jacob," Cara stated. "Think of it this way. Jacob is a man who had a naked woman for the takin', and yet, he was able to keep his commitment."

"And this is helping me how?"

"Just stay with me and spring forward ten to fifteen years—the good body parts start to go south, and some young, perky thing comes along and tries to flirt with Jacob. He's already proven that he can be trusted. It's like Trinity said before; him being faithful to God inevitably makes him faithful to you."

"But I'm humiliated!" Savannah pressed. "He comes off looking like a saint while I look like a slut!"

"Get over it," Trinity chastised. "We all do dumb stuff, and your plan would've worked on 98 percent of the male population. What it proves is that you have one of the 2 percent guys. Besides, you should look at this as progress. Just a couple of weeks ago, a kiss from Brandon sent you off the deep end, and now, for Jacob, you're Lady Godiva. The counselin' must be workin', huh?"

"Uh-uh, I'm not buyin' it," Cara objected. "I've never seen counselin' change behavior that drastically. How exactly did this happen, Savannah?"

"I don't know. I guess I fell apart when I found the skeleton and Jacob …"

"Skeleton!" Cara and Trinity screamed simultaneously.

"Oh yeah, I guess I forgot to mention that, didn't I?"

"How do you forget a skeleton?" Trinity asked, still in shock.

"It's not that dramatic," Savannah said, no longer feeling the excitement of yesterday. "They were breaking through the wall and found a room that wasn't on the blueprints. It took a while to break through, but when they did, there was a skeleton dressed in eighteenth-century clothing lying on a bed. The police are getting back to us with details from the autopsy."

"This house is crazy! And so are you for not mentioning it before now," Cara added.

"I had other things on my mind," Savannah reminded them.

"Oh c'mon. Bein' naked in front of your boyfriend in no way competes with findin' a dressed skeleton," Trinity commented. "Haggerty literally had skeletons in his closets, huh?" she said, laughing. "Who do you think she was?"

"Ruby Lee," Savannah said without thinking as the diaries flashed through her mind.

"Why would you say that?"

Savannah froze. She definitely wasn't ready to tell anyone about the diaries, not even Trinity and Cara. "It's just a hunch."

"Sounds more like a leap," Cara countered. "But can they tell from a skeleton whether the person was white or black and what the person died from?"

"I got the idea they could," Savannah said, remembering the conversation with the police.

"Okay, you gotta show us this room," Trinity stated, getting up from the table.

"And what about work?" Savannah asked.

"You honestly think that I'm goin' to give up seein' where a skeleton was found for a government accountin' job? I don't think so," Trinity snapped. "Now, let's go. Lead the way."

Walking toward the room, they ran into Jacob, and Savannah found herself blushing while Trinity and Cara seemed to be in hero worship mode.

"Hey, Jacob, keep up the good work," Cara stated, winking at him.

"Proud of you, man," Trinity chimed in.

"You told them, didn't you?" he whispered to Savannah.

"What if I did?" She saw no reason to lie. Why should he care?

"I need Savannah for a sec," he said to the women while pulling Savannah aside. "I'm guessin' you guys were headed to the room we found last night, right? It's straight ahead."

"Take all the time you need," Cara stated.

"Unless this is about the house, we don't need to talk now," Savannah stated, still mad.

"It's about the house all right. Why did you tell them 'in the house' about last night?"

"You know that's not what I meant. And I didn't have a choice. Cara saw me in my birthday suit calling after you. Besides, I was the one humiliated, not you."

"But I can just imagine the punch lines that were had at my expense," he said, sounding wounded.

"Why's it humiliating to you? I thought you were being a real man, the kind of man I needed," she said, needling him.

"I did what was best for us, but I don't want to be takin' jabs for it from your female posse."

Calmed by his hurt face, she kissed him. "Good, now we're even," and then she left to join Trinity and Cara.

"What do you think?" Savannah asked, entering the room.

"It's eerie," Cara commented, looking around. "Do you think it was always a secret room? And did this skeleton woman live secretly in it? Or was it built after she died? Was she murdered?"

"Even with the police looking into it, you'll probably never know," Trinity concluded.

"True, but I do think that this house may have some answers," Savannah stated, again thinking of the diaries.

"I'd better go before I'm really fired," Trinity stated, looking down at her watch. "I'll see you guys later. Stay hungry. I'm making salmon tonight. I'll drop it off at the villa because that's more convenient." Seeing their strained faces, she added, "No worries. Brandon won't know."

Everyone left, except for Cara. She stayed. She was thinking that Marcus would probably need to adjust his designs to accommodate the new space, when he appeared.

"Here you are!" Marcus said, peeking his head in. "I've been lookin' for you. You've been scarce these days." Rubbing his finger along her arm, he produced noticeable goose bumps. "We should go out tonight."

Cara pulled away. "I was thinkin' about you too," she said casually, hiding the fact that he could excite her with a simple touch. "But I can't tonight. I'm workin'."

"Aren't you the boss? Rearrange your schedule."

"As the boss, I am rearrangin' my schedule. I'm goin' swimmin'. So, I'll need to work tonight."

"Should I join you for your little swim?" he asked, flashing his sexiest smile. "Are you up for a little skinny dippin'?"

Taking a cue from Savannah, Cara looked away and changed the subject. "Savannah will probably want you to work on designs for the new space. I was just thinkin' 'bout you redoin' it before you came in. Did they tell you they found a skeleton in here?" she asked causally, while trying to hide the heat that he generated in her body. If she was going to keep her commitment of not having sex, she would have to keep him at arm's length.

"Yeah, Jacob told me. That's some crazy stuff, huh? First time I saw this place, I thought it was kind of a spooky place, and each day seems to prove me right." Pulling her close again, he whispered, "I miss you, so this space will have to wait."

"Is that alcohol on your breath? It's not even noon," she said, pushing him away again. When she first met him, she loved the fact that he drank. But now it annoyed her. Things certainly do change. If she hadn't met Jacob, then she would've never known the sexiness of sobriety.

"It was one drink. Why are you trippin'?"

"I'm not trippin'. It's just too early in the mornin' to be drinkin', but it's not my worry anymore."

"Why? You're breakin' up with me?"

"Are we datin'?" she asked, surprised by his sudden possessiveness. "I thought I was just your most recent distraction—the current flavor of the month."

"The blows just keep flyin'. Where's this comin' from? You're mad that we haven't had a midnight rendezvous lately?"

"I'm done with our midnight rendezvous," she informed him, adopting a serious tone. "Don't you know that fornication is frowned upon in the Bible? And I want to stay a virgin until I'm married."

"You, a virgin?" He laughed. "Uh, I seem to remember things differently. Who are you and what did you do with the real Cara? And since when did you start studyin' the Bible?"

"And what's wrong with me studyin' the Bible? You think I'm too much of a heathen? Well …" she said, remembering her wild days, "maybe I was, but I learned from 2 Corinthians 5:17 that 'if any man be in Christ, then he is a new creature, old things are passed away.' The way I see it, because I've now accepted Christ, I'm new again. Like a virgin, touched for the very first time. Which means that the next time you'll experience all of this will be on our weddin' night," she stated, opening her cover up, revealing her well-toned body showcased in a red bikini.

"Our wedding what?" He laughed. "Girl, you must be smokin' somethin'."

"Okay, maybe you won't be my husband," she said, hurt by his words. "Thanks to Jacob, I know how a real man acts," she threw out. "I'll just wait until I find one."

"So, you want me to be Jacob? Is that what this is about?"

"No, I want you to be you," she said, frustrated that he was missing the point. No longer smitten by his dark side, she explained, "I slept with you because I didn't know any better. But you did," she said angrily, now jealous of the fact that Jacob had loved Savannah enough to wait. "You live your life like God isn't real. Why is that?"

"Since when did I start answerin' to you? You don't want to be with me, cool. There are plenty of women who will. I'm out."

"They won't be interested either if they're lookin' for a real man," Cara screamed after him. Then turning toward the wall, she hid the tears streaming down her face.

"Give him time."

Startled, Cara turned to find Jacob standing in the room. Closing her cover-up, she smiled. "I think you've seen enough female flesh for one week. Anyway, I don't have time for Marcus right now," she added, wiping her eyes. "Maybe I need to just date God."

"I'm just sayin' pray for him."

"I'm the newbie in this religion thing. Shouldn't he be prayin' for me?" she asked, upset that Jacob seemed to be siding with Marcus.

"Apparently, you're the one God's chosen to be the witness, not Marcus."

She smiled at that comment, and for a moment, she wished that Jacob was hers. But Savannah was her best friend, and such betrayal was unthinkable. "I've gotta go."

"You'll think about what I said?"

"I'll do the prayin' part, but I can't promise any more than that."

Chapter Fourteen

Back at the villa, Savannah went straight to her room, jumped on the bed, and opened the first diary. "Okay, Ruby Lee, tell me who you were."

**** August 1829 ****

"Massir, Mr. Royce's 'ere to see you," Bell, the main house slave, announced.

"Thanks, Bell," Charles Haggerty said, acknowledging. "Show him to my study. I'll be right with him." Haggerty was on the short and round side, having just crossed over to fifty. He was a wealthy man due to his many investments. Given his nose for a good deal, people often sought him out because of his moneymaking talents.

"Charles, have him wait," his wife, Ernestine, begged. "Tell him you're having dinner." While her husband ran the businesses, she ran the household. She was also plump but in her early forties. She had unkempt, red hair and a smile that was slightly crooked. She was no beauty. Haggerty had married her as a business transaction—not from love. "You never put the family first," she continued nagging. "Would it hurt you to make a stranger wait a minute or two?"

"Don't start, woman," he said, showing his annoyance. "I'm done with my dinner and so are the children." Getting up, he added, "Besides, Mr. Royce is probably here about some financial scheme, and we both know how you enjoy spending the money that I make."

"Charles, don't be that way," she stated, getting up from the table and following him out. "Your behavior towards me is disgraceful and in front of the children too. I deserve more respect."

"You've stayed in this house for fifteen years. That's about all the respect I can muster."

"And why is that? Because of all of those sinful young women that you have smuggled into this house. I even heard you bedded a slave woman, and that's just shameful and indecent," she said, shaking her head at the horribleness of it.

Erupting from her words, he grabbed her by the neck and pinned her against the hall wall. "Don't push me," he replied sternly. "And stop acting like we're some kind of happy couple," he said in frustration. "If you wish to remain in this house as my wife, then I suggest that you stay out of my affairs!"

Rolling her eyes, she walked off. Looking back over her shoulder, she hollered, "Your day's coming, just know that," and then she stomped back into the dining room.

Hunching his shoulders, he headed to his study. Why did Ernestine irk him so? She had never appealed to him in any romantic sense. She was neither soft nor inviting and was often rude to most people, especially the slaves.

Entering the study, his thoughts instantly switched to Mr. Royce. Royce, who was new to the island, came from Europe and didn't really seem to fit in with the rest of the landowners. Being tall and well built with curly, blond hair and vivid blue eyes, the women had definitely sized him up as marriage material. Although usually, he kept to himself, which had Haggerty puzzling over this visit.

"Mr. Royce, I believe this is the first time I have had the pleasure. Whiskey?" Haggerty asked, picking up the decanter filled with his favorite beverage.

"No, I don't really bother with the stuff," Royce said, shaking his head.

Haggerty raised his brow at the response. He'd learned not to trust any man who didn't drink. "To what do I owe this honor?" he asked, pouring whiskey for himself while looking suspiciously at Royce.

"I'll come right to the point. I seem to have come upon a bit of bad luck." Royce's mouth was dry, but having dismissed the friendly gesture of the whiskey, he dared not ask for water. "The doctors have determined that I have a very limited time left here on this earth."

Surprised by the admission, Haggerty stared at the handsome young man. Looks were definitely deceiving, for Royce looked the picture of health, full of youthful vigor.

"I am sorry, Mr. Royce. I can see how that would disturb a man's peace. If there's anything that I can do during this difficult time, I'd be happy to oblige." Then Haggerty took another gulp of whiskey as he continued to stare.

"That's why I'm here. I've noticed that you tend to treat your slaves more, well ... how do I say it ... more humanely than others."

Royce's words made the hair on the back of Haggerty's neck stand up. He didn't want any trouble based on outsiders thinking that he was soft on his slaves. "Mr. Royce, I don't know where you're going with this, but I rule my slaves with a very strict hand. And I don't like the idea of you coming in here telling me otherwise."

"Forgive me," Royce quickly replied. "I meant no disrespect. I simply noted that while you are strict and definitely in control of your slaves," he emphasized, "you see slaves as investments and treat them accordingly."

"Perhaps you should get to the point," Haggerty advised, finishing his whiskey.

"Yes, of course," Royce said, wiping his forehead with his white handkerchief. "I have a slave, a young slave woman, to be exact," he said, looking directly at Haggerty. "I brought her here from Europe. She was afforded certain privileges that are not given to slaves here."

"Such as?"

"She was taught to read and write, and she knows three different languages," Royce eagerly volunteered.

"That's crazy and inhumane. How will an educated slave make it here?"

"Like I said, we came from a different world," Royce reminded him. "I thought I could protect her. Although given my condition, it's pretty clear that I won't be able to do that." Again, looking directly at Haggerty, Royce added, "I implore you to consider taking on Ruby Lee. That's her name."

"I don't know," Haggerty said, unconvinced that Royce was even speaking the truth.

"Please, sir, she wouldn't survive a day on another plantation. She's helpful. She can add and keep books."

"Mr. Royce, if it became known that I had a slave keeping my books, that would be the end of me."

"She can keep babies too. She probably wouldn't make it as a field slave, but she could definitely be a good house slave. She knows and understands that she must keep the things she knows to herself to stay alive."

"Mr. Royce, I feel terrible about the situation that you are in," Haggerty said apologetically. "But you created this problem, and now you want to lay it in my lap. I'm sorry, but I'm not risking my plantation, my family's safety, and my fortune just so that I can help you hide some freak-of-nature slave."

"Will you at least meet her?"

"I don't see the point, but if it closes the matter for you, then I'll meet her."

"Great, I'll fetch her from the wagon."

As Haggerty waited, he found himself pacing. It wasn't that he didn't feel for Royce, it was just too risky. And based on Royce's assessment, he was already viewed as being too kind. For all he knew, this might be some sort of test or joke. Honestly, what slave could speak several languages?

It didn't take Royce long to return with a small-framed woman dressed simply in a long, plain, gray dress with a matching bonnet. She was standing with her head down, which didn't afford Haggerty the chance to get a good look at her.

"Girl, don't just stand there. Show yourself," Royce ordered like a taskmaster, but the emotion in his voice betrayed him.

Ruby slowly loosened the strings on her bonnet, keeping her gaze low. When she finally removed the bonnet, long curls fell out, and then she held her head up almost in a sense of defiance.

When Haggerty saw Ruby, he was mesmerized. She was the most beautiful woman, black or white, that he'd ever seen—a slender, tall, young woman who was a hazelnut-brown color, with black, curly hair that perfectly framed her face. Now he knew what Royce had been up to. She was so beautiful that there wasn't a man alive who wouldn't do whatever she asked. And there was no doubt that Royce had been banking on that reaction.

"Mr. Haggerty, won't you change your mind?"

"If I said yes, when are you proposing that the sale take place?"

"Today," Royce quickly answered.

"No!" Ruby cried out before being silenced by a look from Royce.

"It must be this way," he said sternly. "It is for your own protection. I need to see that you're settled before I get too bad off. You must be strong," he said, keeping his distance. "You can do this." Then, looking over at Haggerty, he added, "That is, if Mr. Haggerty will give you a chance."

"I've been thinking, perhaps it's my Christian duty to step in, given that this dear creature did not ask to be in this situation," he said, trying to find an affable way to eat his former words.

"Right," Royce said, smiling. "It's your Christian duty." *Sure it is,* Royce thought sarcastically.

"Don't do this!" Ruby cried out. "I don't want to live without you," she sobbed, falling into Royce's arms.

"Now, shush, child. That ain't no way for you to carry on," Haggerty stated, walking over. "Mr. Royce ain't the only one who can protect you. I can do it. You'll be safe here."

"Thank you," Royce responded coolly while pulling Ruby off him.

"Call me Charles," Haggerty said, now feeling friendlier.

"Charles, you've made a dying man's last days happier. Just knowing that Ruby will be taken care of lifts a load off me."

"No problem," Haggerty stated. "I guess you'll be visiting again," he said, realizing how difficult it must be for Royce to walk away.

"No," Royce said, sadly shaking his head. "I think it's best if I said my good-byes now. Ruby doesn't need to see me deteriorate down to nothing," he said, staring at Ruby. Turning to Haggerty, he added, "Charles, will you grant a dying man one last wish and let me say good-bye to Ruby alone?"

"Sure. I'll wait outside."

When the door clicked closed, Royce's tears flowed freely. "Ruby, I …"

"Don't say it," she cried, touching his lips. "Don't say good-bye."

Taking her in his arms, he kissed her. "It was wrong for me to create a yearning for love and life and then take it away. And now I've put you in the awful position of not being able to fit in anywhere. But you know how to stay alive if you choose to. Promise me you'll choose to."

"No!" she said, breaking down again. "I won't act like a slave just to stay longer in a world where I don't belong!"

"Listen, Ruby," he said, pulling her close again. "I believe that God has a plan for you."

"God! What God would allow slavery? Make it a crime to be happy or to have a home and a husband. While day after day I'm forced to watch as other people who don't deserve these things get them!"

"I wish there was another way, but there isn't," he confessed. "This is the world that we've been given, but I think Charles Haggerty will be good for you. I will write and explain my reasons." No longer able to resist her, he took her in his arms and kissed her, savoring every moment, every texture, and every taste. "Oh, Ruby," was all he could say. Then he walked out of the office and out of her life forever.

• •

"Savannah, you in there?" Cara said, banging on the locked door.

Closing the diary, Savannah slid all three books under her bed before opening the door. "What's up?"

"What's up with you? And why are you acting weird? And why did you lock your door?"

"I'm not acting weird, and I didn't realize that I'd locked my door," Savannah lied.

"Fine, don't tell me," Cara said, shrugging her shoulders. "Just wait until I know something. Then I'm not gonna tell you."

"Would you stop? I've already told you there's nothing to tell. I was studying some design books and must've fallen asleep. Why were you banging on my door?"

"I was workin' and got hurt." Cara held up her cut finger like a five-year-old. "I was hopin' you had a Band-Aid."

"The villa has a first aid kit. I'll get it."

Just then, Trinity came bustling in. "Oh, I've got a key to the place," she said, seeing their surprise. "I was just gonna drop off your dinner. But since you're here, do you wanna eat?"

"Goodness yes," Cara answered first. "You mentioned food, and my stomach did a somersault. What are we havin'?"

"Sweet-potato quiche, blackened salmon, spinach salad, and mango cobbler for dessert," Trinity announced.

"You're spoiling us and making us fat," Savannah moaned, watching Trinity take out the casserole dishes from the bag.

"Actually, eating healthy, well-balanced meals is the best way to maintain your weight."

"Uh-uh," Cara objected. "Healthy food tastes like straw."

"Not when you know what you're doing." Proving her point, Trinity placed the salmon platter under their noses, allowing them to smell the spices. "That's the spin I want for the restaurant—good food that's good for you. I want to call it Refresh."

"Love it," Savannah stated, going for plates.

"Me too," Cara chimed in, clearing the table.

Pleased, Trinity continued to set out the meal, and soon everyone was digging in. And for a moment, the place went quiet, but once they got full, the conversation resumed.

"Honestly, Trinity, this is the best sweet-potato quiche I've ever had. Wait … what am I sayin'?" Cara asked. "This is the only sweet-potato quiche I've ever had, and it was awesome."

"Ditto," Savannah chimed in.

"Thanks, guys," Trinity said blushing, before changing the subject. "Any more news about the house? Since the skeleton was probably Ms. Haggerty, did you by chance find Mr. Haggerty in another room?"

"It was Ruby Lee, and she'd be quite upset if you confused her with old Mrs. Haggerty."

"What makes you say that?" Cara asked, suspiciously. "Did you find somethin' else?"

"No, I just meant that a slave wouldn't want to be mixed up with the master's wife. That's all."

"Not buyin' it. I can tell when you're lyin'."

"I agree," Trinity jumped in. "Normally, it would be Mrs. Haggerty who'd be upset at being compared to a slave, not the other way around … unless … you know somethin'. What gives?"

"Fine," Savannah said, folding under the pressure. "I found diaries in the chest of drawers in that secret room that were written by Ruby Lee."

"Get out of here!" Cara and Trinity said simultaneously.

"It's true. They're quite old but well preserved. The writing is hard to read, but Ruby does a great job of telling her story. The way she writes, it's like you're actually there."

"I thought Ruby Lee was a slave. How can she write a diary that reads like a novel?" Trinity asked.

"It sounds crazy, but according to the diaries, Ruby Lee came from Europe to Jamaica with a white man name Jack Royce. I got the impression that Jack looked like some kind of Greek god, and he appears to have loved her. He taught her how to read and write and to speak three languages."

"Three languages, yeah right," Trinity said sarcastically.

"I'm not creative enough to make this stuff up." When they still looked leery, she added, "fine. I'll show you." Standing up, she left the table and returned with three large books. She watched Cara and Trinity's eyes grow large. "Now you believe me. And look at this," she said, showing them Ruby Lee's handwriting.

"You think this is for real?" Trinity asked, still in shock.

"I do. Look at the writing and the old-fashion words used. It's gotta be legit."

"Why didn't you tell us about the diaries before now?" Cara asked.

"I was thinking what if the story isn't that great, and I need to edit it." When Savannah saw their expressions, she added, "Okay, I should have told you two. But I don't want anyone else to know, and that includes the guys. I just want to read the diaries and know what's in them. And I should probably tell you about the painting."

"The painting?" Cara and Trinity said again in unison.

"In the secret room, there was a portrait under the bed."

"You know what Ruby Lee looks like?" Trinity asked.

"Not exactly. The picture wasn't well preserved. I'm sending it to the States to have it restored. I know money's short, and this is not the time money-wise, but there was something about it that made me want to make it a part of the opening," she explained. "Because it was in an expensive-looking frame, I naturally assumed that it was a woman from Haggerty's clan. But now, after reading the dairies, maybe it's Ruby Lee."

Cara concurred. "A slave that manages to read, write, and speak multiple languages could definitely have a portrait in an expensive frame."

"Let's find out what happens to Ruby together," Trinity suggested. "We could meet here in the evenings."

"I like that idea," Cara stated. "Besides, I'm gonna need a good distraction since I broke up with Marcus."

"Oh, stop. Y'all just had a little fight," Trinity consoled Cara. "It's not over. I know Marcus, and you're the best thing to ever happen to him. He'll be back."

"What if I don't want him back?"

"But you do, so stop trippin'," Trinity said, smiling. "Now can we read?"

Chapter Fifteen

August 1829

Ruby jumped when Haggerty reentered the study. "Don't be scared, gal. I don't bite," Haggerty said, slowly moving towards her. "I'll take good care of you. Just like that Royce fellow, but unlike him, I won't leave you," Haggerty stated, trying to allay her fears. "Royce told me you can read. I suggest that you let that be our secret." Lifting her face with his finger, he said, "I'll make sure that you get your own room. That way you can read at night but never in public. Do you hear me, gal?"

"Yes," Ruby Lee answered, still not making direct eye contact.

"Around here, you have to say, 'Yes, Massir.'"

"Yes, Massir."

"That's good. Come, let's find your mistress."

Haggerty walked out and called to Ernestine. By her response, he could tell she was still reeling from their earlier encounter. When Ernestine appeared at the top of the stairs rolling her eyes, he added, "I've bought you some help with the children. This is Ruby Lee. Try to be grateful."

"Did I ask for your help?" Coming down the steps, Ernestine took one look at Ruby Lee and hated her. "I don't need her. Let her work the fields."

"She's not working the fields," Haggerty snapped. "She's working with the children. You can put her in that back bedroom that we just cleaned out."

"I will not!" Ernestine replied, flabbergasted by the mere suggestion. "Let her stay with the other slaves. What're you thinking?"

"That I'm still the head of this house, and she'll stay where I tell you." Turning to Ruby Lee, he said, "Follow my wife because she'll show you to your room," and with that he went back into his study, ending the discussion.

Seeing Ruby Lee up close, Ernestine had a good idea of why her husband had purchased the slave girl, which explained why he wanted the girl to have her own room. It was shameful to even think about having intimate relations with a slave. Unfortunately, Haggerty had the upper hand.

"C'mon here, gal," Ernestine said, leading Ruby to the small room that Haggerty had suggested. "You can stay here until I figure out what my husband has in mind for you." Taking another look at Ruby, Ernestine frowned. "Where are you from?"

"I'm Ashanti, from the village of Tirande," Ruby said proudly, although there was really no reason to brag. "My mother was from there, but my father was a white man from Europe."

That little announcement rubbed Ernestine the wrong way. "I hope you don't think that you're white," she responded, rolling her eyes again. How dare this slave claim a white heritage? Black women were used by white men all the time for sexual follies, but that didn't mean that any children born from those unions were white.

"I see you trying to talk like white folks, but you're a good-for-nothing slave. You remember that," she said in a nasty tone, "because I'll have no problem reminding you with the whip."

"Yes, ma'am," Ruby Lee responded.

Walking around and giving her the once over, Ernestine said with a touch of envy, "I'm guessing that the men folk have complimented you. But to me, you look like a slave," she said, ending her inspection. "Perhaps, you've sparked some interest for my husband, but I'm the one who deals with the slaves in this house."

"Yes, ma'am," Ruby Lee replied, still keeping her gaze low.

That small slave-like gesture had Ernestine slamming the door to Ruby's room and marching back into her husband's study. "How dare you bring that immoral creature into our home!" she exploded as soon as she entered.

Haggerty looked up at his irate wife.

"You don't think that I know what's going on here?" she asked, completely appalled by his lack of Christian behavior. "You're trying to commit adultery with that hideous creature, right in front of me, in my own home," she gasped. "It's too horrible to even think about."

"I'd suggest you lower your voice or Ruby will hear you."

"You think I care what Ruby hears? What I care about is your soul— burning forever and ever for the sins you're trying to bring into this house. I've heard of men slinking off and having a cheap thrill with a slave woman, but I have never seen a self-respecting man bringing a savage into his own home to do who knows what with! It ain't right, I tell ya. It just ain't right!" Ernestine sobbed, collapsing into a nearby chair.

"Woman, what are you going on about? I bought Ruby to help with the children. What's so sinful 'bout that?"

"You expect me to believe that your only interest in a slave girl that beautiful is as a nurse maid? Do you really think I'm that stupid?"

"I'll refrain from answering that for the moment," he said smugly. "Although I find it interesting that you called her beautiful, when seconds ago she was a hideous creature. It seems to me that a good Christian woman like yourself should not even be thinking such immoral thoughts, let alone saying them. You might be putting ideas into people's heads that were never there. I brought Ruby here to watch the children, and that's the end of it."

"I'm going to get even with you, Charles Haggerty," Ernestine said angrily. "You just keep pushing me. And don't expect me to be nice to your slave concubine," she screamed at him and then marched out of the room.

When Ernestine returned to Ruby, she jumped back from the door as it opened.

"Don't act like you weren't listening. In fact, I hope you heard what I said," Ernestine announced in a pompous manner. "I don't take kindly to people tempting my husband. I suggest you do your work, stay out of my way, and out of my husband's bed." Once she got her anger out, she said in a gentler tone, "Now, the children, who my husband claims you're looking after, are outside. Go introduce yourself and get them bathed and ready for bed."

"Yes, ma'am."

—⁂—

Ruby could see the children playing in the sand. For a moment, she enjoyed the view herself. The sun was setting, and it looked beautiful hanging over the ocean. She could picture her and Jack walking hand-in-hand along the beach. She now knew that it had been wrong to run off with him. At the time, it was just going to be a little adventure. Then she had planned to return home and suffer the wrath of her mother—who couldn't be all that upset since she had done the same thing, run off with a white man. At the time, Ruby thought that any discipline that her mother inflicted would have been worth it, for she'd always have the memories. And what wonderful memories they were. Jack was so handsome and much more exciting than the men from her village.

But when she returned home, her village had been ransacked by slave traders. Everyone in her family had been either taken or killed. It now haunted her that such a tragedy had occurred while she was out gallivanting with Jack. And now, she'd received the ultimate punishment—alone in a world that hated her.

"Slaves ain't 'lowed to stand roun'. De missus'll get a stick afta yous for sho!'"

Ruby turned to see a dark-skinned, elderly, round woman talking to her. In her experience, she had found that white people didn't like her, but slaves hated her even more.

"Name's Bell. Yo's?"

"Ruby Lee," she said guardedly.

"You 'ere for de chilren?"

"Yes, ma'am."

"You ain't gotta ma'am me. De chilren is Emma and Charles Junior. You gonna 'ave your 'ands full wid dem."

"I've worked with children their ages before. I'm usually pretty good."

"Where yous from? And whys yous talk likes de Massir?"

"Where I come from, there weren't a lot of slaves. I learned to speak from my Massir."

"Well, gurl, you bedder call in dem children. De missus likes dem in bed befo' dark."

"Thanks," Ruby said, grateful to have a kind word from someone.

"No needs to tanks me. I jus' don't likes to sees no slave gittin' beats. Yous got dat look likes yous gonna gits beats a lot." And with that, Bell turned and went back into the house.

Seven-year-old Emma and ten-year-old Charles turned out to be the best part of the Haggerty household. Emma couldn't take her hands off of Ruby's hair, and Charles was impressed with Ruby's answers to his ten-year-old questions.

When Ruby finally got the children to bed and returned to her room, she was surprised to find a book lying on her bed. It was a collection of children's stories. Although she would have preferred something more substantial, she was grateful for even that small diversion. She had also been given a plain white, cotton nightgown and another long, nondescript blue dress. Perhaps Jack was right. Maybe she could have some sort of existence in this place.

Climbing into bed, Ruby lit the candle on her nightstand. She was beginning to read when there was a knock at the door. Sliding the book under her pillow, she was going to say "Who is it?" but before she could get the words out, the door opened, and Charles Haggerty entered.

"You settling in?" he asked, looking through her thin gown.

"Yes, Massir," Ruby responded, pulling the sheet up to cover herself. She could feel her heart racing as Haggerty came over and sat on the bed and placed his hand on her leg, rubbing it through the sheet.

"You know, if you're good to me. I'll be good to you," Haggerty stated, caressing her cheek lightly with his finger. "That's how it works around here. You understand me, gal?"

"Yes, Massir."

"Since it's your first night, I'll let you rest, but I want you to think 'bout what I said," Charles stated before rising and leaving the room.

When the door closed, her tears fell, and hopelessness quickly set in. She doubted that Haggerty would accept no to his sexual requests, and Ernestine was looking for any reason to have her whipped. This left her no choice but to run away. The book she had slid under her pillow she now threw on the floor. It was far too costly. Besides, she needed her sleep. She had a big day tomorrow.

Ruby was awakened at four in the morning by banging. She dressed quickly, without washing, because she saw nowhere to do that. When Ruby opened the door, she was just in time before Bell knocked again.

"Gurl, you up. C'mon gits some food befo' de Massir gits ups. We eats outs behinds de kitchen."

"What about washing up?"

"Yous do dat at night in de ocean when yo works dun. Yous wash dem clothes de same way."

"Thanks, Bell." Ruby was starting to get a good feeling from Bell. After breakfast, Ruby went to talk to Bell alone. "Can I trust you?"

"Trust me 'ow?"

Looking around, to ensure no one was listening, Ruby whispered, "I'm thinking about running away? What'd you think?"

Bell's answer was surprising because it was not verbal but a hard slap across the face, sending Ruby tumbling to the ground. "Gal, don't ever let me 'ear yous say dat! Massir Haggerty's a good Massir. Yous run, we all pays. Yous got it good 'ere. What yous gonna run fer?"

"You don't know what he's asking me to do," Ruby said softly.

"I'se gots me an inklin' of what you talkin' 'bout. Been roun' long time, so I knows dese tings. De Massir tryin' to get you in bed, righ'?"

Ruby nodded her head affirmatively. "Now, you know why I can't stay." Again, she was caught off guard as the back of Bell's hand caught her face. "You ain't Massir! Why do you keep hitting me?"

"'Cause I likes yous, and I'se wants to see yous live. Talkin' 'bout runnin' will get you kilt." This time she whispered. "Dat really what yous want, gurl?"

"What else am I supposed to do?"

"Yous lets dat man sleeps wid you. Dat's what yous do. I don't know whys the good Lord 'llows dem to carry on de way dey do, but yo job's to stay alive no matter what dey do. I done seen how it works. When da Massir takes a likin' to you, your life gits easier in other ways. Trust me. I knows."

"I can't! I just can't!" Ruby sobbed.

"Yous can, and yous will. I'se gonna 'elp. Now, stop de fool cryin' and go gets dem chilren ready. Yous 'ears me, gurl?"

All day, Ruby tried focusing on chores, but it was no use. There weren't enough chores in the world to make her forget about what would be coming that night. Ruby had slept with Jack, but that was different. She had loved him. But it just didn't seem right—a man taking what wasn't given.

Once she got the children to bed, Bell took her down to the ocean, and she washed with the other slaves. Even that seemed unfair, as the men came down to leer and make comments. The darkness of the night, however, came to their defense, blanketing their nakedness.

"You ready, gurl?" Bell asked Ruby as they were drying off.

"To be spoiled by a man that you do not love. Can anyone ever be ready for that?"

"Dere is many a slave folk jealous of yous and would loves to be in yo place. Dere was a time when I'se was young and Massirs came sniffin' afta me. One day, yous gonna wish somebody still saw you as a woman."

"How were you able to do it, Bell?" Ruby now stared at the beaten-down woman. She wondered what story her wrinkles and scars told. How much misery had she endured? And had there ever been any joy?

Bell went silent for a moment before answering, "By not tinkin'. I turned my 'ead off. You can do it."

Back in her room, Ruby waited. She knew Charles would come. And he would probably appreciate that she was now fresh from the ocean. Although this night, she refused to light her candle. This deed would be done in the dark. Staring out the window, her tears fell effortlessly as she wondered about her family. Were they in the same predicament?

Just then, there was a knock at the door. Charles Haggerty entered without invitation, coming into the room like a king entering his courts. Then Ruby did what she'd been told. She turned off her thoughts.

Chapter Sixteen

Savannah's Time Period

The day flew by as the newly delivered furniture was placed in the respective rooms. The smaller rooms on the first floor Savannah planned to use as temporary housing for her and Cara. Since the rooms were eventually to be used for guests, they were properly furnished with flat screens, wireless Internet, and the plushest mattresses that she could find. There were two basic things that she could not scrimp on—aesthetics and comfort. People needed to be wowed enough to pay the exorbitant rates and comforted so much that they never wanted to leave. But for now, the rooms would be home, although it would be weird living where Ruby once stayed.

"Here you are," Cara said, entering the room where Savannah was working. "Ooh, I love these rooms! Each with its own personality, but still everything's cohesive. You are truly gifted. I was thinkin' 'bout the blue room on the end for me?"

"That's fine," Savannah said, continuing to make up the bed. "I was sort of leaning toward this one."

"I can see that. The white furniture is so you, and I love these gold curtains with orange trim. I'd never have put that combination together, but it sure works, along with the orange, gold, and white fabric headboard."

"Thanks." Savannah beamed. She never got tired of hearing people compliment her work.

"Hey, guys," Trinity stated, entering the room too. "The furniture came," she noted, looking around. "Nice. How many rooms are ready?"

"Four," Savannah replied. "Although I've got more furniture arriving at the end of the month. Don't worry; we're on schedule for a Christmas opening. But we should start thinking about advertising, which means we need a name."

"How about the Three Divas?" Cara suggested.

"I kind of like that," Trinity stated. "But after last night, maybe it should be the Four Divas. Ruby Lee should definitely be a part of this."

"Agreed," Savannah piped up. "I also want to hire a marketing team. Maybe we can run our name by them. But first we need to move in and get out of the villa."

"I'm already packed," Cara announced.

"Speakin' of packin', I've been doin' some myself," Trinity shrewdly admitted.

"Really? I didn't know you were moving. Where are you going … Brandon's?"

"Actually … I was hoping here. If we're in this together, then we should be in it all the way. I could save so much money by givin' up my apartment. We're not talkin' forever. I'm marryin' Brandon someday, and then I'll be movin' in with him. But since we're tryin' the no-sex-before-marriage thing, it's probably not best to move in with him right now. And my ovens are comin', and I want to be around to try out new recipes. I'm here most nights providin' dinner anyway."

"Cara, what do you think?" Savannah asked.

"I say yes," Cara said, siding with Trinity. "Truth is we probably want more than two people in this big ole house at night. Old houses have creepy sounds, and just the two of us in here could be scary."

"Didn't mean to eavesdrop, ladies," Jacob interrupted. "But I'm concerned about you all stayin' here by yourselves. Perhaps I should stay too … just temporarily, until you've worked out security. You don't want to take any chances with the Carapones sniffin' around."

Savannah sighed. "Fine, we'll all stay. But what about Brandon?"

"I'll manage him," Trinity quickly responded. "I'll just spend more time at his place. He'll love that." Then rubbing her hands together, she said, "Now speakin' of rooms, which one's mine?"

"I called the blue one, and Savannah wants this one," Cara answered. "That leaves the green and the brown. Personally, the brown room seems rather manly, but that room is right next to this one. I think we should help the love birds keep their commitments of chastity and make sure Jacob takes the green room."

"Good lookin' out, Cara," Jacob said facetiously. "But it's temporary. I don't care which room I take. I'm happy with green or brown."

"I don't care either," Trinity stated. "I'm just happy you said yes, so I'll take the brown."

"Then it's settled. Should we share a moving truck?" Savannah asked.

"Sounds like a plan." Trinity grinned.

Since Brandon no longer had a secretary to announce his visitors, Trinity walked in unannounced to his newly downsized office. The firm had not been happy with Brandon since he couldn't get Savannah's property. It was probably only the goodwill of his late father that kept him employed.

"I'm workin'," he snapped, hoping to short-circuit Trinity's visit.

"If I didn't come by your office, then I'd never talk to you. Besides, my visit has a purpose, but if you're not interested," she said, pretending to leave.

"Okay, you got me. What's up?" he said, taking the bait.

"I'm movin'!"

"Movin'? Why? And where?" he said, finally showing enough interest to get up from his chair and properly greet her.

"Well … I am always at Savannah's … and … it seemed like such a waste of money to keep payin' rent when I was rarely there, especially when I could be puttin' that money into my business, so I'm movin' in with the girls."

"Have you lost your mind? Hello? The Carapones?" he asked, knocking lightly on her head. "Did you forget that they'll do anything to get what they want, includin' burnin' the place down? I warned Savannah. Please tell me that you have more sense."

"This is my dream, and so help me if I find that you're tearin' it apart. Mi kill you miself, you rude, dutty boy!" she said, unleashing her Jamaican accent.

"It's not me, it's the Carapones," he reminded her. "And keep your voice down," he said, closing the office door. "As you know, I'm no longer on the case, so I don't specifically know what they're up to, but I guarantee you it's not good."

"Mi not care 'bout de Carapones. Mi care about opening a business and helpin' to restore a house with so much history. It had its own corpse. How cool is that?" Then looking right at him, she turned serious. "You haven't mentioned anythin' about that, have you?"

"No," he replied, although he could tell that she didn't believe him. Trinity had accidentally let it slip that they had found a skeleton in the house but then had sworn him to secrecy. And despite the fact that it might have helped him improve his image with the Carapones, he never shared her secret. "I don't like the idea of you hangin' around that house, but when I make a promise, I keep it."

"I believe you. It's just that … well … you make me the odd man out. It's always what will Brandon do if he finds out. I'm continually tellin' them that you would never do anythin' to hurt me. I need to know that I'm tellin' them the truth. Am I?"

"Of course," he said, holding her. "Things are just crazy now, and although it may seem like we're on opposite sides, I promise you that when it counts, I'm on your side. I love you," he said, kissing her forehead, which to him was a more intimate gesture than a kiss on the lips.

"I love you too, boo," Trinity stated, hugging him back. Then pulling away, she said, "But I better get goin'. I am movin' after all."

"You want some help?"

"I thought you had to work."

"I do, but I can take a short break," he said, knowing he needed to get back into her good graces. "Wait … don't you have to work too?"

"I took off to move. I'm allowed vacations," she said, smiling at him. "And I don't know about you helpin'. I told everyone that you wouldn't be hangin' around."

"That's cool," he said, shrugging off the fact that he wasn't wanted. "But they must know that it's hard to move alone."

"Do you promise to behave?" she asked, caving. When he nodded affirmatively, she sighed. "Then let's go move."

For Savannah, moving had been simple. The few things from her old apartment in the States were already in the attic, and so it had only taken a couple of hours to pack up her clothes. She'd given the truck to Trinity hours ago, which Savannah regretted the minute she spotted Brandon driving up in it.

"Hey, Savannah," Brandon said, casually strolling into the house with two boxes.

But Savannah didn't speak; she simply nodded with disdain.

"Place looks amazin'."

"Thanks," she responded dryly, not at all impressed with him or his compliments.

"One-word answers—that's how it's gonna be?"

"Yep," Savannah responded, swallowing her anger. She wanted to be nicer, but she was finding it hard to forget Brandon's kissing incident and the fact that he was trying to steal her land.

"Sorry, Savannah," Trinity stated, rushing in. "He's helpin' me move my stuff in, and then he's out of here. I promise."

Seeing Trinity's concern, Savannah softened. Turning toward Brandon, she said, "It's obvious that you mean a lot to Trinity. And she means a lot to us. Obviously, we need to figure out a way to get along. I would, however, appreciate it if you didn't constantly threaten me with the Carapones."

"I've cleared my conscience. I just hate that you've talked Trinity into this madness. I swear if anythin' happens to her while she's here, I'm blamin' you," he said, getting in her face.

"How dare you come in and—"

"Brandon!" Trinity yelled, giving him an evil look. "Savannah, I appreciate your offer, but it's best to keep you two apart. Brandon, can we finish moving my stuff … in silence?" she asked before heading back out.

Once outside, Brandon went off. "I see your friend hasn't learned any manners."

"Excuse you!" Trinity exploded. "Exactly how are you supposed to treat a person who assaults and insults you in your own home? You promised!" she yelled at him again. "I blame that little altercation on you, not Savannah. From where I stood, she was the one extendin' the olive branch, and you were the one bein' obnoxious!"

"You're takin' her side?" Brandon pouted, leaning up against the truck.

"Are you five?" Throwing her hands up in despair, she added, "I don't have time for your childish behavior. Just help me move my stuff so we can leave." Pushing a box in his hands, she piled on more before he could comment further.

Yet, Trinity's regret of bringing Brandon soon turned to admiration. Within three hours, she was packed away. And that would've never happened on her own or even with the help of Savannah and Cara. She was thinking that things had gone fairly smoothly until Jacob arrived pulling a large, brown leather suitcase behind him.

"Jacob's moving in?" Brandon asked, surprised.

"Only temporarily," Trinity quickly explained. "He's concerned about security. Until we can get that worked out, he'll be stayin' here." Looking at Brandon, she could see him fuming. "You know we need Jacob with your vigilante client runnin' around."

"Then I should stay too," Brandon interjected.

"Over my dead body," Savannah replied.

"And that's the problem. Because you act like you're dead, it forces your little boyfriend here to look for livelier options—like my fiancée!"

"That crossed the line!" Jacob said, getting in Brandon's face.

"Brandon, stop embarrassin' me!" Trinity hollered, stepping between the two men. "I gotta return the truck, and you'd better hope that's all I return," she stated before storming out and dragging Brandon with her.

"See, I knew this wasn't going to work," Savannah whined once they left.

"Brandon was just blowin' off steam. Besides, you thought turnin' this house into a B and B wouldn't work either. But you were wrong," Jacob stated, pointing to the lobby. "I don't even think I'm in the same place anymore. People are gonna love it here," he said, reassuring her. "And Trinity will be fine. Brandon's an idiot, but he loves her, and he's not gonna make any real trouble. Now, tell me somethin' else that you're worried about," Jacob said, taking her in his arms.

"All right, Mr. Fix-It, I've done what I know how to do. What about the business part?"

"Funny you should ask that. Last week, Peggy Giles came to my office lookin' for new business. She's the best advertisin' guru in the business. She got me started, and she was wonderin' if I'd put in a good word with you. I'd completely forgotten until now. I'll give you her number," he said, pulling out his cell phone.

"I don't know what to say," she said, completely caught off guard.

"You don't need to say anythin' to me, but I do suggest talkin' to Peggy."

"Right," Savannah said, looking up at him, smiling. "I'll do that now." She started to leave but then turned back to give Jacob a heartfelt kiss. Instantly, his body responded.

"Yeah, you better go right now," he said, pushing her away.

"Exactly how do you intend to stay in control living under the same roof as me, huh?"

"Constant prayer. I have a feeling that I'm gonna be on my knees a lot."

Chapter Seventeen

"Will you keep still?" Savannah said, tired of watching Cara fidget.

"I can't believe you're not more excited. What do you think this Peggy person is like?" she asked, continuing to pace.

"I've only talked to her over the phone, but she must be good. Jacob recommended her."

"And how does lover boy know her? Don't tell me she's an old girlfriend."

"No, he worked with her, and stop planting evil thoughts in my head. Because, unlike you, I'm not excited. I'm just scared. And where's Trinity?"

"Right here," Trinity announced, walking in with a pan and a bowl. "I was baking at Brandon's. Thought we might want somethin' to munch on." Uncovering sweet-potato muffins, she placed them on the table. "I also brought extra batter in case we need it," she said, putting it in the fridge.

"They smell divine," Cara said, inhaling the aroma. "I've never had sweet-potato muffins, but I think I'm gonna love 'em," she said, rubbing her hands together. "And I keep tellin' you that if I can't fit into my clothes, I'm comin' after you with a shotgun."

"Relax—they're low calorie."

"I'm not a believer until I taste 'em." After taking a bite, Cara gasped. "Okay, I don't believe. These are not low cal. They're too good!"

"Yeah they are." Trinity smiled. "And they're definitely goin' on the menu. Sweet potatoes are a super food. And they're great for stress. My mission's to get more sweet potatoes into people's diet. Someday, I want to write a cookbook dedicated solely to sweet potatoes. Maybe I could sell it in Cara's boutique."

"Sweet." Cara laughed. "I'm not objectin' to gettin' more sweet potatoes in me or my store. And they do seem to be calmin' me down." But when the doorbell rang, she shook her head. "Okay, so maybe not totally calmin' me down."

"That must be Peggy," Savannah said nervously. "I guess it's time."

"Hi, I'm Peggy Gil ..." Peggy couldn't finish the sentence. She'd been expecting the typical island décor of palm trees and flowers, but she was totally unprepared for the elegance of this place. The red-and-gold-print runner drew her eyes to the marble staircase and complemented the reds and yellows in the stained-glass window that pictured Jesus and his disciples. The workmanship suggested to her that the glass was antique. Realizing that she was staring, she explained in a light Jamaican accent, "I'm just blown away by what you've done here. I could just picture myself getting married here."

Savannah beamed with pride, immediately liking the pecan-colored short woman sporting a curly Afro. She looked like a size 10 and was wearing a tailored tan suit with a black low-cut top that looked professional and not slutty. She had on a black opal necklace that drew the observer's eye up rather than to her cleavage. In comparison, Savannah felt completely underdressed in jean shorts and a T-shirt. She figured Peggy was just the professional lift that their business needed.

"Glad you like it. You're the first to see it who isn't a friend or part of the construction crew. And your reaction is exactly what I was hoping for—right down to the part about the wedding." Satisfied, Savannah turned to making introductions. "I'm Savannah, and these are my partners—Cara and Trinity."

"Nice to meet you," Cara said to Peggy. "And it's scary how we all think alike. Although we've never talked about having weddin's here, I was just thinkin' that I'd make a good on-site weddin' coordinator. I could do last-minute alterations."

"Then we're three for three," Trinity added. "I was thinkin' 'bout how we might price out small weddin' receptions."

"It's nice to meet all of you," Peggy stated, laughing. "You're all beautiful, smart, and apparently living your dream—your faces just light up when you talk about this place. What do you call it?"

"We were thinkin' about the Four Divas," Trinity piped up.

"Catchy," Peggy admitted. "Do you have another partner?"

"Yeah, but she's dead," Savannah explained.

"I'm so sorry."

"Oh, no, she died hundreds of years ago, so we're good with it," Cara added.

Laughing at Peggy's confusion, Savannah explained. "I inherited this property from a distant relative who was a slave. It's a complicated and interesting story, but without her, I would've never gotten the house. She's what you'd call the ultimate silent partner."

"This place gets better and better. I like the name the Four Divas, but it'll take a lot of branding to equate it with lodging and food."

"Sounds like you know your stuff," Trinity noted.

"Thanks."

"Wait," Savannah said excitedly. "We've been talking about how the property has restored us—how about we call it Restoration, with Refresh being our restaurant and Refined being our boutique."

"That's genius!" Trinity exclaimed.

"I like it too," Cara added. "Refined has the ring of an upscale boutique, and Restoration should be easier to market because it goes right with a stress-free vacation."

"I agree," Peggy said with excitement. "I'm getting branding ideas just standing here. You guys have something very special, and I'm sure I can help you market it," she told them, still looking around. "I know we're pressed for time tonight, but you must have me back for a tour. But let's get started. I have some ideas based on what Savannah shared with me over the phone, which I'll tweak to incorporate the new name. Is there a place where we can talk?"

"Our office is the kitchen," Trinity said. "C'mon back, and you gotta taste one of my sweet-potato muffins. I think it's going to be a regular on my menu."

"Can't wait," Peggy said enthusiastically, but before they got too far, the doorbell rang. "Oh, that's probably my assistant. That girl's always late."

"Vanessa!" Savannah gasped when she opened the door.

"You guys know each other?" Peggy asked, surprised.

"We met at Orion," Savannah explained as a queer look came over Vanessa's face. Immediately, Savannah thought about the swinging doll and the message. They couldn't confirm that it was the Carapones. It could've been Vanessa. Yet, having already been involved in one of her firings, Savannah decided against sharing the particulars of how they met.

"Vanessa was our waitress from Orion," Savannah said, downplaying the events of that night.

"Congratulations on going to Orion, and I guess you'll feel right at home with Vanessa. She's been with me for the last two weeks. I asked her to come. It's easier for her to assist me when she knows what's going on."

Vanessa didn't respond. She just smiled eerily at everyone.

Walking toward the kitchen, Cara whispered to Trinity, "I hope this isn't an omen not to use Peggy."

"I'm sure it's not," Trinity said, although she too was thinking, *Why would Peggy hire Vanessa?*

For the next several hours, they discussed all available marketing options. Peggy made it clear that it was going to take a lot of work to be ready by Christmas, but it was doable. It was also clear that there wasn't enough money left on the line of credit to pay for the marketing and other business expenses. "Savannah, will obtaining additional funding be a problem?"

"When I initially got the line of credit, the bank assured me that I could come back for more. It's just that I hate being in this much debt."

"This place is a gold mine, but it takes money to make money."

"Yeah," Vanessa added, speaking for the first time. "Don't be cheap 'bout advertising because this place could rock just like Orion."

Peggy gave Vanessa a dirty look before resuming the conversation. "As I was saying, one of the major reasons that businesses fail is lack of funding. And you really need to hire a firm to handle your accountings, hire staff, insurance, security, et cetera. This is what it takes to make it in business. I definitely plan to be rich one day, and I intend to do whatever it takes to make that happen. You've gotta have that kind of drive if you're going make it."

"I told you guys we were in over our heads," Savannah moaned.

"What you guys have done is the hard part," Peggy told her. "There are a million little firms that can handle the rest of it. You were right to take a risk on this place."

"You sure?"

"Positive," Peggy reassured her. "As long as you get the word out, and that won't happen without funding."

"Honestly, I don't see a problem getting more funding," Savannah said.

"And I can start payin' rent," Trinity offered.

"I could get a job and start payin' too," Cara added—but only to save face, for she had no desire to get a job.

"Uh-uh, you're worth way more to me as free labor." Savannah laughed.

"I feel so cheap," Cara whimpered.

Still laughing, Peggy stood up. "On that note, I should go. But it's been a pleasure."

Vanessa looked to Peggy for permission to speak, and when Vanessa got the nod, she added, "Yeah, this was fun. You guys have a great place here. I'd love to work here. I mean … if I didn't already have a great job," she said, cleaning up her slip.

Peggy just shook her head. "I'll check with you guys tomorrow to collect the paperwork," she said, packing quickly, wanting to get Vanessa out of there.

"And I'll check with the bank first thing in the morning," Savannah added. "I should probably thank Jacob for setting this up."

"Yeah, Jacob's a sweetie. I had the biggest crush on him. It was all I could do to keep it professional," Peggy said, remembering, "although he never gave me the time of day."

"Join the club," Trinity jumped in. "We've all had a crush on him, but Savannah's the only one who's actually been able to hook him."

"Savannah! You're dating Jacob?" Peggy asked, surprised. She would have guessed that Trinity would've been more his type. Savannah was pretty, but she just seemed so weak—not a woman worthy of Jacob's affections. "I'm jealous. I thought he was in love with his wife … you know about his wife dying?"

"Yeah, and we're not dating. He's helping me with the house. We're just friends."

"They're friends with benefits," Cara teased.

"That's not true. And how did this business meeting digress to this?" Savannah pouted.

"My fault—I'm sorry. I didn't mean to pry. It's just that Jacob seems like the perfect catch, and if he's interested, then why aren't you?" Peggy asked.

"Life's complicated."

"Not that complicated," Trinity teased. "That man is fine, and you need to have your head examined if you walk away from him."

"Feel free to pass his number my way." Peggy laughed.

"Enough of this," Savannah interrupted. "We should call it a night."

"Point taken," Peggy said, catching the hint. "I'll check in tomorrow, and no hard feelings about Jacob." *Although you definitely don't deserve him,* Peggy thought. "Come, Vanessa. Let's get out of their hair." Shaking hands a final time, Peggy added, "This is going to be fun." Seeing Savannah starting to rise, Peggy waved her back down. "Don't get up. We can see ourselves out."

Once they were outside of the house, Peggy let Vanessa have it. "Don't ever interrupt one of my meetings again or I'll fire you on the spot! Your job is to observe, not talk."

"Sorry, it won't happen again."

"You're right it won't happen again," Peggy snapped but then dropped the subject since, other than the untimely outburst, things had gone well. And her luck seemed to be continuing as Jacob drove up in his black BMW. All kinds of dirty thoughts filled her mind as Jacob exited the car. Strange how a white shirt and a pair of blue jeans was all it took to impress her. "You can go," she said dismissively to Vanessa. "We'll talk tomorrow."

"Okay, but first I want to say hi to Mr. Spencer," she said, remembering him from the restaurant.

"Do you or do you not want your job?"

"So it's like that, huh?" Vanessa said, walking off, intentionally throwing her hips to get Jacob's attention. When he splashed a sexy smile, she waved before sashaying to her car.

Peggy was miffed, but it was all forgotten once Jacob approached.

"Hey, Peg." He greeted her with a kiss on the cheek. "You're working late, huh?"

"I'm done working. What about you?" she asked causally, even though just his touch had her emotions surging. "You make construction house calls now?"

Jacob laughed. "No, I'm living here temporarily. I didn't think it was safe for the women to be alone in this big, old house without some security measures. For now, I'm security."

"Is it all work and no play?"

"Obviously it brings some pleasure. Who wouldn't want to stay in a house surrounded by beautiful women with the chance to see other gorgeous women drop by?"

"Good answer. How 'bout you and me acting like tourists sometime. You know, going to Duns River Falls or a romantic dinner?" Lowering her papers, she revealed her exposed cleavage.

"I gotta be honest," he confessed, smiling at the view, "I'm seein' Savannah."

"Really? 'Cause Savannah said that you all weren't dating. That it was only business."

Jacob furrowed his brow. "She said that, did she?"

Seeing the impact, Peggy pushed on. "Yep, that's what she said. Trinity and Cara are my witnesses. You might want to rethink your feelings, especially when there's a woman who is interested," she said, flicking a piece of lint off his white shirt.

"I like a challenge," he said, moving her hand away. "Right now, I've set my sights on Savannah, and I guess you're tellin' me that I need to work a bit harder."

Disappointed, she raised her papers back up, cutting off his view. "Let me know when you're in the market for a real woman," she snapped, and then she stomped off to her silver Audi, upset and humiliated.

—✺—

"Whad 'appenin'?" Jacob announced in his fake Jamaican accent, entering the kitchen. "You met with Peggy?" But his question was met with stunned silence. They had been reading something but stopped. "My bad. Did I interrupt some female bonding ritual?" With the silence still looming, he added, "What? I can't hang with my roomies?"

"Oh cut the crap," Cara replied. "You're only interested in one of your roomies. The rest of us are going to catch the hint and scram," she retorted, dragging Trinity out.

Watching them leave, Jacob was convinced that something was going on. "It seems like I interrupted more than manicures. What's up?"

"You're too suspicious. There's nothing going on." Covertly, Savannah used the dishcloth to cover Ruby's diary, which they'd been reading.

"And you're a bad liar. But I get it. You don't trust me," he mumbled, with Peggy's words still weighing on him. She was definitely hiding something. He thought he was a patient man, but with Savannah, he might've met his match. "I'm goin' for a walk."

"Want some company?"

"Nah, I'll catch you later," and then he slammed the door behind him. Sighing, Savannah went after him.

Peggy grumbled, turning the car around. She'd forgotten her folder. After her last interaction with Jacob, she had no desire to see him again. But the folder was important. When she returned, she saw Jacob and Savannah walking hand-in-hand along the beach, and that had Peggy furious. Intent on getting out of there quickly, she knocked frantically on the front door. When no one responded, she pushed against it and found it open. She was thinking she could just grab her folder without being seen. Yet, as soon as she stepped inside, she saw Cara.

"You're back? What happened?" Cara asked.

"I left a folder in the kitchen. I was thinking I'd just grab it. I didn't mean to intrude."

"You're fine. I was on my way to the kitchen. I'll go with you. Hopefully we won't disturb Savannah and Jacob."

"We're good. I saw them walking along the beach," Peggy said, trying not to show her hurt feelings. "I still can't get over this house," she said, using the small talk to cover her bruised ego. "I've always been interested in old houses."

"Would you like your tour now?"

"Not tonight," she answered, unwilling to risk another run in with Jacob. "I'm too tired," she lied. "Rain check, though, because old houses just seem to bring the past alive."

"I thought the same thing when they found the skeleton."

"Skeleton?"

"Oops," Cara said, catching her slip. "I wasn't supposed to tell anybody about that. Oh well," she said, laughing. "I might as well tell you that we found the skeletal remains of a woman in a secret room."

"You don't say," Peggy said excitedly. "Why's it a secret? I would think that would make the house even more interesting."

"That's not how Savannah sees it. She's convinced that people will think the place is haunted. With us being a new business, she doesn't want any negative publicity. If you didn't notice, she's a pessimist. Somethin' like that could shake her confidence. Which is why we're not gonna tell anybody, right?"

"Right," Peggy quickly agreed. "There's my folder," she stated, entering the kitchen. Once she picked it up, she took a moment to look around. Earlier, she'd been focused on the meeting, and so now she paid attention to the room. "This kitchen's fabulous."

"Yeah, it is, but there's still more work to be done. The appliances aren't due in for several more weeks, although Jacob will probably be finished in here in a couple of days."

The thought of Jacob working with the sweat flowing from his well-defined muscles was not an image Peggy needed in her head right now. Turning her thoughts back to the kitchen, she noticed a sheet on the wall. "What's that about?"

"Another secret." Cara shrugged. "Since I'm already in the doghouse, I might as well continue. It's a secret passage that leads out to a tunnel about two miles out. Watch this," Cara said, pulling the sheet aside to reveal what looked like an ordinary cabinet. Pushing a button, the shelves moved over, revealing steps. "Cool, right?"

"Oh yeah! Why's it covered with a sheet?"

"Savannah's idea to keep it hidden until the door is put up. Crazy, right? To me, the sheet just draws more attention. The door leads to a tunnel outside. Right now, the tunnel creates a vulnerability because you can slip in unannounced. Jacob's installing a security system that if you come in from the outside, it'll sound an alarm. He was gonna just close it off, but Savannah insisted that it remain a part of the house."

"I don't blame her," Peggy stated, watching the shelves slide back into place. "Thanks for showing it to me," she said as they headed to the front door. "Hopefully, once Savannah's up and running, she'll feel more comfortable about releasing some of these details. Maybe I could talk to her."

"No, because you're not supposed to know anythin'. Remember?"

"That's right. But I best be getting home," Peggy said, opening the door. "Thanks again. I can tell that you guys are going to be one of my favorite clients," she said, waving good-bye.

Cara watched Peggy until she was safely in her car, and then she closed and locked the front door. While turning out the lights, her phone rang. "Marcus?"

Chapter Eighteen

"Hey, beautiful," Marcus said in a sexy voice.

"Why are you callin' me?" Cara asked.

"I just wanna talk." When she didn't respond, he added, "C'mon, don't make a brother beg."

"Fine, you've got two minutes," she said, falling down onto the couch, getting comfortable.

"That's gracious of you, but could we talk in person?"

"No!" she blurted out, sitting up in panic. "I'm already dressed for bed," she said, staring down at her pink, fluffy bathrobe.

"Do you have to get dressed to open your front door?"

"You're here!" she said, staring at the door that she'd just locked.

"Yep," and then he rang the bell to punctuate his point.

Cara hung up without responding. Getting up, she went to the door, although she was conflicted about opening it. Letting him in on a night when she was bored to tears didn't seem like a good idea. But she couldn't just leave him outside, could she? "Okay, God's got this," she said, unlocking the door with more confidence than she actually possessed. It wasn't that she doubted God. She doubted her ability to listen to Him. And when she opened the door, she knew she was in trouble. Marcus looked incredible in a black, sleeveless shirt and jeans, and he smelled deliciously irresistible. "Okay, God, this is way harder than the tree test You gave to Adam and Eve," she mumbled under her breath.

"I wondered if you were comin'," Marcus said once she opened the door. Then they stood staring until he asked, "Aren't you gonna invite me in?"

Cara still didn't speak, but she did step aside.

"How've you've been?" he asked while walking inside.

His broad shoulders were tempting her, and she loved his sexy walk. She could feel herself wanting, but she knew she had to resist. "I'm not sleepin' with you," she blurted out.

"Okay." He laughed. "And it's good to see you too."

"Honestly, Marcus, why are you here? Why aren't you out with one of your women?"

"Ouch! You've gotta be the first person to actually become crueler after becoming a Christian. I thought Christians were about love," he said, sitting down.

"I'm cruel?" she repeated, still standing. "You're the one who walked out simply because I wanted you to be a better man. So, why are you here now?"

"You keep asking me that. Do you ever intend for me to answer?" he said patiently, patting the couch for her to sit beside him.

"Go ahead," she replied, even though her body showed that she still wasn't ready to listen. "Explain why you disappeared when all I was asking for was a little respect. I—"

"Woman, do you ever stop talking?" he asked, finally pulling her down to him.

"Fine! Speak!" she said, although she moved to the opposite end of the couch.

"You were right. I've been runnin' from all the things that I believed in. Jacob used to nag me all the time, but it never fazed me. Then you come along and say one thing, and it cuts to the core. I wondered why that was. So, I did some studyin', and I finally came up with some answers. I should say thanks for the wake-up call."

"You're welcome," she said, surprised at his response. "What answers did you get?"

"That I'm in love with you."

"Please, I'm not fallin' for your player lines," she said, standing up, putting even more distance between them. "Religion is new to me, and I'm not that good at it yet. I don't need to be tempted. If you really want to help me, then leave me alone. Go run your lines somewhere else."

"You can certainly throw some blows. Look, I get that you don't trust me, but what I'm askin' for is a second chance," he stated, now standing up too. "I promise you this is not a line to get you into bed. In fact, I love the way you interpreted the 'new creatures' text as a way of being virgins again." He laughed.

"Well … it made sense to me," she said, feeling badly about her lack of knowledge when it came to biblical things. But she was definitely getting better. She now spent at least an hour a day reading the Bible. "It seems to me 'new creatures' should cover all aspects."

"I agree, and I actually graduated with a double major—architecture and religion. Maybe I could help you with your Bible studies."

"For real?" she asked, getting her hopes up.

"Yeah. I want to get to know the new Christian Cara better, maybe introduce her to the Christian Marcus. He's quite the guy, if you give him half a chance."

"I don't know," Cara said, teasing him, having already decided to forgive him.

"C'mon, Cara, we had somethin'. While I can't promise that I'll always stay on the straight and narrow, I'm committed to tryin'. Can't we at least be friends … the kind without benefits?"

"Friends—just friends," she said skeptically.

"For starters … yeah. What do you say?"

"I guess, it would be un-Christian of me not to be friendly, right?"

"Right," he said, encouraging that line of thought. Then he leaned over to kiss her when they were interrupted.

"Look who the cat dragged in," Jacob stated, entering the house.

"Jay," Marcus stated, greeting his friend with a manly hug.

"Marcus," Savannah stated, coming in and hugging him as well. "We've missed you around here."

"Speak for yourself," Cara butted in.

"Stop pretending. The door was open. We know you made up," Savannah stated, laughing. "Obviously, we planned our entrance."

"Then your planning could've been a bit better," Marcus sulked. "I was just about to—"

"Is there no privacy in this place?" Cara interrupted him.

"Not really," Trinity admitted, coming out of the shadows. "We're just happy that the family is back together. You know the old expression— there's a difference between puttin' your nose into other people's business and your heart into your friend's troubles. And I, for one, am tired of seeing Cara mopin' around."

"Thanks for throwin' me under the bus. Now that we're all here, what are we gonna do?" she asked, knowing that she wasn't ready to be alone with Marcus.

"We could read about Ruby Lee," Savannah volunteered. "I told Jacob everything. He was just as hurt as you guys that I wouldn't share this huge find, and when I see it from your perspective, I get it."

"What are you talkin' about?" Marcus asked.

"Remember the secret room?" Cara asked. "Savannah found Ruby Lee's diaries in that same room."

"How's that possible? Wasn't Ruby an illiterate slave?"

"No, she was a prolific writer who tells a great story."

"Seriously? What's her story?"

"We're still finding out," Savannah answered. "But so far Ruby was an educated slave who left Africa with a white lover against her parents' wishes. When she returned home, her village had been raided by slave traders. Then she came to Jamaica with her lover. The lover got terminally ill and sold her to Haggerty."

"That's messed up. How do you sell someone you love?" Marcus asked, bewildered.

"It may have been the only way to keep her safe," Savannah explained. "Apparently, she was a looker. Haggerty fell for her and treated her nice for sexual favors. Ruby's story reminds us of what black women went through during slavery. They probably had it worse than anybody."

"Still do," Trinity jumped in. "And I have a feelin' that her story's gonna get worse, not better."

"Yeah, I got that feelin' too," Cara admitted. "Although Charles Haggerty obviously comes through makin' sure that Ruby's descendants inherited this house."

"Why don't we stop guessin' and start readin'?" Marcus said, knowing he needed a strong diversion.

Chapter Nineteen

August 1829

Ruby awakened to knocking. "Time to work again?" she asked, opening the door.

"Chile, yous funny, it's Sunday. Massir makes us lurn 'bout God," Bell responded.

"Why? We're slaves. The concept of God is lost on us."

"Then yous 'bouts to find God agin. Cause Massir makes sho' we all go. So gits ready."

Ruby dressed quickly, liking the idea of not working, although she had no interest in the white man's God. But that didn't seem to matter to Bell, as she rushed Ruby along.

Baptist missionaries came from England to teach the slaves, even though they had Baptist ministers in Jamaica. They also had nice, big churches, but the service for the slaves was held in an open field. During the slave church service, Ruby stayed close to Bell but only halfheartedly listened as the missionaries preached on Colossians 3:22, "*Slaves, obey in all things your masters according to the flesh; not with eye service, as men pleasers; but in singleness of heart, fearing God.*" At the end of the sermon, he added, "You have a good life here. You have work, the ability to worship, and life and strength. Let us pray for God's continued blessings."

After the prayer, the slaves were allowed to socialize, but Ruby didn't think that was wise. Instead, she chose to walk along the beach, which she regretted the minute she saw Haggerty approaching.

"Shouldn't you be talking with the other slaves?" Haggerty asked, walking up.

"I have nothing to say." Then as an afterthought, she added, "Massir."

"You do understand the importance of keeping up appearances, don't you?"

"Yes, Massir."

"Ernestine's staring, so I'd better go. We don't want to get her spun up. I'll see you tonight. Play the part until then," he said, winking as he left.

"Yes, Massir." Ruby sighed, watching Charles head back to the house. When he disappeared, she looked over at the fields and saw the other slaves and suddenly felt alone. To escape her loneliness, she imagined the ocean waves wrapping around her and taking her into another world. Where she was from, the ancestors watched out and guided you, but here she didn't feel the presence of any ancestors. In fact, she didn't feel the presence of anyone, including the white man's God.

The next Sunday, Ruby followed Charles's advice to socialize. He'd been right. Ernestine had made Ruby's life miserable for the rest of the week after seeing them together on the beach. This time when the missionaries finished their just-live-in-peace-and-love sermon, she tried to remain quiet next to Bell, which didn't last once a young female slave approached.

"Why's Massir so fond of yous?" Noone asked.

"I don't know what you're talking about," Ruby responded, even though she knew exactly what the woman was referencing.

"Yous knows. Yous jus' tinks yous don't have to talk to me 'cause I works de field."

"Noone, leave dat gal 'lone," Bell intervened. Turning to Ruby, she added, "Chile, don't mind Noone, she dun been out in de sun too long. 'Er brain's fried."

"I's not talkin' to you, Bell, I's talkin' to 'er." Noone gave a disapproving look toward Ruby.

"But I's talkin' to yous," Bell countered. "Leave dat gal 'lone."

"Den yous tells me why she actin' like a mistress, talkin' funny an all."

"I can't help how I talk," Ruby broke in, not appreciating being discussed in the third person. "And I've done nothing to get the Massir's attention. I don't want any trouble. I'm just here for slave church, even though they don't speak the truth."

"Wha'cha mean?" a tall, muscular, young male asked. "I'm Sam, and I wanna know wha'cha mean by dey don't speak de truth."

Ruby was in awe. Sam reminded her of the young men from her village. Men she had snubbed. She should have learned from her mother, who had suffered greatly because of her indiscretion, and so had Ruby, for it wasn't easy growing up with your father always being referred to as the blue-eyed devil. Perhaps, that was why she'd found Jack's blue eyes so captivating.

"You hear me, gurl. I asked wha'cha mean?"

"My former Massir used to read the Bible to me," she said, stretching the truth. "That's where I learned about Moses. He was sent by the white man's God to free his people who had been enslaved by an African king."

"Dat Bible of deirs talks 'bout an African king?"

"It does," Ruby replied, "but it doesn't end well for the king. He refused to let God's people go, and God sent trouble until he did. That's how I know that the white man's God does not approve of slavery. He doesn't just tell his people to live in peace." Changing the subject, she asked, "Are you Ashanti?"

"I am. Whad 'bout yous?"

"I am too," she said and then smiled at Sam, suddenly feeling closer to home. "I left home when I was young, but when I came back, my village had been hit by slave traders," she said regretfully. "Being Ashanti, you should know that our ancestors would not be happy with us just keeping the peace, and neither is the white man's God."

"Gurl, wha'cha doin' stirrin' up tro'ble," Bell chastised.

"Leave 'er. Tell me more 'bout wha'cha tink slaves should be doin'," Sam said.

"Oh, I don't know," Ruby said flippantly. "I just don't think our ancestors would like it if we just accepted slavery."

"We got no choice! You wanna end up dead," Noone said, snarling at Ruby. "Sam, don't mind dat devil woman."

"I 'grees, Sam. Dis fool talk gonna gits people kilt. Ruby, dat's what yous wants?" Bell asked.

"I'm not telling anyone what to do," Ruby stated. "But I remember freedom."

"Easy for yous to say when yous sleepin' wid Massir," Noone snapped. "Yous gets whatever yous wants, cause the Massir gits whats he wants every nigh'."

"I'm not sleeping with Massir," Ruby said with attitude. "He's sleeping with me," and with that, she walked off, figuring that was enough socializing.

For the next couple of weeks, things went smoothly because Haggerty was away on business. Even Ernestine seemed nicer. Although Ruby had continued to go to slave church, after the last interaction, she had gone back to being unsociable, figuring it was safer. This would, however, be the last Sunday before Haggerty returned, and she was anxious to spend it staring into the ocean. Sometimes she would stare so hard she would see her family in the waves—see them washing clothes and swimming to cool off from the heat. Her half-brothers laughing as she imitated the chief, which was considered very disrespectful. Back then, she hated her village life. But now, if she could, she'd turn back the hands of time and erase every idle word, every foul thought, and every careless complaint. She'd had no idea how good life had been back then, but she knew it now. Now that she had nothing—not even the will to live. All that was left was staring in the ocean and remembering. And that was her plan. Yet, Sam disrupted that plan by raising his hand when the missionary asked if there were any questions.

"I understand dat in dat book yous read is de story of Moses and 'ow he freed 'is people from slavery. Dat true?"

"Boy, where'd you hear that?"

Immediately, Ruby's heart sank. If Sam mentioned her name, it could mean lashes. Looking with pleading eyes to Sam, she hoped he would not say where he had gotten that story.

"I 'eard the white chilren talkin' 'bout it," Sam replied. "I's just wondered if dat was true, since I's never heard yous talk 'bout it."

"Uh … well … that story is in the Bible," the missionary admitted nervously. "The point of that story is that slaves are never to take it upon themselves to be free. They must wait for God to send a Moses. That's it for today," he said, quickly packing up his books and notes before departing.

Ruby could feel her heartbeat slowly decreasing as the meeting broke up and people started talking. Looking up, she could see Bell's disapproving face for telling Sam the Moses story in the first place, and Bell was right. They needed to stay alive, not to rock the boat. Perhaps the boat hadn't been rocked too much this time. Now, Ruby was even more intent on getting to the ocean and was quite annoyed when Sam stopped her.

"I done told everybody 'bout yo Moses story."

"You shouldn't have. Follow the words of the missionaries. I was wrong to tell you otherwise."

"I believes yo words was right. De missionaries talk 'bout God not carin' whether you slave or free. Dat God loves us all. I'se been tinking 'ow de missionary can say dey love God but treats slaves worst dan animals. Cain't be right. I grew up Ashanti, I know like you that I cain't lets down the ancestors."

"No, Sam. Bell was right. It's about not starting trouble."

"Too late. You taught me dat sometimes troubles come."

"Trouble won't come unless you invite it," Ruby reminded him.

"Tanks to yous, I's invited it. Tanks to yous, everyone 'grees dat it's wrong to be slaves."

"That is not my doing," Ruby insisted.

"Yeah it is. Do you know your name?"

"Course, it's Ruby Lee," she said with impatience.

"Nah, your name's Moses." And with that, Sam turned and walked away.

Chapter Twenty

Savannah's Time Period

Trudging toward the kitchen, Trinity yawned. Mornings were always difficult, especially after a long night. Pouring orange juice, she thought about Ruby Lee being a Jamaican Moses. "You go, girl!" Trinity said, toasting the air with her orange juice glass.

Searching the minifridge, she looked for breakfast. Spotting leftover muffin batter, the idea of sweet-potato pancakes came to mind. Keeping very few supplies on hand, Trinity checked for syrup. Luckily, she had both maple and corn, but seeing the barren shelves had her wishing for a fully stocked and functioning kitchen, although it was beautiful, rivaling any other part of the house. There were dark blue tiles that looked like marble and light blue walls with an ocean wave border. In the center was a large, square, blue granite island with the middle cut out, allowing her to teach or to work with other chefs. Over the island was a rack that artistically displayed the pots and pans, but with the push of a button, the rack descended, providing access to the cookware. Savannah had called it practical art, and it was Trinity's favorite feature. On the walls would soon be the large restaurant-sized ovens, refrigerators, freezers, and warming trays. And she couldn't forget the cabinet that slid over to reveal a hidden tunnel, making her workspace even more enchanting. The kitchen had become more than a place of employment; it had become home.

"Morning," Cara said, shuffling in, holding her head. Moaning, she slumped down into a chair. "I need coffee."

"Caffeine's not good for you. Eat some of these sweet-potato pancakes. That'll wake you right up."

"Yes, Mother," Cara stated sarcastically, even though she did skip the coffee. "Did you say sweet-potato pancakes? Why am I not surprised?"

"I keep tellin' y'all that sweet potatoes are a super food," Trinity replied, undeterred by the sarcasm. "And next time, we'll have to stop readin' before 2:00 a.m. I feel lousy too."

"Try 3:00 a.m.," Cara corrected, still slumped over the table.

"Three? Did you hook up with Marcus?"

"Seriously, is that all you think about?" Cara asked, giving her a sour look. "No, I stayed up doin' research. After hearin' Ruby's story, I was curious about slavery in Jamaica. And you'll never guess what I found."

"What?" Trinity asked, flipping her pancakes that were now smelling up the kitchen.

"There was a slave rebellion in 1832," Cara said, sounding scholarly, "partially instigated by the missionaries that came to the island. Baptist missionaries told the slaves to wait for emancipation, but the slaves rebelled by refusin' to work. It was instigated by Sam Sharp."

"Ruby's Sam!" Trinity gasped, looking up from her pancakes. "Ruby's diaries are linked to real historical events."

"I can't say it's Ruby's Sam for sure," Cara admitted. "Ruby doesn't give Sam a last name, but the timing suggests it's possible," she said, grabbing juice out of the minifridge. "Ruby Lee could truly be a Jamaican hero."

"Get out of here!"

"It's true. It all started because Sam strategically burned a trash house," Cara explained while pouring juice. "But other groups got involved, and it turned violent. After that, they just started burnin' everythin'. The rebellion was put down, and parliament eventually freed the slaves, but not before several missionaries and slaves suffered."

"You think Ruby suffered ... I mean as a result of the rebellion?"

"She was found in a secret room."

"Good point," Trinity admitted. "Now I can't wait to see what happens next in the diaries."

"What diaries?" Brandon asked, strolling in. "The door was open, and I see that all the boyfriends, except for me, are now stayin' here," he stated with disapproval. "Why's Marcus sprawled out on the couch? And what diaries are you guys talkin' about?" He stopped talking to kiss Trinity's cheek.

Trinity frowned. Brandon was supposed to stay away and not mess things up for her. "We're readin' the *Diary of Anne Frank*," she lied. "And

Marcus isn't stayin' here," she clarified, knowing his jealousy. "He was just here late last night and spent the night on the couch. Speakin' of men, why are you here?"

"Yeah, Savannah's gonna go crazy if she sees you," Cara said in support.

"Luckily, Savannah and Jacob aren't here. They left this morning to go to the bank," Trinity explained while buttering the pancakes.

"Since the ice princess is out, can I have some of whatever it is you're cookin' that smells so good?"

"I guess," she said, even though she really wanted to send him packing.

"Man, it's hard to sleep in this place," Marcus said, entering the kitchen in his bare feet. After taking a moment to say a personal good morning to Cara and hailing Brandon, Marcus complained, "Between the talkin' and the delicious smells, a brother can't get his Zs on. Trinity, what're you makin' that smells so good, and do I get some?"

"Sweet-potato pancakes, and yeah, I've made enough for everybody." Trinity set the table and placed the pancakes in the middle. After a quick prayer, everyone dug in.

"Why are Savannah and Jacob missing this feast?" Marcus asked, when he finally came up for air.

"They went to the bank," Trinity replied.

"Savannah's extending her line of credit to pay for advertising," Cara explained.

"Good luck with that," Brandon retorted, taking in the last bite before pushing his plate away.

"And what does that mean?" Trinity asked.

"Those were the best pancakes that you've ever made."

"Don't change the subject. What did you mean by 'good luck.'" Although Trinity looked like she might hit him, she just leaned over to take his plate. Noticing him wavering, she added, "Mi just fed you, so talk, dutty boy!"

"Fine." Brandon sighed. "You're gonna find out anyway. The Carapones located the bank that Savannah's been usin' and applied some pressure to stop her fundin'." Seeing them about to attack him, he added, "Hey, don't hate on me. I told you the Carapones played dirty."

"Savannah's gonna be crushed," Trinity said, horrified.

"Just a temporary setback," Cara assured them. "God's got this—Mark 11:24, 'You can pray for anything, and if you believe, you will have it.'"

"Looks like we've got another Jacob on our hands," Brandon said with a sneer. "A real Bible-quotin' Christian. Is that what you've become? What happens when God has other plans and things don't go the way you pray?"

"I get that being a Christian isn't all sweetness," Cara snapped. "Still I hold on to Romans 8:28, 'All things work together for good for them who love the Lord, and are called according to his purpose.' This text suggests that God's using every situation for our good. I could be wrong, but I don't see any good comin' from the Carapones gettin' this property."

"What Kool-Aid have you all been drinkin'?" Brandon asked. "The Carapones are crazy. They're gonna have this property. The only question is when, not if."

"I don't know," Marcus jumped in. "I've started drinkin' the Kool-Aid, and I kind of like it. Like you, I did everythin' I thought I was grown and sexy enough to do," he said, looking over at Cara. "But after it was all said and done, I still felt empty. Meeting Cara reminded me of what I used to be. Perhaps it's time to come back into the fold. Maybe we should be boys again—me, you, Jacob. Maybe we—"

"You demon!" Savannah screamed, entering the kitchen. "How dare you show your face here! You and your vigilante client may control the rest of Jamaica, but this is still my property. I want you gone!"

"Bank turned you down?" Cara asked.

"Yeah, thanks to Brandon's clients! The bank wouldn't say it, but I know the Carapones were behind them refusing to increase my line of credit." Getting in Brandon's face, she looked at him, disgusted. "Did you make the call to cut off my funding?"

"As a matter of fact, I did."

"I knew it!" she exploded again. "Get out!" she repeated, attempting to attack him, but Jacob held her back.

"How's gettin' mad at Brandon gonna help?" Trinity asked.

"Whose side are you on?" Savannah snapped, not wanting to hear anything positive about Brandon. "I need air." Pulling away from Jacob, she stormed out of the kitchen, and Jacob went after her.

"Now what was that about us being boys?" Brandon asked.

Chapter Twenty-One

Standing up, Brandon straightened his suit jacket. Only he and Trinity remained in the kitchen. Cara and Marcus, not being able to stomach him, had left right after Jacob. Looking over at Trinity, he knew her heart was breaking. "I'm guessin' that was my cue," he said, shrugging his shoulders. "You were right. I need to keep my distance." Pulling her up into a hug, he whispered, "But I miss you. What about hangin' with me tonight?"

"Mi dun't know 'bout tonight, but mi was wrong for tellin' ya to stay away." Switching to her American accent, she asked, "Will you go to church with me this weekend?"

"No one wants me around, and that includes God." Since the break with his boys, he hadn't opened a Bible or even said a prayer.

"And whad dat mean?" she pressed him. "I know somethin' gwann on wid you! Tell mi! If we're to be married, then there should be no secrets between us."

Catching the "if," he proceeded cautiously. "Trust me, you don't want to know," although he could see that she wasn't going to let this go. "If I tell you, then you'll hate me too. Fact is—I hate myself." Falling back down into his chair, he rested his head in his hands.

"Talk! Dutty boy, talk!" she said, sucking her teeth. "I mean it! Mi not gonna stop harassin' you till you do!" But instead of talking, he squirmed uneasily in his chair. Kneeling down beside him on the floor, she whispered, "You know you can trust me."

"I killed a friend!" The admission came out louder than he intended. But it came out. He'd been looking down but now looked up for her response. Since all he got was a blank stare, he continued his confession. "It was rainin'," he said, remembering. "I wasn't speedin' though." He needed her to understand that none of this was intentional. "I was tired, havin' put in a sixteen-hour day. I'd turned up the radio … to stay awake. Then this car came out of nowhere. I hit the brakes but couldn't stop. I swerved, but it was too late. After the impact, I was a bit shook up. But otherwise, I seemed fine. I went to check on the driver, and that's when I saw … Kimberly."

"Jacob's Kimberly! You're the one who hit her!"

"Afraid so." Again, unable to face her, he concentrated on the floor—a floor that was made of a deep blue marble swirl. As much as he disliked Savannah Hartford, she was a talented designer. The things she picked just seemed to work. There must've been a thousand different shades of blue to choose from, but somehow she had managed to pick the perfect shade of cobalt blue—a blue that allowed him to think.

"She was hurt bad," he said, continuing the story. "There was so much blood. I called 911 and was goin' for help, but she grabbed my hand and wouldn't let me leave. She didn't want to be alone. I told her she'd be fine, but there was too much blood. So, I knew … knew she wouldn't be fine."

Glancing up, he saw the fear in Trinity's eyes, and surprisingly, that kept him talking. "Kimberly died in my arms. She passed away peacefully, but I panicked. Unsure of where to go or what to do, I found myself back at the firm. That's where I ran into Sean, the managin' partner. Sean said he'd take care of it, and he did, which is why the firm threatens me every time I try to leave."

"Brandon, you poor ting," she consoled. "At least dat explains your unfaltering loyalty to that evil firm. But for a lawyer, you're kind of stupid, aren't ya? You just described an accident, not murder!"

"Before I met you, both Jacob and I were in love with Kimberly, but Jacob won. The crash could've been viewed as me saying if I couldn't have her, then nobody could."

"That's absurd! Where'd you get such a ridiculous idea?"

"Sean."

"But that's crazy. Can't you see dat? He took advantage of your fragile state," she said, in a soft, relaxed accent.

"No," he said, not wanting to be comforted. "All I see is the fear in her eyes, blood everywhere, and then her body peacefully going limp. That's all I've seen for the last three years."

"Baby, you gotta let this go," she said, rubbing his back.

"How? How do I forget that I'm the one who killed Kimberly?"

"You did what?" Jacob hollered, storming into the kitchen.

"Let me explain," was all Brandon got out before Jacob pulled Brandon up by the collar and slammed him hard against the wall. The pain vibrated through his back and neck.

"You killed Kimberly!" Jacob ranted, knocking him against the wall.

There was an automatic instinct to retaliate, but Brandon's conscience restrained him. "It's not what you think. It was an accident."

"That's crap! I'm out of here!" Jacob finally released Brandon and turned to leave.

"Jacob! Wait!" Trinity called out. "You didn't hear the whole story."

"I heard enough!" Jacob thundered back, steadily moving toward the door.

"Jacob! Please."

"Let him run like he always does," Brandon threw out.

"Like I always do," Jacob said, turning around. "Bro, I think you got that backward; based on what I just heard, I'm not the one who runs." He saw Brandon start to move. "What? You wanna pick a fight? You wanna piece of me?" Grabbing a knife off the kitchen table, he lunged at Brandon.

Trinity stood by silently.

"Jacob," Savannah gasped, reentering the kitchen. "Stop! Please!" When he didn't listen, she jumped on his back. But by simply twisting, he sent her flying into the wall, which allowed Brandon to reposition. Yet, within seconds, Jacob had wrestled Brandon back into the same position.

"Jacob!" Savannah screamed again. "What's wrong with you? You're scaring me!"

Although her screams had no effect on Jacob, they did bring Marcus and Cara running in. With Brandon and Marcus working together, they were able to subdue Jacob and get the knife from him. Then punches started flying between the three men.

The women watched in horror until Cara ran out and returned with a small handgun. Firing a single shot into the wall, she stopped the fight. Once she did, all attention focused on her. "Well … I couldn't just sit by and let y'all kill each other, could I?"

"Baby," Marcus said in a soothing tone. "Give me the gun." Needing no persuading, she quickly handed it over. "Where'd you get a gun?"

"I bought it for protection against the Carapones. Who would've thought I'd need it for you guys? What happened here anyway?"

There was an awkward silence before Jacob answered. "Brandon killed Kimberly." Now everything made sense. Their friendship ended after Kimberly's death. He had always believed that it was due to Trinity's ill-advised advances, but now he knew it was because of Brandon's guilt.

"Seriously, man, you were gonna cut Brandon?" Marcus asked.

"What would you suggest happen to a murderer?"

"Jacob, it wasn't like that," Trinity finally said. "It was an accident! Do you have any idea what Brandon's been through?"

"Brandon!" Jacob hollered, rising from his chair. "What about me!" he said, getting in her face. "What about what I've been through! She was my wife!"

"But you weren't the only one who loved her!" Trinity hollered back, not at all intimidated. "Brandon loved her too. Give him a chance to tell you what happened."

"I know what happened," Jacob said, moving back. "He was drinkin', ran my wife off the road, and then he ran like the coward he is!"

"I don't drink," Brandon reminded Jacob. "It was rainin'. The music was blastin'. And Kimberly came out of nowhere. I called 911. I was goin' for help, but she begged me to stay. She died in my arms," he said, looking over at Jacob. "I've relived the scene a million times, wonderin' what I could've done differently. I didn't want her to die! I loved her too."

"Now what?" Cara asked, cautiously.

"The murderer should turn himself in," Jacob said coldly.

"Forget you, Jacob!" Trinity blurted out. "You're not the only one who's hurtin' here! But aren't you the one always quotin' scripture? Why aren't you doin' that now?"

"Which scripture would you like?" he snapped. "The one about turnin' the other cheek. Not happenin'. I've been goin' out of my mind wonderin' who did this to Kimberly. And all this time, it was Brandon! And he said nothin'!" Jacob then slumped back down in his chair, putting his head in his hands.

"Can you blame him?" Trinity asked. "I would've kept quiet too. Sometimes, you can be a hypocritical religious bully! You're happy pointin' out other people's faults. But obviously, you're not ready for translation either!"

"Leave it, Trinity," Brandon interrupted. "I'll just go."

"Wait. Before you go, I have a text that fits this situation," Savannah offered.

"You have a Bible text?" Cara asked, shocked.

"Yeah, I've been struggling with issues of forgiveness, and 1 John 4:20–21, has helped. I'll have to read it because, unlike Cara, I haven't memorized the entire Bible." Grabbing her phone, she pulled up the text. "'If anyone boasts, I love God and goes right on hating his brother or sister, thinking nothing of it, he is a liar. If he won't love the person he can see, how can he love the God he can't see? The command we have from Christ is blunt: Loving God includes loving people. You've got to love both.' This suggests that God's love requires us to forgive."

"Well done," Jacob replied, clapping his hands as he stood. "The student has now become the teacher." Turning toward Brandon, he added, "Sorry, bro, but everything in me wants to tear you apart." Grabbing him by the jacket, Jacob pulled him close. "You took everythin' from me that night. So I'll never forgive you!" Then he walked out. And this time, Trinity didn't stop him.

"It seems the tables have turned," Savannah said once she caught up to Jacob, who was heading to his truck. "At the bank, you told me the Bible story of Job. You said he lost his health, his kids, and his wealth but never his faith."

"Not now," Jacob said, continuing his pace. "What do you want me to say?" he asked as she continued to run beside him. "I'm a hypocrite. Trinity was right. That's why I'm leavin'," he said, pushing past her.

"Leaving? To go where? For the past three years, you were heading to heaven. Where are you headed now?"

Jacob had opened the door to his truck, but her question had him closing it. "Savannah ... look ... I'm ... sorry."

"No need to apologize," she said, forcing him to face her. "Back there, you showed you were human. Proving just how powerful your convictions are—turning you from a lion to a lamb. You truly believe in this whole heaven thing. You've even got me believing. Someday, I hope to meet Kimberly. Sit down on streets of gold and talk about what we loved most about you."

"That's a weird thought," he said, releasing a slight smile.

"Why weird? I think it's comforting, having the hope of seeing your loved ones again." Although Jacob dropped his eyes, she continued. "And it makes you think about things differently. Now, you've got to worry about what Kimberly thinks, since you'll see her again. And do you honestly think that Kimberly will be happy finding out that she was responsible for killing your friendship with Brandon? Kimberly's good now, but Brandon's not. Are you really going to let your love for Kimberly seal Brandon's fate?"

"You're good," he said, still in denial that these arguments were coming from her.

"Well, you can't help but be good when you have a great teacher." She smiled.

"I didn't teach you that," he said, shaking his head.

"Oh, the ego," she said, laughing. "I was talking about Abigail."

"Abigail?"

"Yeah Abigail, Nabal's wife," Savannah explained. "You're not the only one who can apply biblical stories to modern-day life. Abigail used some powerful psychology on King David to keep him from killing her husband. I just tried that same psychology on you."

Jacob let out a robust laugh before grabbing Savannah and kissing her.

"That must've hurt," she said, touching his swollen lip.

"Not really," he said, kissing her fingers. "In fact, the only thing that I feel right now is my love for you … and Brandon."

"You've got a thing for Brandon? Should I be worried?" she teased him. Then seeing Brandon coming out of the house, she wondered if her little talk would actually hold Jacob.

Kissing her forehead, he moved her aside. "I gotta go."

"Wait," she said, holding on to his arm. "Are you sure you're okay? You've forgiven Brandon that quickly?"

"No," Jacob admitted. Then he smiled at her. She'd seen him at his worst and hadn't run. That meant a lot to him. "But one day I will," he said, forcing a smile. "Until then, Brandon needs me to act like I've forgiven him, and for Kimberly's sake, that's what I plan to do."

Seeing Jacob approaching, Brandon held up his hands to stop him. "Don't wanna fight. I'm doin' what you suggested—turnin' myself in."

"Brandon, don't!" Trinity yelled, running out of the house. "Jacob, tell him not to go!"

"Can't do that. Brandon needs to notify the police. It's the only way he'll be free, although I don't think that he should go alone." Turning back to Brandon, he added, "I can go with you, if you want."

"You'd do that?"

Swallowing his pride, Jacob admitted, "You and Marcus are my boys." He didn't want to admit it, but he'd missed Brandon. Although he wondered how would he ever reconcile his friendship or get over the fact that Brandon had killed the love of his life? But with God, he realized, all things were possible. After saying a prayer for strength, he said, "C'mon, let's do this."

"Hey, wait for me," Marcus yelled, jumping off the porch. "I'm coming too."

Chapter Twenty-Two

When Savannah stuck her head in the kitchen, she couldn't believe her eyes. The table was laden with food—rice and peas, corn pudding, candied yams, collard greens, fried plantain, fried snapper, ackee and saltfish, festivals, and a lemon cake. "Trinity, you must've cooked nonstop!" Savannah said, not believing her eyes.

"I had to do somethin'. I've been callin' Brandon all day, but he won't answer."

"Same thing with Jacob," Savannah replied. "And sorry for not being here today. I had appointments—Cara too."

"It's fine. I wouldn't have been good company anyway," Trinity admitted, still frying chicken. After turning down the fire, she faced Savannah. "What if Brandon gets convicted? He's a pretty boy. He wouldn't last a day in jail." She laughed nervously, cleaning her hands on a dishtowel.

"He's not going to jail. The most they have him for is leaving the scene of the crime, which technically he didn't do. He called for help and stayed until she died. That's not the definition of a hit and run." Now, threatening people, that's a crime—and one that Brandon was actually guilty of, but Savannah didn't think this was the time to bring that up.

"Sorry this happened, but honestly, coming clean is for the best. Brandon needs to officially put this behind him."

"I keep tellin' myself that," Trinity replied, turning her chicken over. "Still, I'm scared. I'm still gettin' back into the groove of trustin' God."

"Based on this feast, I'm guessin' we've heard good news," Cara said, coming into the kitchen.

"This feast is from nervous energy because Trinity hasn't heard anything from the guys. You heard from Marcus?"

131

"Not a peep, but I've been prayin' all day." Cara then stopped to taste a plantain. "I think they're gonna be fine. Better than fine. I bet they'll be friends again," she stated, chewing.

"That'd be nice," Trinity confessed, taking the chicken out of the pan. "It's hard datin' the guy that everyone hates," she said, joining Savannah at the table.

"We don't exactly hate him," Savannah stated. "We just want different things for this property."

"Speakin' of hurtin', what did y'all think of Jacob's little explosion?" Cara asked, now sitting down at the table too.

"Scary and sexy all at the same time." Savannah laughed. "Why is it that we're always attracted to the bad boys? Jacob looked so good beat up."

"I'll second that," Cara threw in. "In fact, they all looked pretty good beat up. We must be some sick chicks," she said laughing.

"Maybe so," Savannah agreed. "But I think we like seeing that brute strength, although it's no fun when he uses it on you. My neck still hurts from slamming into that wall. I don't even think he touched me. He just flexed, and I went flying."

"Yeah, that was funny." Trinity laughed, finally releasing some of her built-up tension.

———※———

Brandon took a moment to observe the women before making his presence known. Trinity looked lovely. He still couldn't believe how she'd had his back. "Based on your jovial mood, it doesn't look like I was missed," Brandon interrupted, finally making his presence known. He didn't get two steps into the kitchen before Trinity was in his arms.

"What happened? I've been so worried," she said, holding on to him tightly.

"According to the law, I'm a free man, although you wouldn't know it from this chokehold you have on me," he teased Trinity as he pried her arms loose before continuing. "The police believed me since it jived with the evidence, and Jacob really came through. When the husband says he believes you, it goes a long way."

"Thank God," Cara chimed in.

"Trinity, you cooked a feast just in case it was good news?" Jacob asked, grabbing a chair and sitting next to Savannah.

"Uh-uh," Brandon jumped in. "Cookin's my baby's copin' mechanism. And judgin' by the dishes on this table, she was pretty worried," he said, pulling Trinity back into his arms.

"You've no idea. But the good thing about my copin' mechanism is that we have dinner."

"And I'm starvin'. I say let's eat," Marcus chimed in, grabbing a chair.

"This day started off pretty bad with us eatin' a meal," Brandon said, stalling. "Perhaps we shouldn't push our luck with another one."

"I disagree," Savannah countered. "It's fitting to celebrate with a good meal. Anyone for a toast?" she asked. "I think there's lemonade in the minifridge."

"We used to toast with champagne." Cara laughed. "I guess times have changed, but there's still the elephant in the room. Brandon may be cool, but he still works for the enemy."

"Not anymore," Marcus said. "We stopped by the firm before we came here. And he quit, just like that. We even helped him pack."

"You quit," Trinity repeated in shock. "That's an answer to a lot of prayer. Now, we can really start buildin' a life."

"Not the life we planned," Brandon pointed out, finally sitting down. "You think they're gonna let me practice law? No. Sean's probably gonna make sure that I'm blackballed at every major law firm. Basically, you're gettin' excited about bein' homeless."

"You bet I am," Trinity said enthusiastically. "I was always taught that happiness is not havin' what you want but wantin' what you have. And I have everythin' I want right here."

"I appreciate all the lovey-dovey stuff, but can we eat now?" Jacob asked, rubbing his hands together, surveying the variety of dishes.

"I agree," Cara seconded. "Brandon, would you say grace?"

After the prayer, everyone dug in. Trinity smiled, seeing the group all together. Finally, Brandon belonged. "Perhaps later we could do a little readin'. I mean, if that's all right for Brandon to join us?"

"Yeah, I guess," Savannah replied hesitantly.

"Appreciate the offer, but I've already read *Anne Frank*."

"Small white lie," Trinity confessed. "*Anne Frank*'s not what we're readin'. We're reading Ruby Lee's diaries. Savannah found them in the secret room, and they're fascinatin'."

"You told him about the secret room?" Savannah asked, alarmed.

"It just slipped out, but he never told anyone. Right, Brandon?"

"I gave my word, didn't I? These diaries, have they been authenticated?" Brandon asked, now relieved that the attention was being diverted from him.

"No, but I know they're real," Savannah replied.

"This house is just full of surprises." The biggest one was that it had provided him the chance to come clean and get his best friends back.

Chapter Twenty-Three

December 1829

Sitting on the back porch, Ruby Lee mended clothes while watching the children play. Things seemed to be back to normal. Charles was back from his trip, Ernestine was back to being evil, and she was back to days and nights filled with misery. Thinking about her plight, she didn't even notice that Sam had come up to the house. It took him several hails before she even acknowledged him.

"What're you doing here?" she scolded him when she finally heard him. "Aren't you going to get in trouble and get me in trouble?"

"Yous knows yous a pretty ting?" Sam said, smiling, flashing his perfect white teeth.

"What kind of fool talk you doing now?" she asked, seeing his well-defined muscles gleaming in the sun. "The kind of talk that will get us killed. What about Massir? What if he hears you making nice words with me?"

"You a slave, aintcha? I'm 'posed to makes words wid my own kind. What? Yous off de table cause yous belongs body and soul to de Massir?"

"He owns my body, not my soul. Nobody can own a soul, not even Massir," she replied, hoping that was true. Seeing Sam grinning, she felt the need to explain. "Everybody thinks it's my fault that Massir comes sniffing after me. But I don't want his attention. I just don't know how to get rid of it."

"What 'bout my 'tention? Yous likes dat?" Sam said, nudging her.

"I'm a slave. I'm not allowed feelings."

"Dats why I'se come here," Sam explained. "Tanks to yous, we gonna make a move. We gonna refuse to work. It's times dey treats us likes we human."

"You must be plum crazy! They'll kill you," Ruby whispered, fearing for Sam.

"Dey gonna kill all dey slaves? Den who's gonna do de work? Not dem." He laughed.

"You're crazy, and I want no parts of this foolish talk that you're doing. Nothing good can come of it," she said, dismissing him and returning to her sewing.

"Sam, you got business up at the house?" Haggerty stated, walking out on the porch.

"I'se sent to tells yous dat de sugar crop's ready."

Charles wrinkled his brow. "You can go on back now. I'll be out there directly."

"Yes, Massir," Sam said, nodding his head to acknowledge. Then turning back to Ruby, he said, "I'll be seein' you." Then he winked at her and headed up the road.

Haggerty frowned. "I didn't know you and Sam were friendly," he said, casting a disapproving look at Ruby.

"We're not friendly," she corrected him. "I was just following your advice—talking more to the slaves like you suggested."

"I meant the slave women," Haggerty clarified. "Not the men." Lighting his pipe, he added, "I don't want to see you talking to Sam no more, you understand me, gal?"

"Why?"

"You back talking me?" he said, surprised at her response.

"No, Massir," she quickly responded, casting her eyes down toward the ground.

"I don't need to explain myself to you," he said in a softer tone. "Just do what I say," and then he walked back into the house.

Ruby sat back down disgusted. Sam was everywhere. How was she going to stay away from him? And now that Sam was forbidden, it made him that much more appealing. Massir would have done better if he had never brought the matter up, Ruby thought.

The rest of the day was uneventful, except for the fact that her stomach stayed unsettled, which had her deciding to skip dinner. Bell, however, would have none of that. She kept insisting that Ruby eat. That is, after chastising her for getting Sam all stirred up.

The news was spreading through the slave quarters that Sam was going to refuse to work. Bell thought he was as good as dead if he went through with his plan. But that was Ruby's point; it was Sam's plan, not hers. She could not be responsible for his actions simply because she mentioned one story.

The next couple of weeks went badly. She was feeling worse, and although Bell kept plying Ruby with food, she just kept throwing it up. And Ernestine had no patience or sympathy when Ruby threw up on the hallway floor. Ernestine hit Ruby six times with a broom handle before having her clean it up. Later that night, when she went down to wash, the welts from the broomstick burned.

"Yous ain'ts carryin' da Massir's chile is yous?" Bell asked.

"Why would you ask that?" Ruby asked in a panic. The thought of having a child terrified her.

"Not keepin' food down is a sure sign dat deres a baby on de way." When Ruby looked at her with a puzzled expression, Bell added, "Yous ain't had no chilren?"

"No."

"Wells, I'se dun had my fair share. I's knows dat not keepin' food down is a sign dat a baby's comin'. Yous better tell de Massir. He'll helps yous."

For the rest of the evening, Ruby wondered about being pregnant. Back in her village, having a baby meant a huge celebration. Yet, here, all she wanted was to pull out whatever was growing inside of her, if anything. Bell could be wrong, Ruby thought. She could just be sick. Maybe she'd caught what Jack had, and she wouldn't have to dream of walking into the ocean anymore. She could rely on the sickness to end her life.

When Haggerty came in for his nightly visit, Ruby announced without warning, "Bell thinks I'm pregnant."

"What?"

"I've been throwing up for a couple of weeks. Just today, I got lashes for it."

"Ernestine hit you!" Shaking his head, he muttered under his breath, "That woman! I just want to get rid of her, but there would be too much talk. Are you hurt?" he asked, turning his attention back to Ruby.

"My back stings a bit from the saltwater, but Bell says it's the best thing for it."

Ruby sat still as he examined her back. Gently, he touched each welt as he cursed silently. "We got to get you out of here. If you are pregnant, things will only get worse. I've got to hide you."

"Hide me? Hide me where?" Ruby asked, alarmed.

"I have the perfect place." Sticking his head out of the room to ensure that no one was watching, he led her to the front of the house where she watched him open the wall before pulling her inside.

Speechless, she watched him light candles before the wall closed behind them. "I don't understand," she said, looking confused. "How'd you do that?"

Laughing, he continued lighting candles. "This is a secret room. It was built by my great-great-grandfather when the house was constructed in the 1700s. My father pointed it out to me before he died. I couldn't imagine my life without this place. One day, I sent everyone out and fixed it up as my private study. Before you arrived, I used to spend hours in here. You can stay here until I can figure out what to do with you and the baby. You'll have to stay inside during the day, and then you can come out at night. I'll simply tell Ernestine that I sold you. This way you won't have to work during your pregnancy."

Haggerty then stepped out to get supplies, and Ruby looked around in astonishment. It was as if she had stepped into another dimension—one that she despised. The room was very manly with a large desk, couch, and a wall of books. There were no windows, which made her feel trapped and hot. And that had her wondering how she would last a couple of hours, let alone for the rest of her life in this room. The idea of being cut off from the sun seemed like a fate worse than death.

Haggerty returned with two empty basins, a blanket, and a couple of pillows. "We can make this space really cozy," he said. "I suggest sleeping during the day and saving your need for the outhouse at night. Ernestine must believe our ruse or she'll be your worst enemy." Looking over at her, he could see the fear on her face. "Trust me, this is only temporary."

"Please, Massir, don't make me stay here!"

"Come now," he said, holding her. "And in here, it's okay to call me Charles."

"I can't live without the sun," she panicked. "It's so stuffy. I can't breathe."

"There are vents," he said, stopping to show her how they worked. "But when the vents are open, the sound travels. Even when the vents are closed, you still have to be careful because the walls are paper-thin. You don't know the things I've learned by just sitting in this room listening," he said, laughing. "Soon, you'll know all of the secrets of this house."

"I can't do this! Just kill me and get it over with!"

"Now, stop the fool talk," he said angrily. "What would you have me do? Watch you get whipped on a daily basis? Let you suffer Ernestine's wrath when she discovers you're carrying my child?" Calming his anger, he stated, "It's not ideal, but it'll keep you safe."

Pulling away from him, she fell down onto the couch, completely defeated.

"This really ain't so bad," he encouraged her, setting up the blankets and pillows.

Eventually Ruby settled down and fell asleep. When she awoke, Haggerty was gone. He had left fruit and biscuits on the desk, but she wasn't hungry. Besides, how would she relieve herself? Of all the things that she had been through, this was the worst. With little effort, she gave in to her fears and frustrations. She cried for herself, Jack, her mother, her father, the elders, her unborn baby, and even for Haggerty. He obviously cared about her, but circumstances didn't allow him to treat her like a woman. Because by all accounts, she wasn't a woman—she was a slave. She still had the responsibilities of a woman though, for growing inside of her was possibly a child, and where would that child grow up? In a secret room, never knowing what it was like to belong somewhere? That thought made her cry again. She cried until she fell back to sleep.

When she woke up this time, she could hear the hustle and bustle of the house, and surprisingly, she missed it. She wondered who was looking after the children. And what was Bell doing? And what had she been told, if anything?

Ruby listened as people came to talk to Haggerty. She had always wondered what it would be like to be a fly on the wall, and now she knew. It was as if she didn't exist. She seemed more like a ghost trapped inside the walls.

After a couple of hours, she got hungry. But how could she eat with no access to an outhouse? She used one of the basins to pee, but now the smell of urine filled the air, and that made her want to vomit. So she used the other basin to do that. But now she was trapped in a room that smelled of vomit and pee. Again, the tears came, and again, she didn't stop them. She cried until she once again drifted off to sleep.

When she woke up, Haggerty was back. The smell was gone, and the two basins were now clean and sitting beside the desk. Haggerty had a bowl of soup waiting, but she had no appetite. Yet, with Haggerty's insistence, he got her to take a little soup and a couple of apple slices.

"You were right. This isn't working," Haggerty admitted. "The smell drifted out to the rest of the house, and now Ernestine is convinced that there's a dead rat in the wall. She swears she heard crying, and some of the slaves claimed they heard it too. They think the house is haunted. Ernestine's going out tomorrow. That'll give me the chance to take you to your new home."

"New home?" Ruby asked with concern.

"I have a piece of land on the other side of town, but I had people living there," he explained. "I've managed to relocate them. Now, you can stay there. I'm sending Bell with you. That way you won't be alone."

"Really?" Ruby sat up excitedly. "I won't have to stay in this room anymore?"

"Just one more night, and then you'll be back out in the sunshine. Now, you still won't be able to go prancing about, but it won't be like this."

Without thinking, she threw her arms around Haggerty and hugged him.

"That's the most emotion I've ever seen from you," Haggerty said, smiling.

"Sorry, Massir. Did I cross the line?"

"There are no lines in a secret room," he said, smiling at her.

"I'm just relived not to be living in this tomb anymore." She sighed in relief.

Charles laughed. "For me, it was solace; for you, a tomb. Well," he said, still smiling, "I think everyone's sleeping, so you can go outside now."

Chapter Twenty-Four

Savannah's Time Period

After Ruby's story last night, Trinity started the morning off in a good mood, until she read the morning headline, "New B and B Haunted," next to a picture of Restoration. Obviously, the Carapones were at work again! When she called her partners, she discovered that it was even worse than she thought. The story wasn't just in the local paper. It had run on *Good Morning, World*, an international TV news program.

Entering the house, she found Savannah and Cara in the kitchen, and without thinking, Trinity dropped her stuff, washed her hands, and started pouring flour into a bowl.

"Trinity, what are you doin'?" Cara asked.

"Whatcha mean? We're strategizin', aren't we?"

"I mean with the bowl. You're cookin'?"

Looking down, Trinity didn't even remember getting the bowl. "You know I have to cook when I'm nervous," she said, laughing. "I'm not even sure what I'm makin'." Thinking for a minute, she said, "Maybe some cookies. Everything's better munching on warm cookies, right?"

"You are so right," Cara agreed. "Keep stirrin'. I'm feelin' hungry already."

"We're laughing, but this is serious," Savannah interrupted. "If no one comes to our grand opening, then we're out of business. And how did they find out about the skeleton, Brandon?"

"No," Trinity snapped. "See, mi knew you were gonna go and blame mi man. He didn't do it! I just came from confrontin' him." Seeing their

141

disbelief, she added, "Mi know dat Brandon's a rude, dutty boy with no broughtupsy, but he didn't do dis ting."

"Did anybody else tell?"

"Me," Cara said, raising her hand like a schoolgirl. "It slipped out to Peggy. But c'mon, she's our marketin' person. What incentive would she have for tellin' the Carapones? Brandon's got more reason to sell us out than Peggy."

"Mi tellin' you he didn't do it!" Trinity said, sucking her teeth at their mistrust. But just as quickly as her anger rose, it subsided. "Mi sorry 'bout Brandon's role in all of dis, and if you don't want mi in the business no more, then just say so."

"Of course we want you!" Savannah consoled Trinity.

"Yeah, I didn't mean anything by what I said," Cara seconded.

"And for the record," Savannah threw in, "you're not responsible for Brandon's actions. You're as much a part of this business as me and Cara. I'm the one who made the mistake. Run a business—what was I thinking?"

"Seriously, Savannah," Cara cut in. "You can't honestly be second-guessin' the move. It was the right move for all of us. Like sisters, we're gonna fight, but we've changed. We're not the same people we were a couple of months ago. The only thing that truly needs adjustin' is your pessimistic attitude. Proverbs 15:15 says, 'When a man is gloomy, everything goes wrong, when he is cheerful, everything seems right.' We just need to figure out our next move. We're smarter than the Carapones, and more importantly, we've got God on our side. 'For greater is he that is in me, than he that is in the world.' And didn't Psalm 23 say, 'He prepares a table in the presence of mine enemies'? We're gonna have the ultimate table here at Restoration, and the Carapones will be jealous with envy."

"Well, mi pretty sure King David wasn't talkin' 'bout Restoration when he wrote dat, but hey, it works for mi. So now that we've had our sermon, how do we save our business?"

"I called Peggy. She's on her way over," Savannah replied.

"Great," Trinity said, dumping her dough on the table. "Now, you're talkin' like a fearless leader. We need to fight this."

"Why?" Savannah sighed. "Even if we somehow get through this hurdle, what about the next one?"

"God's got an answer for that too," Cara replied. "Mathew 6:34 says, 'Don't be anxious about tomorrow. God will take care of your tomorrow too. Live one day at a time.' To me that means don't think about the next hurdle until it comes."

"Since we're sharin' our feelin's, mi might as well tell ya dat Brandon's back at dat firm of dutty criminals," Trinity informed them.

"Really," Cara commented, grabbing the spoon to taste the dough that Trinity was now forming into circles, their prior argument now forgotten.

"What happened?" Savannah asked, also tasting the dough.

"Don't know," Trinity confessed. "Mi tink he was scared to be out of work. Dat's his biggest fear," she explained. "But he didn't even try. He was away from dat place for less than a day. He claims he wants a more strategic exit and dat he could be a spy for us with de Carapones."

"Honestly, Trinity, I love that idea," Savannah admitted.

"You're right. His reasons for goin' back sound great. The problem is mi don't tink 'we' make sense anymore."

"Don't say that," Cara interjected. "We have the perfect little group here. We're all friends, and now our men are friends. It just works."

"You and Marcus work, and Jacob and Savannah are over the top. Yet, I'm the one who's engaged without a weddin' date. Why? Because Brandon's always waitin' to get the right amount of fundin' or find that openin' he's been lookin' for to leave the firm. When Brandon did actually leave, I thought it meant our time had finally come," she said, licking the spoon. "Which is why, even though it's for good reasons, it's such a slap in the face. And don't forget the way we met. Mi findin' Brandon in a lip lock with Savannah. Mi tink de writin' dun been on the wall for a long time. Mi just refused to see it, and now, mi eyes are finally open," she said reflectively. "I do love that he's back with his boys. And maybe that'll help him cope when I leave his dutty butt," she said, mixing accents.

"God will work it out," Cara said.

"Cara, I love you." Trinity laughed while putting her cookies in the oven. "There was a time when Brandon was everything. But this," she stated, looking around the kitchen, "is home to me now, and he can't even support it. Maybe, for now, the business is enough."

"What I see is how Brandon looks at you. How he fought to be around you. Just pray about it."

"Done," Trinity stated, just as the bell rang. "Is that the cavalry?"

"Sounds like it. I'll let Peggy in," Savannah offered, still dazed from the news.

When Savannah left, Trinity looked at Cara's sullen face. "You know I'm okay with me and Brandon not bein' together. And I need you guys to be okay with it too."

"Course, Trinity, you're my girl. And you're right. We don't need men. But they do make it more fun. Besides, when Marcus and I broke up, you were our cheerleader. I just want to be that for you."

"You and Marcus are different. If you were five years down the road and he was showin' no commitment to marriage, then mi would say kick dat brother to the curb. Men show love by bein' able to make a commitment, and mi definitely not feelin' de love from Brandon."

"Hey, guys," Peggy stated, entering the kitchen. "Sorry about this latest setback, but I gotta be honest," she replied, joining them at the table. "This publicity is bad, and without the funds to counter it, it may be time to hang it up or at least move to a new location."

"I can't move!" Savannah shrieked. "If this doesn't work, it's over."

"Are you sayin' there's nothin' we can do?" Trinity asked, looking directly at Peggy.

"I wish I could do more," Peggy was saying when the doorbell rang again.

"I wonder who that is," Savannah stated. "Maybe it's someone selling something. I'll get it." When Savannah returned, it was with a visitor. "Peggy, it's for you. He says he's a colleague of yours."

Surprised, Peggy turned to see Jamie. "It's Jamie Parker, one of our PR guys," Peggy said, introducing the tall, blond, lanky Caucasian man. "What are you doing here?"

"Saving your butt. I tried calling you but couldn't get through. I heard about your dilemma, but all I saw was an opportunity. I've tentatively scheduled Restoration to appear on *Good Morning, World.*

"Shut up!" Cara squealed.

"With that kind of international exposure, I'd say your troubles are over."

"Blouse and skirt!" Trinity squeaked.

"It's for this Friday. I know that's quick, but you have to strike while the iron's hot. Now, you can still say no; either you or the show could cancel. But I know they're not going to pass this up. We just need a hook to keep them on the line."

"We have the perfect hook," Cara said excitedly. "The woman whose skeleton we found is a Jamaican hero. She sparked the slave rebellion of 1832, and she's written these diaries that read like an autobiography explaining everything and—"

"Cara!" Savannah yelled.

"Oops! I forgot. We were supposed to be keepin' it a secret."

"What's she talking about?" Jamie asked.

Giving Cara a disparaging look, Savannah explained. "We found diaries in the same room with the skeleton. Peggy knows. Cara let it slip to Peggy too." Savannah watched as Peggy squirmed in her seat from that disclosure. "The diaries suggest that Ruby Lee may have played a pivotal role in the Jamaican slave rebellion."

"That's incredible. Have you had the diaries authenticated?"

"No, but they were in a sealed room. And the police did confirm that the skeleton was a mulatto woman," Savannah replied. "Here, I'll show you," and then, she left to get the diaries.

"Jamie," Peggy said, turning to him. "I don't know what to say."

"You don't need to say anything. We gotta look out for each other— right, kid? You always come to me when there's a problem. I don't know why you didn't do that this time."

"When they told me the Carapones were behind this, I thought it was hopeless. By reputation, the Carapones are unbeatable. Thank goodness you had my back on this one," Peggy stated, smiling, but internally she was fuming. He was definitely going to hear about this later. He'd made her look bad in front of the client, and in advertising, image was everything.

"Well, Cara—I got your name right, didn't I?" Jamie asked. When she nodded, he continued, "That's quite the hook. Everyone's going to want to come here. You'll be booked for years."

Savannah reentered carrying three large books. She then showed them to Peggy and Jamie, who were amazed as they skimmed them.

"If you can get them authenticated, these books could make you a fortune," Jamie noted.

"Oh, I'd never sell them."

"You wouldn't have to sell them. You could rent them to museums and other historical organizations. But with these babies, I'm pretty sure we're on for *Good Morning, World*. Do I have permission to go ahead with this story?"

"I don't know," Savannah responded hesitantly. "I'm not sure it's smart to tell the whole world. Someone might steal them, like the Carapones."

"You're right. If this story goes public, you should keep the diaries in a safe place," Jamie concurred. "But I'm telling you, this is the story to bring people into this place. And a simple lure is all you need because once inside, they'll be in love. You've done an incredible job. That chandelier, the colors—when you walk in here, you feel like you've been transported to some royal paradise. You add in that historical piece, and you're going to be laughing all the way to the bank."

"He's right, Savannah," Trinity said, agreeing. "This is a great opportunity to put Restoration on the map. And Ruby Lee's story should be shared."

"I guess." Savannah sighed. "But me on TV, that's completely out of my comfort zone."

"It wouldn't be just you. It would be all of you guys," Jamie pointed out. "Maybe you could have one spokesperson."

"I nominate Cara," Trinity interjected. "She's cute, bubbly, and would make a great spokesperson. That is if Savannah doesn't mind."

"Mind—please, it would be a relief."

"Thanks, guys. I've always wanted to be on TV. You know I got an A in my speech class. Not sure if that qualifies me."

"Believe me, it qualifies you," Savannah confirmed.

"Good," Jamie responded, pleased. "I'll set this up, but I'll need you to sign the paperwork authorizing me to represent you. It includes my fee, which is standard for the industry."

"If you can get us on *Good Morning, World*, I don't care what your fee is." Savannah laughed. "I can't believe it. Our work showcased on a world stage, and now that I don't have to be the spokesperson, I'm hyped!"

"This turned out better than expected, huh? You ladies are so lucky," Peggy joined in, preparing to leave with Jamie.

"We prefer blessed," Cara added. "By the way, where's your assistant?"

"Oh, I had to let her go. Nice girl, but she's got a lot to learn. In fact, it was only after I fired her that I learned that she'd been fired from Orion. You guys met her at the restaurant. Did you have any problems?"

"I think we're the ones who got her fired," Cara confessed. "She had such a bad attitude, but when I pointed that out ... well ... let's just say that she didn't like the feedback. Her management heard about the altercation and another incident that had occurred that same night, and that was the end of the road for her."

"I had no idea. And then I show up with her at the initial meet and greet. I'm so sorry. It gets worse. I believe Vanessa may've been the one who told the papers about the skeleton. As my assistant, I mentioned it to her, but I specifically told her not to say a word."

"You did what?" Cara said, enraged. "I trusted you!"

"Like I trusted Vanessa, but I didn't know about the bad blood. I fired her just because my gut told me she was up to no good. I love what you're doing here. There's no way I'm going to intentionally jeopardize that."

"No point crying over spilled milk now," Savannah jumped in. "Like you said, you didn't know, and there's no harm done. And even if there was, you've definitely turned it around. C'mon, I'll see you guys out."

When the three of them left, Cara turned to Trinity. "Who is this Vanessa? Some spawn of Satan?" Slumping down in her chair, she admitted, "I don't know what happened. First, I let stuff slip to Peggy and then Jamie. And now, I've let Vanessa the vampire hurt us. I'm hopeless. And I think your cookies are burnin'."

"Oh no!" Jumping up, Trinity grabbed a potholder. "They're not burned," she stated, pulling them out of the oven. "They're golden brown just like I like 'em," she said, placing the pan on top of the stove.

"We don't even know how Ruby's story ends," Cara said, still whining.

"Which is why we need to finish the diaries before our interview on Friday," Trinity suggested, inhaling the smell of her cinnamon cookies. "We can munch on cookies while hearin' about Ruby. Consider it prep for the show." Blowing on a cookie to cool it down, she took a bite and smiled. "Yep, they're good. I've done it again—created the perfect cookie."

"Can I have one? So you don't have to be the only one givin' yourself praise?"

"Don't leave me out and only give one to blabber mouth over there," Savannah said, reentering the kitchen.

"Savannah, I'm so sorry. I don't know what happened," Cara started rambling.

"I'm kidding," Savannah said, smiling. "It's fine. Really, I'm okay. I told Peggy that too. I'm actually glad that Ruby's story's gonna get out. It should be told, although I seriously think that Vanessa needs to be in somebody's asylum." After blowing on a cookie, she took a bite. "This cookie's awesome. It's hot but good."

"Thank you." Trinity beamed. "Cara and I thought they'd be good for story hour."

"Story hour?"

"We should finish the diaries before Friday. We need to know how the story ends. Think of it as prep for the interview. Besides, I want no distraction when my kitchen appliances come in. After that, you won't be able to pry me out of this kitchen."

"Oh I forgot," Savannah said. "The appliance store called, and they're still backlogged. The appliances won't be in for another two months. They were thinking the end of November."

"November! No fair! That's too close to the openin'! This is killin' my dream!"

"Not killing, just postponing," Savannah clarified. "Besides, given what's happening, I'm beginning to believe that we're gonna have the best opening ever. Your appliances will be here, the Carapones will go away, and we'll be rich because everyone in the world will be trying to come to Restoration to hear about Ruby!"

"Somebody pinch me," Cara stated, looking over at Savannah. "I know that's not Ms. Pessimistic talkin'," she replied, laughing, and everyone else joined in.

"Am I'm interruptin'?" Jacob said, coming in. "Were you sharin' some juicy gossip again?" He stopped when he saw the cookies. "Those look good. Can I have one?"

"I should say no," Trinity said, passing him the pan. "Especially since you think so little of us. Do you honestly think that's all females do is gossip?"

"Pretty much, and when the men folk aren't around, then it's usually about us. But when you're beautiful and you make cookies that taste this good, you can do just about anything you want," he said, chomping on a cookie.

"Nice comeback, pretty boy, but you need to respect the new stars in the house."

"Stars?"

"Yep, big stars since we're going to be on *Good Morning, World*," Cara piped up.

"No kiddin'!"

"It's true. Vanessa tried to dis us on national TV, but it backfired. Now, we're gonna get to tell our side of the story. Our PR guy, Jamie, seems to think this is gonna send our business through the roof. It's the Joseph effect at work again."

"The Joseph effect?"

"Yeah, Cara, I don't understand either," Savannah jumped in. "Joseph is about people running away—right, Jacob?"

"What's your Joseph effect, Cara?" he asked, ignoring Savannah.

"Joseph was sold into slavery by his brothers, and then all of these horrible things started happenin'. But because of that, he became one of the biggest leaders in the land. His brothers ended up beggin' for food, leading to his iconic phrase, 'What you meant as evil, God used for good.' That's what happened here. Vanessa meant to help the Carapones put us out of business, but God put the Joseph effect on them. And instead of putting us out of business, they're actually growin' it."

"I get it," Jacob said, laughing. "You've an interestin' way of interpretin' scripture."

"I keep tellin' y'all that my interpretations may not be perfect cause I'm still learnin'. Anyway, we were about to finish reading the diaries. We want to know what happens to Ruby before our interview on Friday. You want to join us?"

"Can't. I've actually accepted another job that starts tomorrow. I was hopin' to get as much done today as I can. I want to be confident that things run smoothly in my absence."

"You're leaving," Savannah pouted. "Another job is now taking precedence over me."

"Nothin' could ever take precedence over you," he said, winking at her. "I'm not leavin' you," he clarified. "I'm leavin' as site manager because your job's basically done—at least from a construction standpoint. In fact, I think my guys will be out of here by Friday, apparently just in time." Pulling Savannah into his arms, he added, "But I do like the fact that I'll be missed."

"You two have surpassed my nausea level," Trinity complained. "And besides, everything you just said was hogwash."

"How's it hogwash?" Jacob looked at her, confused.

"Are you the boss?" she taunted him.

"I'm the boss, but I have to set a good example for the men."

"I agree," Cara chimed in. "Sounds like hogwash to me too."

"Obviously, there's no winnin' with you two. Okay, I'll join your story hour, but can we at least move it to a backroom? I don't want my crew to see me slackin' off."

"Works for me," Cara quickly answered before he changed his mind. "We'll reconvene in Savannah's room in five."

Chapter Twenty-Five

December 1831

Haggerty kept his word. Ruby now stayed in a house he owned with Bell as a companion. Ruby spent her days reading, cooking, cleaning, and caring for the most beautiful baby boy—hers. "Shush, child, no need to make all that fuss. Mama's right here. I'm not going anywhere," she said, holding him in her arms.

It was as if little Billy understood because he stopped crying. But after a while, he started fussing again, signaling it was time to eat. She nursed him and then placed him on a quilt, but that didn't last long. "You little blue-eyed devil … you knew I wanted you to stay on that quilt!"

"Why, when he's a free spirit like his mama," Haggerty stated, coming in laughing.

"Charles," Ruby stated, turning to see him and Bell standing in the doorway. "Look, Billy. Your daddy's here."

"And I come bearing gifts," he announced, handing her a brown paper package.

"A present for me," she said excitedly. "What is it?" she asked, examining it. "Too big to be a book."

"I can give things beside books," he stated grumpily.

"Oh, I didn't mean anything by that," she quickly assured him. "I love the books that you bring me. They're my world." Staying at the house had changed their relationship. They were no longer master and slave. They were friends. Now she could freely discuss the books she read, although Haggerty usually wanted very little to do with the Bible, which was now her favorite book. Based on her studies, she no longer saw God as the white man's God.

"Don't just stand there. Open it," he urged her.

Ruby quickly tore at the paper. Gasping, she pulled out the most beautiful yellow dress with buttons, flowers, and embroidery—not a dress for a slave, which was confirmed when Haggerty started laughing.

"You know I nearly got beat up by Ernestine," he said, still laughing. "I ordered that dress from the general store, and Suella, the store clerk, thought that it was for Ernestine and told her so. For the last couple of weeks, she's been acting real nice. I had to do a lot of covering up when she kept waiting and nothing happened."

Ruby laughed too, even though she wondered how Suella could have ever thought that Ernestine could fit into a dress that small. "Why buy me such a pretty dress when I never leave the house? No one will ever see it," she said, pointing out the impracticality.

"Because you deserve a dress like this, and I deserve to see you in a dress like this. And I've got another surprise," he said with a twinkle in his eyes. "I've got a trusted friend who paints, and I want him to paint a picture of you in that dress."

"Charles, no!" Then seeing his disappointment, she tried to explain her reticence. "It's just that ... we've been so careful. How do you know you can trust this painter?"

"He's my best friend, even saved my life once. You can't get more loyal than that."

"I don't know," she said. "I really like this world that you've created for me. I just can't go back to that secret room or to Ernestine."

"That's not going to happen," he assured her, lighting his pipe. "But I need a picture to put in my private study. I can't get out here as much as I would like, and I want to be able to see you at any time. And I thought that you would look lovely in yellow."

"I do love it," she said, looking at the dress again. "And if you trust this guy, then I guess I should too." Just then, Billy caught her eye. "Come see Billy trying to pull up," she said, motioning Haggerty over. "I haven't been around many babies, but our baby seems really smart. Bell said so too, and she's been caring for babies for forever."

"You're looking happier these days," Haggerty said, going over to the baby. "You're happy aren't you, Ruby?"

"I'm content, which is more than I expected being a slave."

"You're not a slave—at least not while you're here," he said, gently caressing her face.

Putting her hand over his, she smiled again. "Bell's a slave, isn't she?" Ruby asked, looking over at Bell, who was cooking at the stove, not listening to them.

"But Bell's different. Being a slave is all she knows."

"How can I consider myself free when the people around me aren't?"

"Well, neither you nor I can do anything about that," he said. "Now, why don't you go put that dress on? I'll look out for Billy," he stated, reaching down to pick up the baby who seemed happy to see him.

The dress was definitely lovely with a high collar made of white lace that came down to the shoulders. There were large puffy sleeves at the top, but the end of the sleeve from the elbow to the wrist was made of white lace that fit snuggly around her arm. The softest and prettiest yellow fabric was on the bodice, and a beautiful white satin sash cinched the waist, emphasizing the bottom of the large skirt that had appliquéd flowers.

Even with just a small broken mirror to view her image, she liked what she saw. Pushing her shoulders back, she stood as tall as she could. Still, it was hard to imagine such a dress belonging to her. Touching the pearl buttons that were on the sleeve, she admired the intricate pleating on the bodice. Haggerty had brought her an underskirt to make the dress billow out. Spinning around, she felt like a flower. She recalled Luke 12:27. "Consider how the lilies grow. They do not labor or spin. Yet I tell you, not even Solomon in all his splendor was dressed like one of these."

When she stepped out of the room, she took both Haggerty and Bell by surprise. While Ruby didn't have the best view in her small broken mirror, there was no denying the admiration that came from Haggerty.

"You look insanely beautiful." Coming over, he kissed her. "Turn around and let me see you." With perfect grace and beauty, Ruby slowly turned, like a princess used to being gawked at in fabulous frocks.

"I'se believes I's dun seen an angel," Bell exclaimed in her broken English.

"Wow, I'm starting to see why I'm here," a man announced, walking in. Seeing Ruby's frightened expression, he quickly explained. "I saw Charles's buggy outside and thought it would be all right to come in."

"Jacque, so glad you could make it," Haggerty intervened. "This is Ruby Lee. Ruby, this is Jacque Milan, your painter."

"Nice to meet you, Mister Milan sir," she stated, transitioning into slave mode.

"The pleasure is all mine," Jacque stated, kissing her hand.

"Ruby, I filled Jacque in about you, so you can be the same way with him as you are with me. I mean … with respect to not having to pretend to be a slave," he clarified. "Jacque, are you here to work? I don't see any painting supplies."

"They're in the wagon," Jacque said, still staring at Ruby. "I'll bring them in, if that's all right."

"Yeah, the sooner you get started, the sooner you can be finished," Haggerty said, slapping Jacque on the back. "I'm really looking forward to this portrait. I'll help you carry your materials in." He then handed the baby to Bell. "You stay with Bell," he told the baby. "'Cause we don't want you throwing up on your momma before her picture's been painted."

"I can't believe this!" Ruby exclaimed when the men left. "First this dress, and now a painting. It's too much to take in."

Bell smiled. "I'm 'appy fer you. Good to sees yous smile. Dis one got you so busy always movin' roun'," she replied, looking down at the baby. "Gonna take 'im out. Let yous git your picture painted in peace." And with that, Bell skirted out as the men came in, carrying the painting supplies.

"I'm gonna leave you to your work," Haggerty said, after he laid down the last of the supplies. "I'll check in on you later." Before leaving, he kissed Ruby lightly on the lips, intentionally marking his territory.

"Where do you think we should do this little project?" Jacque asked once Haggerty left.

"I don't know. That sounds like something that you'd be the expert at deciding."

"I love a woman who's willing to take direction."

"Oh," she said, after thinking a moment. "It might work well on the back porch, for pretty surroundings, and the light would be better than in the house."

"I love a woman who knows what she wants." Then looking over at her, he asked, "Are you sensing a pattern?"

"You love women?"

Letting out a hearty laugh, he said, "You know, I like you. I was going to say that I'm an agreeable gent, but I like your pattern better. Shall we get started?" he asked, bowing before her, allowing her to lead him to the porch.

Sitting still was hard for Ruby, but getting used to Jacque was easy. Over the next few weeks, they talked about history, literature, and society at large. Apparently, Haggerty had shared that she was well read. And so Jacque didn't hold back in starting some provocative conversations. And she loved it. To have someone to converse with, to argue with, and to laugh with was unbelievable. He reminded her of Jack, except he wasn't as handsome.

Jacque was tall and lanky, and he kept his dark brown, straight hair a little too long so that it fell into his eyes. So much so that she wondered if he could see well enough to paint her portrait. But what he lacked in looks, he definitely made up for in charm, making her wonder what type of woman he attracted. From what she had seen, he probably had all of them swooning. For the first time, Jacque had her wondering what it would be like to be a white woman. To look at a man, find him interesting, and then to send out cues, signaling that it was safe to approach. It was what she missed most—love, on her own terms.

"You're awfully quiet today," Jacque stated, noticing her serious face.

"Just thinking what it would be like to live under different circumstances."

"It kills me that you have to live this way. When Charles first told me about moving you here, I thought he was crazy. Then after meeting you, I realized that he would've been crazy if he hadn't stepped in. You guys are risking a lot, but then you've got no choice." Seeing her squirming, he added, "Now, there you go moving around."

"Sorry," she apologized. "But I never thought about what Charles was risking."

"He's risking a lot, and so are you," he reminded her. "Ernestine can be quite vengeful," he warned her. "I used to wonder why Charles wanted a painting of you. To me, it was just asking for trouble. Then I met you, and I understood. You were meant to be painted ... preserved. I'm just lucky that I'm the one that gets to do it."

"You are always full of compliments."

"Which will be coming to an end," he said, packing his supplies. "I think one more session, and I'll have what I need. Then I'll finish everything at my place." Draping a covering over the picture, he started collecting his brushes.

"Isn't it time for a peek?" she asked, moving closer.

"Absolutely not!" Then looking at her suspiciously, he added, "You haven't peeked already, have you?"

"No, I haven't," she assured him. "I just thought that by now …"

"Don't even think about it," he stated sternly. "I promise it won't be long, and then I will unveil the masterpiece."

"And then what?"

"What do you mean?"

Dropping her eyes, she moved away from him before speaking. "Will you still visit?" she asked hesitantly. Then gaining more courage, she turned to face him. "Will we still have the opportunity to have our discussions? I love talking about the Bible. You bring such insights."

Smiling, he intentionally moved toward Ruby. "I wish I could. Unfortunately, there's one thing that I've learned about men folk," he said, now close enough to touch her but intentionally refraining. "It's that you don't mess with their women folk."

"Oh, I didn't mean it that way," she stated, now embarrassed.

"I know you didn't," he said, moving away from her to finish collecting his painting supplies. "But that's how Charles would see it. Now, I've got a purpose. After that, anytime I showed up, it would be suspect. But I do have a great book that I think you'll enjoy. It's where a lot of my ideas come from about the Bible. I'll bring it to our final session."

"That would be great," she responded, hiding her disappointment as he grabbed his stuff and sauntered to the door. Standing in the doorway, she watched him climb into his wagon and grab the reins. The horses responded without hesitation, whisking him away, and immediately, she missed him.

Walking back to the porch, she found herself staring at the sheet-covered canvas. It seemed strange that after so many sessions she still couldn't see it. She longed to take a peek, but she had given her word.

"Chile, what you doin' out 'ere. Time to eat 'cause 'fer you know it dat baby gonna be cryin for 'is food."

"Bell, what do you think my painting looks like?"

"I dunno. Probably looks good. He sho' been workin' 'ard on it."

"You think I should take a peek, even though I said I wouldn't?"

"Nah, yous should keeps your word."

"But, Bell, you could lift the cover since you didn't give your word."

"Dat's smart, Ruby … I sho' could do dat. Yous wants me to?"

Ruby nodded her head yes, and Bell lifted the sheet. When Ruby saw it, she was unimpressed. It wasn't that the picture was bad. It just didn't look like her. She recognized the dress and the porch but not herself.

"To me, it don't look dat much like yous," Bell concluded. "Maybe he didn't sees you wid all dat 'air in 'is face."

"Bell, I think you're right. If he's going to keep painting, he should consider a haircut. You can cover it back up. I don't want to see it anymore. Let's eat."

It was a couple of days before Jacque returned for the final session, and he was in rare form. He talked nonstop, told jokes, and even sang. Ruby didn't think she had laughed so much in her whole life. But the laughter didn't last. It seemed like the shortest session ever. Watching him packing up for the final time, she was filled with remorse. She was truly going to miss him, although she did wonder how he made it as a painter. "The people around here, do they consider you a good painter?"

"I do well enough," he said, being modest. "I keep a roof over my head and food in my belly. Why?" But before she could answer, he asked, "Did you peek?" Putting down his brushes, he walked toward her. "I can tell by your guilty smile that you did," he said, holding her hostage against the wall, his hand slipping around her waist. "Madam, do you have a defense?"

"It was Bell who looked. I just happened to be there."

Bringing her even closer, he asked, "Did you instruct Bell to do it?"

"I can't seem to recall," Ruby said, laughing.

"Convenient amnesia—is that what you're going for?" She was so lovely. He felt the need in him rise up. "Why do I have to be such a good friend?" He sighed and then released her.

She was surprised by the shiver that ran down her spine when he had pulled her close. It had been such a long time since a man had made her feel like a woman. For despite Charles's wishes, she felt like a slave. But in Jacque's eyes, she saw desire, and she knew that he had wanted to kiss her, and in a different time and place, she might have let him, and maybe she would even have kissed him back. In this world, however, that was not an option. "I liked the picture," she said, changing the subject. "It just didn't look like me."

"That's because it's not finished. When I'm here, I'm putting down the structure, the bones of the picture. But it's the small details that make the picture you, and I do that back at my place without witnesses. I work until it's perfect. Don't you worry. When you see the final product, you will not be disappointed. I promise," he said, coming over and kissing her on the forehead. "Next time I see you, it'll be with the finished painting."

It was three weeks before Jacque returned, and this time he came with Haggerty. Ruby was excited, although she wasn't sure that she should be. Deciding to be optimistic, she held her breath as he unveiled it.

Haggerty's face also showed his anticipation, but she could read nothing in Jacque's. And her expectations grew as he took his time unveiling the canvas. When the portrait was finally revealed, she was in shock. It was nothing like the picture she had seen earlier. It was just like her, or at least the woman she had always wanted to be—happy, young, and full of life. It had all kinds of details—the kind of details that made it not just a picture but made it her.

"Jacque, you did it!" Haggerty exploded in delight. "You captured her! I've never seen Ruby like this—young, vibrant, carefree, and laughing. Ruby doesn't laugh."

"You're telling me," Jacque agreed. "I had to work hard, saying and doing all kinds of bizarre things to get those expressions out of her."

"So you were just goading me for the picture?" she asked, remembering his antics. "Well," she laughed, "it worked."

"In this picture, you look like you crossed over from contentment to happiness," Haggerty stated, winking at Ruby.

"I think you're right." She smiled back at him.

"Yous beautiful." Bell smiled, and even Billy seemed to coo when he saw the picture.

"Thank you, Bell and Jacque," Ruby replied with a full heart. "I've never had my picture painted. Charles, thanks for setting all this up and for the dress."

"It was definitely done with my interests in mind," he stated and then leaned over and whispered in her ear, "Now I can see you whenever I want."

"But can't I keep it for a little while … please! I've never had a painting before. I just want to take some time to stare at it."

"I guess, for a little while," he said, kissing her. "I gotta get back, but I brought you these," he said, pulling out the rosebuds he had been hiding. "Your favorite flowers. I never forgot that you told me you liked them because they remind you of fresh starts. This is like a fresh start for us."

"Thank you, Charles." Instantly, her heart lifted, not from the rosebuds, although she loved them, and Haggerty, for bringing them, but it was from the hope that Jacque might stay once Haggerty left. She wanted to thank

Jacque alone. Perhaps this time she might have the courage to kiss him. But her hopes were quickly dashed.

"Coming, Jacque?" Haggerty asked. "I've got your payment and some things I want to discuss with you."

Sadly, Ruby watched them leave. Having caught Jacque's eye, she figured he had wanted to stay too. Her heart broke watching them get into Haggerty's wagon, but it was for the best. *Ruby, you're a slave, and Jacque is out of reach*, she told herself. Then she noticed three books that had been left on the table—commentaries on the Bible. She smiled—at least one part of Jacque would remain.

Chapter Twenty-Six

Savannah's Time Period

"Why'd you stop?" Cara and Trinity asked in unison.

"Phone's vibrating. It's Peggy," Savannah explained, grabbing her phone. "I'd better take this." Not getting the best reception, she stepped outside.

"Aw, man," Cara grumbled. "I was all into Ruby's story."

"I know. I loved Jacque," Trinity admitted. "He's romantic in a dismissive sort of way."

"Women," Jacob smirked.

"So, you're tellin' me you weren't into the story?"

"The story's good. I just didn't need a tissue every two minutes like you two."

"Whatever," Trinity said, giving him the hand. "Point is I don't wanna work. I wanna keep readin'."

"Maybe we won't get picked up by *Good Morning, World*," Cara offered. "And then we could keep readin'."

"Fat chance," Trinity replied. "This is the story of a lifetime. GMW is not passing this up."

"If you get the interview, then you should definitely serve these cookies," Jacob suggested, munching on one. "You should also give them to your guests when you open."

"Jacob, you're a genius!" Trinity said, leaning over and kissing his forehead. "That's a great idea. It's a recipe from my grandma, and you're right. It's perfect for when you're feeling a little frazzled—a nice pick-me-up that's not too sweet. I could probably get some cute bags to put them in," she said excitedly. "Okay, I'm back. We'll have to pick up with Ruby after our TV debut. I was hopin' to finish before Friday, but it doesn't look like we'll have the time."

"Well, I'm not back," Cara moaned, still lounging on the bed. "My heart's still with Ruby. At least now we know how a slave got her portrait painted. I can't wait to see it."

"There's a portrait?" Jacob asked, standing up and stretching.

"Savannah found a portrait in the secret room, which she sent off to the States to have restored. She didn't tell you?"

"Maybe because no one was supposed to know," Trinity reminded Cara.

"But Savannah told about the diaries," Cara said. "I just assumed the secrecy thing was over," she rambled on. Looking over at Jacob, she saw his sullen face. "I'm sure she's gonna tell you."

"No worries," he said dismissively. "I gotta go."

Cara watched him slink out of the room. "Savannah's gonna kill me! What's wrong with me? Why do I keep lettin' things slip?"

"Technically, it's not your fault. It's Savannah's. She continues to build these walls to keep Jacob out. I know he's Jacob the Understanding, but he's a man. Eventually, he's going to get tired of bein' pushed aside."

"Yeah, but she's been through so much."

"I'm just sayin', the victim thing only works for so long. What happened to her anyway?"

"Savannah hasn't told me a thing," Cara said, shaking her head. "But knowin' her like I do, I'm guessin' that it's nothin' serious. She probably got dumped. That's all it would take for her to stop trustin' men. Maybe your doctor will help."

"We're on for Friday," Savannah said, returning. "Jamie's coming over to walk us through the details. The GMW staff arrives on Thursday. They've asked to stay here. So, we'll have our first guests."

"Will they need dinner or breakfast?" Trinity asked.

"I'd plan on it. Oh, you guys, it's really happening. Soon the whole world will know about Restoration." Sitting on the edge of the bed, she sighed happily. "It's so surreal. I think I'm going to faint."

"No time for that, honey," Trinity reminded her. "We've got work to do. You need to decide which rooms they'll stay in, get linens and everything else that they'll need."

"You're right, which means we're going to have to stop reading," Savannah said, looking at them sadly. "Besides, Jacob already headed out."

"Did Jacob say anythin'?" Cara asked.

"Not really. He just waved good-bye. Why?"

"No reason," Trinity broke in. "She's just being nosey." Then Trinity gave Cara a look to shut her up. "Okay, chop, chop, everybody. Didn't you say Jamie would be here soon?"

"All right, everyone in the kitchen when Jamie comes," Savannah stated, heading out.

When Savannah left the room, Cara whispered to Trinity, "You don't think I should tell her about what happened?"

"You can. Just not until after the interview. You know how Savannah obsesses. Right now, it's best to have her obsessin' over Restoration."

"Good point."

When the GMW team arrived, Savannah was a bundle of nerves. Although she had made a list and crossed everything off, she still felt like something was left undone. Despite her apprehensions, the night went smoothly. As hoped, both the reporter and the cameraman gasped when they entered. Trinity cooked a scrumptious dinner, which she served in the dining room, using her own china because the dishes for Refresh hadn't come in. Savannah selected two rooms with the nicest view and handpicked the bed linen and towels. She even procured fancy soaps and lotions. She was nervous and excited to have their first guests.

"How'd you sleep?" Savannah asked, the next morning when the reporter entered the lobby.

"Fabulously," Margo Shantz responded.

Margo was everything that Savannah imagined a TV reporter would be. She was tall and thin, and her red hair set off her brown designer pantsuit and complemented her porcelain skin.

"You guys certainly have a jewel here," Margo said, admiringly. "I thought that this place was something last night, but when the sun came up, it became a whole new wonder. You're going to make a mint here. We've already gotten some good footage. When people see this place, they're going to be flocking to your doors."

"You think so? I must tell you that I'm a little nervous."

"No need to be. You're in good hands. It's not a live piece, so we can take our time—get things right. It'll be fun. I think your segment's scheduled to air on Monday's show," Margo explained. Still seeing Savannah's nerves, Margo added, "Really you can trust me. You sold me on this place last night. I'm going to make it—and you—look incredible." When Cara and Trinity walked up, Margo immediately included them in the conversation. "I was just telling Savannah that you guys have a gold mine here."

"Cara will be our spokeswoman for the interview," Savannah threw in.

"Sounds good."

"I'll be the spokesperson to an extent. If there are questions about designs, then I'm turnin' it over to Savannah, and only Trinity can talk about the delicious dishes that she creates. But I can definitely talk about Ruby."

"I thought you were going to do everything," Savannah stated with alarm.

"Cara's right," Margo jumped in. "Part of the charm of this place is you three. You each light up when you're talking about your respective parts. Don't worry. You'll be fine."

And she was right. After about two hours, they were done, and there were very few retakes. Even Savannah was surprised at how comfortable she felt explaining her designs and the inspirations behind them. Trinity was required to pack a food-to-go bag, and Cara was overjoyed because Margo bought a dress.

—⟫⟫—

On Monday, they all sat glued in front of a fifty-eight-inch flat-screen TV that the guys had pushed into the kitchen. When the segment was over, Cara announced, "I'm available to take autographs now."

"I'm glad to see this didn't go to your head," Marcus teased.

"Of course, it should go to my head. I'm an international star. Isn't *Good Morning, World* seen around the world?"

"Don't know, but it's a big deal no matter what," Jacob admitted.

"Which is why 'we' guys have decided to treat 'you women' to a night out," Brandon announced grandly. "Initially, I was against this little project because of the Carapones, but given the publicity, the Carapones will be forced to give up. And that's why 'we,'" he said, pointing to himself, Jacob, and Marcus, "wanted to take you out."

"To Orion?" Trinity asked excitedly.

"Sorry, babe, I don't roll that way anymore. I'm back at the firm, not back in the fold." Raising his eyebrows, he added, "Which proves you're hooked on the firm perks."

"No. I just wanted to go before Refresh becomes so popular that I don't have time to visit other restaurants."

"Right," Brandon replied sarcastically. "Your humility is overwhelmin'."

"Mi dream big. Mi don't deny it. And mi dream about you certainly came true—you goin' to church wid mi. That felt good."

"Here, here, man. I agree. Props for comin' back to church," Jacob added.

"Okay, don't start harassin' me. Let's just keep it cool," Brandon replied, blushing.

"Oh hush up," Trinity interjected. "You ought to be glad that somebody is interested in your soul. Besides, this is our moment of glory, not yours. I only raised the church thing because everythin' that has happened makes me realize that I'm ready for the next step—mi tinkin' 'bout havin' some picknies. Family—the whole works."

"I know," Cara jumped in. "Restorin' this house has put me in the family mood too."

"That's our cue," Marcus laughed, getting up from his chair. "It's getting too dangerous up in here."

"What about you, Savannah? Any family urges?" Jacob asked.

"Me? Oh no! Too overwhelmed," Savannah answered. "Unlike my partners, I'm not ready for marriage and family."

"Jacob, man, how'd you get so lucky not to be on the female clock?" Brandon joked.

"Forget you, Brandon," Trinity pouted.

"I was only kidding, boo," he stated, pulling her into a hug. "I have to go. I've got a potential client coming in. So, I'll make it up to you tonight. I promise."

"Yeah, tonight you guys will love us again," Marcus assured them. "I've got to hit the road too," he said, kissing Cara before grabbing his suit jacket.

"Me too. New job site," Jacob explained before heading toward the door.

"Jacob? Aren't you forgetting something?" Savannah asked.

Stopping, he looked around. Patting his pants for his keys, he answered, "No. I got everything." He looked at her, confused.

"You forgot this," she stated, throwing her arms around him and giving him a steamy kiss. Feeling his body respond gave her a sense of power.

"Yeah, I guess I was missin' that," he said, with a smile.

"Okay, you guys win couple of the year," Brandon stated, patting Jacob on the back.

"Yeah, way to go, dude," Marcus seconded, slapping him on the back as well. "I mean, how can the rest of us compete?"

"I gotta go. I wish I didn't," Jacob said with regret before stealing another kiss.

"Oh, get a room," Cara hollered, and then started laughing, "Oh I forgot, you've got forty of them."

"Corny," Savannah replied, giving Cara a grim look while waving good-bye to Jacob.

"And you're so horny." She laughed once Jacob was out of earshot. "What was that all about?"

"She was savin' her man." Trinity laughed. "Didn't you see Jacob's face fall when Ms. Heartless was like, 'I'm too overwhelmed to think about marriage, Prince Charming'?"

"You guys are cruel. I didn't mean it that way. It just came out wrong."

"Sweetie, I'm tellin' you," Trinity stated, in a motherly tone, "you're playing a dangerous game. Unlike the fools we're datin', you actually have one that likes the whole home-life thing, and you're actin' like a nun in a nunnery."

"I'm not that bad."

"Yeah, you are, but you've been warned. But on another note, we should take the day off. Have a beauty day to get ready for our dates."

"Trinity, do you even go to work anymore?" Cara asked.

"Yeah, I do, which is why I need a day off, since I've been working two jobs."

"Well, I'm on board," Cara said, "but Savannah's always a hard one to convince."

"Actually, I'm on board too. Makes sense to take a vacation before the real work begins. In the next several weeks, Trinity's appliances come in, and I need to interview for our open positions. Speaking of which, you'll never guess who applied for the front office clerk." Too excited to wait, she answered, "Vanessa."

"Vanessa!" Cara shrieked. "In addition to the skeleton leak, we can't even rule out the swingin' doll. Just how quickly did you trash her application and have a good laugh?"

"That was going to be my response, until Jacob told me that Vanessa is Alice's oldest daughter."

"No way! You mean, Alice who works at the villa?" Cara said in shock. "But how's that possible? Alice is so nice. How did she produce a devil child?"

"I have no idea, but now I feel I have to hire Vanessa. After all, we did play a role in all of her firings. Maybe she just needs the special touch of Restoration. And you're the one always quoting that with God nothing's impossible."

"Fine," Cara snapped. "I just hope Vanessa the Villain doesn't burn the place down before she gets restored."

"What about your preopening fashion show?" Savannah said, thinking it best to change the subject.

"I'm pretty far along. I just need to talk to Trinity about what we're eatin'."

"I'm on it. I'm thinkin' of some cool appetizers."

"I'm thinking that we should sell tickets to offset the cost," Savannah suggested. "We could include a tour of the hotel. Cara, you could give away an outfit. And, Trinity, you could give away a catered dinner. That way we can charge about $150 or more because we'll need to pay for security."

"Why, when we're dating three good-looking, hunky men?" Trinity asked. "But I love all the other ideas, and I say we get started on them first thing tomorrow. Today should be for us. How about we start with a swim?"

"You're on," Savannah stated, but then she stopped when her phone rang. "It's the Restoration line," she said excitedly. "Someone's calling!"

Grabbing her laptop, she pulled up the reservation database and booked a room. When she got off the phone, all three women screamed and hugged each other. It was official. They were in business. Then, as if on cue, the phone rang again. And again, it was the Restoration line, and everyone listened as Savannah gave out information.

"Enough," Trinity interjected when Savannah got off the phone this time. "Put a message to go to the website. This is proof that we need today because it may never come again."

Savannah didn't think she'd ever get used to the idea of the ocean being her back and front yards. And it felt so good just to take a moment to enjoy it. It was the perfect de-stressor.

"This view is priceless," Cara stated, dropping down beside Savannah on the sand. "It's like living a fairy tale."

"Well, speakin' of fairy tales, shouldn't we start getting ready for ours?" Trinity asked.

"How long does it take to get ready for dinner?" Cara asked.

"A long time when we're talkin' 'bout Orion," Trinity added.

"But we're not goin' to Orion," Cara grumbled.

"Oh but we are. I know Brandon, and I can always tell when he's lyin'. His eyebrows quiver. It's a dead giveaway."

"Why didn't you say somethin'?" Cara asked, sitting up excited.

"I thought it would be fun to surprise you guys."

"Unbelievable, we get to go back to Orion," Cara said excitedly. "Then you're right. We need to start gettin' ready. Last time, Brandon paid for us to go to a high-class salon. This time, we're on our own."

"Not exactly," Trinity said, smiling. "Have you seen what I can do with a flat iron?"

"I hope my yellow dress still fits," Savannah said, smiling at the thought of putting it back on.

"Yeah ... you could wear that," Cara agreed. "Or ... you could follow me back to my sewing room and wear a Cara original."

"Cara, really!" Trinity jumped up, screaming. "Your collection's finished. We've been dyin' to see it. You've been so secretive."

"I'm a perfectionist." Then, looking over at Savannah, Cara added, "I'm no different from you, Savannah. Except for the lobby, which you couldn't hide, you kept the rest of the rooms a secret until they were completely finished, even the side rooms where we're stayin'. But now I'm ready to unveil my line."

"You have enough gowns for all of us to wear one tonight?" Savannah asked.

"Yep. In fact, I've got six. So you can choose. Whatever dress you pick, I'll just make some quick alterations. Then that can be what you're modeling in the fashion show."

"Oh cool, we get to model," Trinity stated excitedly.

"I can't model!" Savannah said, panicking. "That's completely out of my comfort zone."

"Savannah, you're killin' me. You've been out of your comfort zone since we got to Jamaica," Cara said, shaking her head. "Here's the deal, either you model or we can spend money that we don't have to hire models."

"Okay, I'll model. Who'd have thought I'd be a property owner, an entrepreneur, and a high-fashion model? If I weren't living my life, even I wouldn't believe it," Savannah said, laughing. "So, is it time to go shopping?"

—⁓—

Cara beamed, watching her evening gowns being admired. As she hoped, Savannah and Trinity loved all of them. They had the hardest time making a selection. But because she knew which dress would be perfect for Savannah with her more slender frame, and which dress would make curvy Trinity stand out, she guided them to the right looks. For Savannah, she chose a teal, off-the-shoulder, goddess dress. For Trinity, Cara opted for a fitted lavender dress with a plunging V-neck. And for herself, she selected a gold embellished halter dress. Given her expert skills, it took only an hour before she had made the necessary adjustments.

"Okay, my turn," Trinity piped up. "Hair and makeup time," she announced. "Be prepared to be transformed." And then she marched them toward her room.

Three hours later, the women emerged looking stunning, and an hour later the guys arrived. The three women watched as the men provided their own personal fashion show by merely stepping out of the limo one by one. All of them were wearing tuxedos, but the tuxedos were all different. Jacob exited the limo first. He was wearing a well-tailored, classic, blue tone-on-tone patterned tuxedo with a thin, blue tie and white shirt. Brandon was next. He was wearing a more modern black tuxedo with an interestingly cut white vest, white shirt, and white tie combo. Marcus was the last to leave the limo. He was wearing a black classic tuxedo with a black and pink striped bow tie against a pink shirt. Each man looked like he had just stepped off the cover of some fashion magazine.

"Pinch me, somebody," Cara said, drooling. "Are we not the luckiest women in the world?"

"They look like the eye candy tonight, not us," Savannah pouted.

The men were just as mesmerized by their glamorized women. "Baby, you definitely know how to dress a woman," Marcus stated, taking Cara into his arms. "You did good, babe," he said, kissing her.

"Well, that's the best compliment that I've received all day."

"I guess we're just chopped liver, huh?" Trinity stated, with Savannah backing her up.

"No, but it's just special when your man notices," Cara said, smiling up at Marcus.

"Well, the bottom line is that we look amazin', and the people at Orion will think we're stars," Trinity added.

"I thought I told you that we weren't going to Orion," Brandon said, frowning.

"And I thought I told you to stop lyin' to me because I can always tell."

"Nothin' gets by you, huh?" He sighed. "Fine, let's go to Orion."

"Doesn't this evenin' just make you think of Psalm 37:4? 'Delight yourself in the Lord and he will give you the desires of your heart?' Course, if you ask me, God went way beyond the desires of my heart," Cara laughed.

Jacob laughed too. "Honestly, Cara, that text didn't come to mind, but now that you've said it, you're right on."

"One more thing would make this night complete—finishing Ruby's diaries," Savannah suggested.

"Then let's do it," Brandon responded. "We'll need to drop off the limo and pick up our cars first, and then we'll come back here and spend the evening with Ruby Lee."

"Okay, I heard the sarcasm, but what else can we do—since we're all on sexual diets?" Cara reminded him. "And Ruby's story is far better than anything on TV or video."

"Speak for yourself," Brandon said gruffly.

"What? You'd prefer TV or you're not on a sexual moratorium like the rest of us?"

"Shut up, Brandon," Trinity jumped in. "Oh my goodness, you talk too much. If you must know, we fell off the wagon three weeks ago," she confessed. "But the point is that we got back on. So, he who is without sin, let him cast the first stone."

"We're not judgin'," Cara responded. "We're all hot-blooded adults and understand the struggle. I say congrats for gettin' back on the wagon."

"We wouldn't have to be on the no-sex wagon if we set a date and got married!"

"Okay, let's table this conversation before nobody's speakin' to each other," Brandon stated, corralling everyone out of the door. He took this as a sign that he needed to be extra careful tonight to stay on Trinity's good side.

Chapter Twenty-Seven

March 1832

Ruby loved rocking little Billy—it made her content, perhaps even happy. But it had her wondering what he'd grow up to be. She wished she could take him back to Africa, where he could grow to be a man. Perhaps she could start dropping hints to Haggerty, she thought, while lying Billy down in the cradle.

Billy seemed so peaceful rocking back and forth, but to her, the synchronized sound was depressing. With Bell in town and Billy now sleeping, Ruby could feel the loneliness creeping in. To raise her spirits, she put the yellow dress back on. The soft fabric felt good against her skin as she admired the lace and pearl buttons. Her whole mood shifted as she buttoned the dress. Spinning in the dress, she allowed her body to match the lightness of her heart.

"Yous in a good mood," Bell said, entering the house. "But it's gonna change when yous finds out whad don 'appened."

"Bell, what are you going on about?"

"Las' nigh' Sam started some kinda rebellions with dem slaves from cross de island. Dey burnt up everytin' dey saw. Nows de massirs burnin' mad. Dey whippin' every slave. I'se had to git out of dere."

"And Sam?" Ruby asked, worried.

"Dey was beatin' Sam when I'se lef. Dey was tryin to git 'im to say who got 'im to do dis ting."

After hearing that, Ruby went straight to bed, too overcome with grief to do anything else. And the next day, she was no better. She feared for

Sam and for herself too. She was haunted by the fact that Sam blamed her, and maybe Haggerty did too.

"Chile, you been mopin' roun' 'ere for de longest. Why don't you puts de yellow dress back on?" Bell asked. "Id usually makes yous smiles, dun it?"

Going into her room, Ruby pulled out the special dress and stared at it. Normally, her heart would leap just at the sight of it, but today, the dress held no magic. Still, she put it on, wondering whether she would ever wear it like a real woman—out in the world for everyone to see.

"Chile, did it work?" Bell asked, coming back into the room and seeing her staring in the broken mirror. "Do yous feels better?"

"Not really."

"Well, it dun't madder; yous still needs to eat. C'mon, I's dun fixed yous some fish soup. It's good an 'ot."

Reluctantly, Ruby sat down to eat. Mainly because Bell kept pestering. And it didn't take much coaxing after the first spoonful. The soup was hot and flavorful and instantly boosted her energy. "The soup's good, Bell. Thanks," Ruby said, cleaning her bowl.

"It sho look likes it 'elped. Now, 'ow 'bout yous tellin' me one of dem stories from de Bible book."

"The story I'm reading now would only depress you."

"Well, tries me anyways. I's don't depress easy." Bell laughed, her big belly jiggling, making Ruby laugh too.

"I've been reading about how God sent His Son to save man. You know Christmas and God being born by the Virgin Mary."

"Course, I's knows dat story. But I never knew whad become of dat baby God?"

"He grew up. And for three years, he told the people how much God the Father loved them but not their ways. They didn't want to hear that, though. So, they killed Him. Beating Him bad—like they beat Sam," Ruby said reflectively. "Then they hung Him on a cross. And all God's Son said was, 'Forgive them, Father, for they know not what they do.'"

Facing Bell, she added, "Sometimes, I believe that God wants so much more for us, but our massirs are under Satan's control and can't help themselves. So, we should pray for them. But then … there are times … like when I heard about Sam, that I just want to kill them. I've got such hatred in me. I don't believe I can forgive like God's Son did."

"Dat's a lots to ask of a 'uman bein'. Do God really wan' dat from people?"

"I think so," Ruby answered. "And I've got this funny feeling that I'm gonna get a chance to find out. I'm afraid they're coming after me. I can feel it. I think Sam's dead."

"Yous dun't knows dat," Bell said, reassuring Ruby. "He gots beats … dat's all. Slaves git beats all de times, and dey survives. Sam's strong. He could've survived."

"Survive, for what?" Ruby asked, now standing up and staring out of the window. "This ain't no life. As slaves, we're denied even the simplest of pleasures. But God's going to give us a new life. That's why He went through all that torture. He bought us a new life," she explained, looking at Bell again, smiling. Ruby thought of Isaiah 53:5—*"By his stripes we are healed."* "God was able to get through the torture because He knew what was on the other side. You think I'm strong enough to do that, Bell?"

"Yous talkin' crazy," Bell said, getting up from the table to clear it. "Massir Haggerty, he gone protects ya. Dat man loves 'im some Ruby Lee. Yous gonna be fine. Yous just wait and see." Then looking puzzled, she asked, "Ain't dey got some nice stories in dat Bible?"

"Well, actually that is a nice story," Ruby said, laughing again. "God went through a painful death so that when we die, it won't seem like death at all. It'll be like we're sleeping. Then God's going to come back to this earth, wake us up, and take us to heaven. In heaven, we'll have beautiful white robes that'll make this yellow dress look like a rag. And we're gonna have our own personal crown with lots of jewels."

"Everybody?" Bell asked with interest. "Or just da Massirs?"

"Everybody. There'll be no slavery in heaven. Everybody's going to be free. But only kind people will be there. Evil slave owners won't go unless they confess their sins."

"Now ya talkin crazy agin," Bell said. "Do you sees any of de Massirs roun' 'ere confessin' 'bout dem bein' mean to a slave?"

"No, I don't," Ruby said, shaking her head. "That's why this is a nice story. They won't be there. Otherwise, we wouldn't have a bit of peace," she said, laughing again, but maybe a bit too loud because after that, she heard the baby whimpering. "Uh-oh, there goes Billy. I better go see 'bout him before he really starts wailing."

As soon as Ruby Lee left the room, Haggerty came rushing in. "Where's Ruby? We gotta get her out of here. Quick, grab some supplies!"

"Massir, what's wrong?" Bell asked, seeing his fear. "You scarin' me."

"You're right to be scared," he said, still rushing around. "Everybody done gone plum crazy over this rebellion with all the property damage, and now they're looking for Ruby. They think she had something to do with it."

"Why'd dey tink dat?"

"Cause Noone told them so. When I overheard what was going on, I headed over. I've got to put Ruby somewhere else. Hurry, Bell, we ain't got much time." Then pausing, he called out, "Ruby Lee!"

"Charles," Ruby answered, coming out, looking more relaxed. I was just cleaning up the baby. Are you staying for dinner? Bell made some delicious soup."

"Ruby!" Charles shouted again. "Things have happened. It's not safe here."

"What things?" Ruby asked, her heart now pounding. "What's going on?"

"You know 'bout the rebellion?"

"Bell told me," Ruby admitted hesitantly. "But what does that have to do with us?"

"Sam was my slave. I'm being held responsible. Noone told everybody that you were the one who gave Sam the idea."

"That's a lie! I simply told him the story of Moses," she said frantically. "He came up with the whole rebellion thing all by himself. Where's Sam? He'll tell you."

"Sam's dead, and now they're looking for you. It's only a matter of time before they figure out that you're here. We need to put you and the baby some place safe."

"And Bell?"

"It's going to be hard enough hiding you and the boy."

"You're not taking me back to that secret room are you? I can't go back there. I just can't," Ruby sobbed, moving away from him.

"I'm not taking you back there; with the baby crying all the time, that would never work. Maybe you can stay with Jacque one night," he said, thinking out loud. "Ernestine knows about this place. She'll tell them. We have to go."

"Go where, Charles?" Ernestine asked, walking into the house.

"What're you doing here?" he asked nervously.

"I followed you, along with these here boys." As soon as she said that, three large white men entered the house.

"You had no right to do that." Perspiration was now forming on Haggerty's forehead.

"What's going on here, Charles?" Mark, one of the three white men, asked.

"Why's that any of your business!"

"It became my business once your slaves participated in the rebellion," Mark responded. "Ernestine believes that this woman is Ruby Lee. The one identified as being involved."

"This is Ruby Lee," Haggerty admitted, "but she hasn't been involved in any rebellion. She's been here at this house. She doesn't even have contact with other slaves anymore, except for Bell."

"She used to," Ernestine pointed out. "And you said you sold Ruby."

Looking only at the men, Haggerty explained, "Ruby Lee hasn't been around other slaves in months, and since when does a man tell his wife every time he changes his mind about his property."

"Then what are you doing here?" Ernestine asked.

"Like I said," he responded, still looking at the men, "it's nobody's business what I'm doing here, although it should be pretty obvious that I'm using the girl to breed. In fact, she's holding one of my investments now. But when she's pregnant, she's not good for much else. She gets the morning sickness, and it lasts all day."

"I can see how there could be benefits to having a slave woman that looks like that," Mark snickered.

"Exactly," Haggerty said, encouraging him. "And you can understand why I didn't want the little woman in my business," he whispered to the man. Then they both laughed.

Ruby stood frozen. Afraid to move, to think, to breathe—her nightmare was coming true. She knew that Ernestine had no love in her heart, and Ruby wasn't getting a good feeling from the men who had entered with her.

"If what you say is true, then we should take the baby back to the slave house to be raised with the other slave babies," Ernestine said, motioning to Mark to grab the child.

"No," Ruby yelled out. "He's mine! You've got no right!"

"Charles, what's this slave saying?" Ernestine asked, for the first time noticing the yellow dress. The dress immediately clued her in on what was going on. "It seems to me you're here keeping house—sinning in the sight of the Lord. If you're in love with this woman, it proves that you were too soft on your slaves, and you were the reason for the rebellion. So is she a slave breeder or your personal lover?"

"I already told you what she was," Haggerty barked.

"Then give me the baby," Ernestine insisted.

"Why, he can't work yet."

"The child needs to learn at an early age that he's a slave," Ernestine continued. "And why do you care where a slave baby stays?"

"I don't! Take the baby!" he snapped angrily.

But Ruby screamed and held onto Billy.

"I'll fix this later," he quickly whispered to Ruby. "She'll have the child killed if you don't let go."

Ruby let go but not because of Haggerty's words. It was because she was no match for Mark, the man who had come to fetch Billy. Falling to the ground, she tried to drown out the cries of her child. Billy had been her only reason for living. How could they take him from her?

Satisfied, Ernestine took the baby from Mark. Yet, when she looked down, her satisfaction turned to horror. It was like looking into the face of one of her children. This was no slave man's child. This was Charles's child, and the thought kindled her anger. "Bell, take the baby and wait in the wagon," Ernestine ordered.

"Why don't you take the baby yourself on your way out," Haggerty suggested.

"'Cause I'm not done," Ernestine snapped. "Now, Charles, these men rode out to check on you. The least you could do is offer them some hospitality," she said, her eyes searing through him like fire. "I'm a Christian woman myself, but unlike me, I know that these men have a carnal nature. If this slave woman is for breeding, then these men should be able to have a little fun with her, don't you think?" Turning to the men, she asked, "Boys, would you like that?"

"She is pretty," Mark answered.

"She ain't available in that way," Haggerty replied in anger. "I don't want you destroying my property."

"It ain't gonna stop her from breeding to entertain these men. You're acting like you're in love with this slave woman," Ernestine spat out.

"It does seem suspect," Mark stated. "Perhaps we should tell the other property owners about your slave lover, especially since she's been linked with the rebellion."

"Fine. Do what you will to her," Haggerty said, caving. "Just don't kill her. She's a good, strong slave, and I paid a lot of money for her."

—m—

Haggerty saw the fear in Ruby's eyes. With his own eyes, he tried to tell her that this was the only way. Then he watched as the three men moved toward her. He watched as she fought back. He watched as they tore at her beautiful, yellow dress. He watched as they dragged her to the bedroom. And even when he could no longer watch, he could hear her screams. Everything inside of him died, hearing her cries of terror fill the room.

Looking over at Ernestine, he felt nothing but contempt. Grabbing the collar of her dress, he pulled her up to him. "How could you do that to another human being?" he said, in a voice raspy with emotion. Then he let her go but only long enough to grab a lit candle off the table, which he put to her throat. It satisfied him to see her eyes grow large with fear.

"Charles, what are you doing? You're scaring me," she said, shaking from the fire being so close to her skin. "Do you really want to go to jail for killing me? Then who's going to look after your little slave lover?"

He was about to set her on fire when her words jarred him. She was right. Ruby Lee would need him. "I want you out of the house," he snarled, suddenly changing his strategy. "When I get back to the main house, there should be no trace of you."

"I can't just leave. I'm your wife!"

"Not anymore! You've got one hour to get out!"

"Charles, that's not enough time to get me and the children packed up. Be reasonable."

"The children aren't going, just you," he said in a chilled tone. "You can either go quietly or I'll swear that you slept with every man in Jamaica, including the slaves."

"Charles, please," she cried. "Don't do this! You can't tell me that a slave woman means more than me!"

"Ruby means everything to me, whereas you're dead to me. And if I see you again," he said, holding the flame closer to her cheek, "I'll make sure that you're dead to everyone else, and that's a promise." Then he blew out the candle and threw it at her.

Jumping from the sting of the hot candle, Ernestine's tears tumbled out. Unmoved by her emotions, Haggerty grabbed her one final time. "I hope you rot in hell for what you've done to Ruby." Then releasing her, he stepped aside. "Now, get out!" He watched her run toward the wagon. As she was about to get in, he yelled, "Get your filthy carcass off my wagon! Walk! That'll give you time to think about what you've done to Ruby!" He then watched Ernestine stomp off down the dirt road.

By now, Ruby Lee had gone silent, but he could still hear the men pleasuring themselves, and it sickened him. No longer able to stomach the evilness of the irascible men, he left and went down to the wagon. "Bell, I'm going to take the baby to Jacque," he said, getting in the wagon. "I want you to stay and help Ruby. Tell her the baby's safe. Bell," he said, stopping her momentarily, "tell Ruby that I had to do this to save her life." Then he released Bell and took off.

Bell hid behind the house waiting for the men to leave. After about an hour, they came out laughing, but she didn't move. She waited a few more moments to ensure they wouldn't come back, and then she went to see about Ruby.

Chapter Twenty-Eight

Three weeks had passed since Ruby's attack. Ernestine had been shipped back to America, without the kids, and Noone had been whipped within an inch of her life and sold to another plantation. But none of it phased Ruby. She now spent her days writing in her diary and reading the Bible, searching for answers. She thought she understood God, but after her attack, she felt like she didn't know Him at all. Still she kept reading. And it was with a sense of urgency because she knew she wasn't well. Although fearing for Billy, she was relieved to be dying.

Lying in her bed, she could hear Haggerty enter the house—his sturdy boots hitting the floor, his rough movement of the chairs announcing his arrival.

"How is she?" Haggerty asked Bell, taking a seat.

"She ain't no bedder. I'se tried everytin', but she eats nutin'."

"She still won't see me?"

"No, Massir. I tink dem mens brok 'er 'eart. I tinks she's dyin'."

"Don't say that!" he said, fighting back the tears. "You told her 'bout Billy, didn't you? You told her that I'm protecting him."

"Yous protectin' 'im likes yous protected 'er?" Bell innocently asked.

"How dare you question me!" he screamed, raising his hand to Bell.

"You righ', Massir," Bell quickly stated. "I dunno nutin'. I's just a slave. Dun't beats me," she said, backing up and lowering her eyes to the ground.

That familiar slave gesture hurt him more than if she had slapped him across the face. "Sorry, Bell. I didn't mean it. I'm just not myself these days. I'm sick over what's happened. I've got to see Ruby."

"It's yo 'ouse, yo slave; yous dos what you wants."

Haggerty slipped into Ruby's room. She looked thin and close to death. "Ruby," he whispered, but she never responded. Sadly, he turned and left the room.

"I'll try back tonight," Haggerty told Bell before exiting.

After Bell closed the door behind Haggerty, she muttered, "I knows more dan you, Massir. I knows you'd done lost dat gurl." Bell busied herself with making soup for Ruby. She had tried everything to get Ruby up and moving around, but nothing had worked. "Chile, how's you feelin' today?" Bell asked, going in Ruby's room.

"The same, but, Bell, I need you to do something for me."

"Soon as yous do sometin' for me. I needs yous to eat so yous gets back up on yo feet."

"Bell, eating is for the living," Ruby explained. "I'm dying, and you don't feed death. I'm writing a note for Charles in my diaries. Promise me you'll give them to him when I'm gone. And take care of Billy. Tell him he was the prettiest baby ever. And, Bell, thank God for you. You're the best friend I've ever had." Gripping her arm, Ruby pleaded, "Bell, I need to see Billy. Talk to Charles."

"I'se talk to 'im, but yous gotta stop dis fool talk 'bout dying. Yous young and strong. Yous gonna make it. Yous just gotta believes dat."

"I don't want to believe," Ruby said, shaking her head. "Please, do as I say and get my baby boy. I want to see him before my final sleep."

Bell found Haggerty in the field. The minute he heard Ruby's request, he dropped everything, got Billy, and took him to her, no longer caring what people thought. He had seen the look in Bell's eyes and figured that Ruby didn't have much time.

He watched from the corner of the room while Bell helped Ruby to hold Billy. She was so weak that Bell had to control the baby. Ruby played with the baby until her energy gave out. Her tears flowed freely when Bell took him away.

"Don't worry, Ruby, I'm just gonna feeds 'im," Bell reassured Ruby. Then turning to Haggerty, Bell said, "Massir, you gonna let Billy stay, ain'tcha?"

"Course, Billy's home," Haggerty said, coming closer. "He needs you to get well," he said, patting Ruby's leg through the sheet, the same way he'd done that first night she arrived. "You're his momma, and he needs you," he told her. "I'm not gonna let what happened to you and Billy ever happen again. I'll go to my grave protecting you and Billy. You hear me, don't you, Ruby Lee?" But Ruby never responded, and with nothing left to do or say, Haggerty slowly walked out of the house.

Bell looked down at Billy and shook her head. "I believes your daddy's mad at da wurl. Dat's too bad."

Chapter Twenty-Nine

Savannah's Time Period

"It stops?" Cara said, with disappointment. "Just like that?"

"Yeah," Savannah stated. "I read everything there, and ... I'm ... sorry. I need air," she said, rushing out.

"She's takin' it hard," Brandon stated, watching her run out. "Aren't you goin' after her?" he asked, looking over at Jacob.

Jacob's gut was telling him no, but since the question seemed more like an indictment, he went. And he knew exactly where she'd be—sitting on her favorite rock, staring out at the ocean. "Mind if I sit down?"

"Go ahead," she said, but inside she was screaming, *Go away.*

Her lackluster welcome had him deciding against engaging in conversation. Instead, he sat silently beside her.

"You're not going to ask me why I came out here?" she asked after a few moments of silence.

"Why? Would you tell me?" he asked, staring at her, knowing that made her nervous.

"Do we really have to go through the whole I've got trust issues?"

"When would you suggest we talk about it?" he responded, surprised that he'd kept his cool. Normally, she pushed his buttons, but today he only felt sorry for her. "You're hurtin', and I can't even sit silently beside you for support." Watching her turn away, he used his index finger to turn her face back toward him. "I'm not stupid. Somethin' happened to you. I'm guessin' it was somethin' sexual, and whatever scab grew over your emotional pain just got ripped off by Ruby's story. Am I warm?"

"Hot. How'd you know?"

"There were signs," he said, now understanding the hurt that had been in her eyes when he rejected her advances. It had been her way of taking back her sexuality. "And when you ran out just now, that's when I knew that Ruby's story … was somehow yours. You know, I didn't want to come out here," he said, facing the ocean again. "I wanted you to have your space." Rubbing his hands together, he added, "But I caved under the pressure. A good boyfriend would go runnin' after his upset girlfriend, right?" Since she didn't answer, he answered for her. "That's what that group in there thought," he said, looking back over his shoulder at the house. "I came out here to save face. But honestly, are you even my girlfriend?"

"What is this, third grade? Do we need a label? Why can't we just be?"

Standing up, he pulled her up to him. "It's because I'm not in the third grade that I need to know where this is heading. Exactly what are your intentions, young lady?" Then he stopped to laugh. "Now, why do I sound like the woman in the relationship?"

"Look, I'm sorry. I'm so messed up. I wanted to tell you," she said sadly. "I've been to therapy, I've prayed about it, and still I can't get the story out."

"It's not your fault," he said, hugging her. "I'm just not the one. From the moment we met, I've loved you, but I also hated you because of the barriers that you throw up. I thought I'd be able to break them down. Turned out I was wrong," he said, shaking his head. "Although for the longest time, I kept tellin' myself to just try harder. But hearin' Ruby's story changed my mind. She had no one in her time of need. Not Bell, who couldn't relate, and not Haggerty, who didn't help her. When you ran out, I wondered who you'd confide in and if I was stoppin' you from meetin' that guy."

"Jacob, no! You've got it all wrong," she blurted out. "And I'm going to work through this. You'll see."

"And that's my point," he said sadly. "You shouldn't have to work through things alone." Placing his hands in his pockets, he shuffled his feet. Letting out a long sigh, he knew he'd miss those gorgeous eyes that seemed to bore straight through him, that silky hair always blowing in the wind, and that soft skin that smelled of jasmine. It'd been refreshing to have a woman who challenged him. Normally, women went overboard trying to please him, but not her. "Someday, you'll find that person who you can open up to," he said before taking one final look. She was definitely a beautiful woman—just not his woman. "Bye, Savannah," he whispered softly, and then kissed her on the forehead. And like Charles Haggerty, Jacob ended their relationship the way he had started it.

—⁙—

"Jacob!" Savannah called to him, but he just kept walking. "Jacob! This is crazy!" she hollered again, but he never stopped, never even looked back. Collapsing onto the rock, she burst into tears. Minutes later, Trinity and Cara joined her.

"Girl, what happened?" Trinity asked.

"He's gone. And don't you dare say I told you so."

"Gurl, mi not kickin' you when you down. And no need to bawl out over dis ting. Mi wanna know if you love him."

The question took Savannah by surprise. For the first time, her response of "go ahead and leave" didn't work. She'd let Jacob in just enough that it hurt when he pulled out.

"Well?" Trinity pressed.

"Jacob's right. Maybe he's not the one for me. He thinks with the right guy, I won't have any trouble opening up.

"That's the dumbest thing I've ever heard," Trinity replied. "Men don't know if they're 'the one' until we tell them." Then hesitating, she added, "Wait, mi tinkin' you never told Jacob about your past."

"Then you tinkin' right." Savannah said, mimicking Trinity.

"Why? I sent you to therapy!"

"I don't know!" Savannah said, equally frustrated. "The words just never came."

"This ends tonight. You're goin' to go to his house and tell him."

"I can't!"

"Yeah, you can. I don't know exactly what happened to you, but it's pretty clear some guy hurt you. And now, you're lettin' that hurt—hurt your chances with Jacob."

"Apparently, it's in my blood. Terrible things happened to Ruby. She died with her life ruined. Maybe that's my fate too."

"I don't think so," Cara jumped in. "First of all, Ruby went through the worst thing a woman can go through. I'm sure you can't relate. And even so, Ruby understood that Satan is the real culprit. So things aren't always what they seem."

"That's exactly what Grandma Nene said about the African princess story and I …" Suddenly, Savannah paused. "Oh my goodness … Ruby … she's the African princess." Seeing their confusion, she continued. "Don't you see? Ruby fell for Jack and not the men from her village. She snubbed her village and its practices. Haggerty, a slave owner, fell for her, gave her a room, and then a house." With her eyes now gleaming with excitement, she continued. "Her love being savagely torn away must have been Billy being ripped from her arms. Even the part about her crying in the walls was true. It was when she was in the secret room. Grandma Nene was right. It wasn't folklore, which means that the second part must be true too. This house must be the wealth that generations were promised. Haggerty must have shared his plans with Ruby's son, Billy, and told him to pass it on," she said, thinking out loud. "And I was wrong about Haggerty," she said, now allowing herself to be honest. "He must've truly loved Ruby. When I examined the wallpaper in the secret room up close, I noticed pink rose buds—Ruby Lee's favorite flower. He turned his secret man cave into a custom-designed tomb. Now, that's love."

"Which shows God answered Ruby's prayers," Cara noted. "You knew Ruby's story before we ever came to Jamaica. Her story was carried down, and her son, the blue-eyed devil, was protected and has his own line of stories."

"Haggerty must've have taken Billy to North Carolina," Trinity concluded.

"Why?" Cara asked. "Slavery had ended in Jamaica. Why take him to North Carolina where it's still going on?"

"I agree," Savannah said. "It must've been a later relative that moved to North Carolina, and if the blue-eyed devil grew up here in Jamaica, it makes his story more plausible. For Billy never would've gotten away with all the stuff that he did in North Carolina. It must've been Billy's children or grandchildren that moved. The only piece that's still puzzling is that Grandma Nene said that the wealth would come with a letter. I always thought it was Brandon's letter, but that doesn't make any sense. Haggerty didn't know about Brandon."

"Maybe not Brandon," Trinity offered, "but some lawyer would've been involved."

"Grandma Nene said that the letter would be more valuable than the treasure. I don't see that being the case for any attorney's letter."

"I've got it!" Cara announced. "The house did come with a letter—the diaries!"

"Right, and the diaries do mean more than the money."

"And given that Ruby was victorious. It suggests that she found her answers and just didn't get the chance to write it down," Cara suggested.

"Aren't you the same one who thought things were turning around for Ruby?" Savannah smirked.

"Maybe I missed the boat on that one, but that doesn't mean I'm wrong this time."

"Cara, you're not helpin'," Trinity butted in. "Bottom line—it's time for your family to evolve. Perhaps the story was carried down just so you could do somethin' different. Unlike Ruby, you need to forget and move on from the past because it's keepin' you from a good man. Learn from Ruby. She gave up on a man who was tryin' to give her a good life. Are you really gonna let history repeat itself? If you love Jacob, prove it—tell him what happened to you. You saw how he reacted when you told him about the diaries. Imagine how he'll feel hearin' 'bout your past."

"Fine, but I'll wait for him to come back here."

"Jacob's not comin' back," Cara piped up. "He sent a text to Marcus to see if he could stay at the house for the rest of the week. That's how we knew somethin' was up. Guess he figured you needed your space."

"Then he's really gone!"

"He's not gone, because you're gonna go fight for him," Trinity stated, pulling her off the rock and giving her a little push. "Now, go! You owe it to yourself."

"By the way, was Peggy here?" Cara asked.

"No. Why?"

"I thought I saw her car pullin' off as we headed down."

"That was probably Jacob getting away from me."

Chapter Thirty

"Door's open," Jacob yelled, hearing a knock. He'd been watching TV on the couch but turned it off when Savannah entered.

Walking in, she saw unlit candles, champagne glasses, and an uncorked bottle of sparkling cider. "Am I interrupting something?"

"Nope," he answered, admiring her wardrobe change to a red wraparound dress from the sweats she'd slipped into when they were reading the diaries. If this was ammunition to fight for their relationship, it was working.

"Well, clearly you're expecting someone," she said suspiciously.

"Yeah … you," he said, getting up and walking towards her.

"So you were playing me?" she snapped, ready to go off on him.

"Basically," he said, using his sexiest smile to calm her down. He wondered if she even had a clue what she did to his emotions. He'd convince himself that he could be content with a life without her, but when she walked in, his need for her became clear.

"Why you ba—"

"You might want to rethink your adjectives," he said placing a finger to her lips, "You should know that my parents tied the knot before the doctor cut the cord." And since he'd caught her off guard, he continued with a kiss—a kiss that took her several seconds to regain her composure.

But once she recovered, she went off. "You self-righteous man, don't think for one minute that I'm staying for your little charade," she said, heading for the door.

"Okay, I'll rephrase. I was hopin' you'd come, but there was a chance that you wouldn't. Please, forgive the drama—since that's usually reserved for your gender," he said, enticing her again with a smile.

His words stopped her and had her turning from the door. Surprisingly, his smile settled her. "Oh please! Men are full of drama," she said, collapsing into one of his dining room chairs. "Besides, I'm the one who owes you an apology," she admitted. "And before your cocky attitude, I was prepared to give it."

"Don't need an apology. I just want you to be happy. And tonight, I realized that might not happen with me."

"No, you're wrong! I've never been happier," she said, choking up.

"Really," he said, laughing. "Because you don't sound or look happy, but I get what you're sayin'. You're happy with the house, your business, your girls, and our friendship. Problem is that I'm lookin' for more, and I don't think you are."

"Not true. It just that … well," she said, lowering her eyes. "Until now, I've been afraid to want more. But that's changing, which is why I came here tonight—because I don't want to lose you."

Jacob sighed, glad that his instincts had been right. "I don't want to leave. I just need to know how I fit into your life. This isn't just about you. I want to do what's best for both of us."

"I understand," she said with her words, but with her body she moved further away from him. "What I'm about to say, I haven't told anyone," she confessed. "And I mean no one—not Grandma Nene, not Cara, absolutely no one. I haven't even been honest with myself," she noted, walking toward the window. "There was this guy—Eric Statler. He was gorgeous, and I was infatuated. Grandma Nene was not a fan, but I was too in love to listen. Despite Grandma Nene's disapproval, I went out with him." A cold chill ran down her back as she recalled Eric sitting there drooling over her.

"During the date, he apparently put something in my drink," she laughed nervously, "and stupid me, I was concerned about looking weird by getting sick on the date, instead of thinking this nutcase just drugged me. But he played along. He was like, 'Sure I'll take you home.'" Stopping for a moment, she swallowed the lump that was now forming in her throat. "But he didn't take me home … at least … not to my home," she added, still staring out of the window.

"He took me to some frat house and he … he," but her voice failed as the memories came rushing back—the keys on the desk, the Bob Marley poster, and the shoes in the corner. Eric was looking directly at her, and he was not alone. There were so many hands—reaching, grabbing, stroking, gripping, and pulling. She wanted to stop the memories, stop the story, but she knew she couldn't—not if she was going to keep Jacob. Turning away from the window, she looked at Jacob for support. "Eric raped me, along with two of his friends!" There. She had said it. Searching Jacob's face, she looked to see if it was enough. Seeing his eyes, she knew it was. "That's why I ran out tonight. Finding out that the exact same thing happened to Ruby was too much to take."

After relaying the story, she was shaking. Jacob wanted nothing more than to tear this Eric Statler to pieces, but more hatred was not what she needed. He waited a moment before reaching out, not sure of how she would respond. Surprisingly, she collapsed into his arms and cried unashamedly. Holding her, he stroked her hair. "I believe slaves like Ruby that accepted Christ have a special place in God's heart. More so than anyone else, they understand total dependence on God. And I've read that the trials of this earth, no matter how bad, will pale in comparison to the riches and blessings of heaven. First Corinthians 2:9 says, 'No eye has seen, no ears have heard, no mind has imagined the things that God has prepared for those who love him.' I don't have the answer to why bad things happen to good people, but I have the hope that God is in control. And one day, He'll explain the greater good for the trials that we suffer. Until then, we just have to trust that He is preparing us for heaven." Pushing her back to peer into her eyes, he added, "I'm sorry that happened to you and Ruby, but it's time to let go of the hurt and the anger. The first step is forgiving."

"I can't," she sobbed, gripping Jacob's shoulder tighter. "Everyone keeps telling me that—like it's a rope that I can drop. Those guys don't deserve forgiveness! They should suffer forever!"

"Forgiveness is not for them. It's for you. I learned that from Brandon." It was no secret it had taken him a while to forgive Brandon, but once he did, it was like a weight lifted off him.

"But those men's faces ... I just keep seeing them, and the hatred just rises up in me. How do I stop the way I feel?"

"By practicin' feeling somethin' else—you gotta feel somethin' besides hatred."

"Maybe you're right. I really do want to put this behind me. When I first met you, I didn't even believe God existed, and now I know He exists, and I'm even learning to trust Him. Although I'll be the first to admit that I've got a long way to go," she said, sniffling.

"If you'd like some company on your journey, I'm available."

"Oh really? 'Cause a couple of hours ago, you were kicking me to the curb."

"I never kicked you to the curb." Then seeing her about to object, he added, "But how 'bout I give you a sacred promise that I'll always be there for you?"

"What's a sacred promise?"

"Hold that thought," he said, leaving the room. Returning, he came over and held her hand. "A sacred promise is one that you make before God and a bunch people, on your wedding day." Getting down on one knee, he pulled out an engagement ring.

Savannah went silent, staring at the large chocolate diamond encircled by smaller diamonds that he slid on her finger. "It's beautiful," she finally got out. "But what does this mean?"

"That I want to marry you," he said, stating the obvious.

"You sure? 'Cause I've got issues."

"Nobody's perfect, not even me. But I'm willing to try if you are," he said, winking at her.

Jacob made it seem so easy, but her doubts were always there. What would happen if for once she ignored those doubts? "Okay yes."

"You're sure?" he asked, surprised by her quick response.

"Yep. I mean it'd be a shame to break in someone new now," she said, teasing him.

"Is that all I am ... a habit you can't kick?" he said frowning, taking her in his arms.

"You're a habit I choose not to kick. There's a difference," she pointed out. "I guess I've finally fallen for you, Mr. Spencer!"

"Goodness knows, I worked hard enough, Ms. Hartford," he said, smiling.

"I love my ring," she said, staring down at the glistening rock on her finger. "Is it mine? Or Kimberly's?"

"Yours. Kimberly was buried with hers," he said, breaking away and heading toward the table.

"When did you buy a ring?" she asked, still mesmerized by the sparkling diamond.

"The first time I saw you in that yellow dress," he replied, popping the cork of the cider. Topping off her glass, he added, "The next day, I was walking past a jewelry store, and I saw that ring. It had your name written all over it. I just had to pray that I'd be able to use it someday."

"But why me?" That question had always troubled her. "I've met at least two women who were interested in you. Trinity and Peggy, and I have no doubt there've been countless others. Why choose me? 'Cause in the looks department I can't hold a candle to Trinity."

"You underestimate yourself, Miss Hartford. But you're right, it wasn't your looks. Don't get me wrong; my heart did a somersault when you turned around that first day in that yellow halter top and hip-hugger jeans," he said, smiling.

"You remember what I was wearing," she said, impressed.

"It's seared in my memory. The light touch of makeup, that silky, long hair, and you were showin' just enough skin to make a man wonder. Oh yeah, you would've turned any man's head, but that's not what got my attention. It was your dismissive attitude. You weren't afraid to speak your mind. And your reaction to me was so different from other women. You made me want to know more. Your beauty turned out to be just the icin' on the cake. And then I started seein' all the different facets of you. One minute you were a witch, the next you're a compassionate friend. At first, you're this weak and timid person, but then you transform into a powerful businesswoman wieldin' $2 million deals. And that's why I fell in love with you—not because of the way you look, or the way you think, or your talent in design, or even your ability to transform—but it was all of you."

"Well played, Mr. Spencer. Is that how you thought about Kimberly?"

"She challenged me too but differently. She was the first woman to open me up to the idea that physical beauty was not enough. Because before her, mi head turned at every pretty ting in a skirt," he said with his fake Jamaican accent.

"Does that make me Leah?"

"Huh?" he asked, confused, as he filled his glass.

"In the Bible, Jacob had two wives—Rachel and Leah—Rachel, whom he really loved and Leah whom he settled for. I've seen the way you talk about Kimberly. I'm guessing she was Rachel, which makes me Leah?"

"I do believe that I've created a biblical monster," he said, laughing again. "Let's just say that I've surpassed my namesake because I had two Rachels, although I do believe that the biblical Jacob really did love Leah. But if it's any consolation, and it may not be manly to admit this, but when I first saw you in that yellow dress, you brought me to tears. So, just like Jacob cried the first time he saw his Rachel, so did I. That never happened with Kimberly."

"That's not in the Bible!"

"It's in there, I promise you," he said, recorking the bottle. "Rachel brought her man to tears, just like you." Walking over, he handed her a glass of cider. "Don't be jealous of Kimberly. There's room for both of you in my heart."

"How poetic," she said, sipping the cider. "And I'm not jealous. From everything you've told me, I really admire Kimberly. I'm just letting you know that I'm not her. I'm just Savannah."

"Lucky for you, that's who I want," he said, clinking champagne glasses with her.

"Yep, lucky for me!"

Chapter Thirty-One

"Still staring at the ring—must be love," Brandon teased, entering the lobby. "I for one am glad that Jacob Spencer's off the market—again."

"Yeah, he was a real threat," Savannah smirked. "Looking for Trinity? She's in the kitchen, putting the final touches on the food. Something wrong?" she asked seeing his worried expression.

"Afraid so." Sticking his hands in his pockets, he paused a minute. "Why am I always the bearer of bad news?"

"At least now you're on our side," she said gratefully. "What is it this time?"

"The Carapones," he said, frowning.

Savannah frowned too. She hadn't heard that name in a while. "I thought their fixation with us was over."

"Me too after your TV debut, and especially once they got a new CEO. But I overheard Carapones' men talkin'. They're plannin' some kind of attack on Restoration tonight."

"Tonight!" Savannah panicked. "But tonight's Cara's fashion show! Why do something when the place is full of witnesses?"

"More impact maybe, I don't know. What I do know is that you have to cancel. You can't risk anyone gettin' hurt."

"How do we know that someone will get hurt?" she asked, twirling her ponytail in frustration. "And is this even a viable threat?" They'd had false alarms before from the Carapones. "Show starts in two hours. There's no time to cancel."

"Hey, babe." Trinity strolled in. Throwing her arms around Brandon's neck, she kissed him lightly. She was definitely back to being impressed by his looks, and his dark suit and striped bow tie were definitely talking. "Hey, why do you two look like somebody died?"

"Because someone might," Brandon answered.

"Okay, you're scarin' me. Tell me what's goin' on." Trinity looked first to Brandon and then to Savannah.

"The Carapones are plannin' some kind of attack on this place tonight," Brandon finally responded.

"Tonight! But tonight's the fashion show!"

"Perhaps that's the point. People die, and then—bam—this place closes before it opens."

"Brandon's right. We've got to call this off," Savannah said, thinking practically.

"Call it off!" Trinity exploded. "Why? We have the heads-up. We've paid for security—right, Savannah?"

"That's right. We're expecting them any minute."

"Bredren whad gwann," Jacob said to them, walking in, in his blue tuxedo.

"Brandon's canceling our fashion show—dat's whad gwann," Trinity pouted.

"Not following," Jacob answered Trinity, although he stared at Savannah. His chameleon woman had changed once again. This time she had transformed into a mesmerizing Barbie doll with dramatic makeup, hair pulled back in a ponytail, and wearing a white, cotton, sleeveless dress. He couldn't help but smile at the thought of his awkward Savannah being a runway model.

"The Carapones are plannin' some kind of attack on Restoration tonight," Brandon explained. "For everyone's safety, I suggested they cancel the show."

"And I suggest we cancel that suggestion," Trinity interjected. "Why can't we be like Cara and have faith? Why do the Carapones always get to win?"

"What do you think, Jacob?" Savannah asked, considering him now as a partner. "We do have a security company coming. The guests could be confined and controlled."

"What about the tour?" Brandon reminded her. "Isn't that still on?"

"Yeah, but the tour can be structured. Everyone watched."

"Call the police, ask for guidance," Jacob recommended. "If the police say go forward, then do it. But if somethin' happens, you look like a concerned owner who took proper precautions."

"Makes sense," Savannah responded, just as Peggy joined them.

"Hey, guys." Peggy entered the lobby, dressed in a fitted, black, one-shoulder evening gown that fit like a glove. "I came early to help," she said, hoping no one picked up on her lingering stare of Jacob. "I just ran into Cara," she said, but then stopped. "What's wrong?"

"The Carapones are planning some kind of disaster for Restoration tonight," Savannah answered.

"You're canceling then, right?"

"Why should we?" Savannah said with attitude. Why did everyone expect her to just roll over? Peggy of all people should be encouraging her to fight.

"Then what are you going to do?"

"Call the police and ask for advice," Savannah announced, and then she walked off showing that the matter was settled.

When the police arrived, they suggested full-scale security searches. Although the women weren't thrilled with the idea, it seemed a logical compromise. And with the exception of the Carapones' threat, the night was a huge success. All seventy-five guests were impressed when they walked in. After the tour, twenty people signed up to stay at Restoration. Cara sold everything in her trunk show. And Trinity booked a catering event and gave away a ton of cards. She was also grateful for Peggy's help of running back and forth to the kitchen, allowing her to stay with the guests.

Despite the night's success, they were more relieved when it ended without incident, which had Savannah wondering if the Carapones had anything planned at all. The officer, however, still found the threats credible and suggested that they spend the night elsewhere.

Peggy agreed. Pulling Brandon aside, she whispered, "You'll talk them into leaving, won't you? The Carapones scare me."

"Then you've got good instincts. Don't worry. I can reason with them."

"Good! Then I'll leave you to your work," Peggy said, hugging him good-bye.

Savannah, who had been hovering in the shadows listening, came out when Peggy left. "So, we can be reasoned with, huh? And what's Peggy's interest in all of this?"

"Oh you heard that," he said, laughing it off. "Don't be too hard on Peggy. She's just worried … me too. There's no reason why we can't move this party to the villa."

"I'm not leaving," Savannah said stubbornly. "It's my business—my home. Do I just step aside and let the Carapones have their way every time they issue a threat?" she said, walking into the lobby.

"Mi for fightin' the dutty boys," Trinity joined in. "I didn't like riskin' other peoples' lives, but I'm willin' to stand up wid mi own. I'm ready to tell these Carapones to come hard or go home."

"And what will you do when they come hard? This place is brick and mortar and can be rebuilt," Brandon pointed out. "Somethin' happens to you, you can't be rebuilt."

"Then we'll use this," Cara said, laying her gun down on the middle of a wrought-iron coffee table.

"Violence for violence. Is that the answer?" Trinity asked Cara.

"Dr. King said, 'If you're not willing to die for something, then you're not fit to live.'"

"You're pullin' out King," Jacob retorted. "This isn't a civil rights movement, it's a business. And isn't it selfish to put a business above your personal safety? Don't we men have a say?"

"Y'all should stay and protect us," Trinity replied, falling down onto one of the couches.

"Why, when you can move to a place where you don't need protecting?" Brandon replied. "Just pay the security guards extra to spend the night."

"The security guards left before the police," Savannah said. "Besides, if we were in danger, wouldn't the officer have stayed?"

"I don't think you can interpret his goin' home to his family as a reason to ignore the threat. And let's not forget, he told you not to stay." Looking over at Trinity, Brandon could tell that she'd already checked out of the conversation, and that floored him. He couldn't understand her complete disregard of the Carapones. Maybe it was because she hadn't seen their handiwork up close, whereas he had.

"While y'all debate, I'll make hot chocolate. Anyone want some?" Trinity asked, standing up again.

"Ooh, I love your hot chocolate," Cara cooed. "Count me in."

And then a "yeah me too" was heard by everyone in the room.

"I'll help you," Cara offered. On her way out, she added, "Whatever's decided, we'll be fine. I've already turned this over to God. Y'all should start trustin' Him too." With that announcement, she followed Trinity into the kitchen.

"I guess she told us," Jacob said, shaking his head. "Bro, your girl definitely has a connection to the Man upstairs."

"Yeah, I got the Christian Energizer Bunny," Marcus smirked, leaning against the reception desk, his suit jacket now long gone—his bow tie hanging untied around his neck.

"But she's right, isn't she?" Savannah jumped in. "When God's involved, you don't have to worry, right?"

"Yeah, but you still gotta use common sense," Jacob argued. "We're sittin' ducks here."

"But if we don't stand up to the Carapones, then everything that we've worked for at Restoration is for nothing. We leave tonight, we might as well sell the place tonight too," Savannah said defiantly.

"Hate to interrupt," Cara said, coming back in, "but Trinity said to come back to the kitchen 'cause she's not haulin' the hot chocolate in here. And, Savannah, you know the diaries are in the kitchen, right?"

"Yeah, I was putting them in my car because of the Carapones' threat. Peggy suggested it but then distracted me. Just to be safe, I'll put them in the car when I head back there."

"Come back in about five minutes," Cara advised.

"Tell my baby we'll be there," Brandon said for all of them. "I can already taste her hot chocolate." He wondered what Trinity would look like as they got older. Every time there was trouble, she was either making food or drinks.

"Shall I kiss her for you too?" Cara teased him as she exited.

"Keep your lips off my girl. I'll handle that part." He laughed when Cara turned around and stuck her tongue out before leaving again. "You all make a great team," he said, resuming the conversation. "Everyone with a different personality, and still it works. But that's my point. You guys do amazin' stuff, but you can do it anywhere."

"You're wrong," Savannah countered. "Here's where I feel empowered, here's where Ruby Lee lived and started a revolution, and here's where we've all been changed. It was even here that I met Jacob. But it's more than sentimentality. It's about God calling us to do a work here. It's about—" But her statement was interrupted by shattering glass hitting the floor like a mini rainstorm.

"What was that?" Marcus asked, speaking first.

"Don't know, but we should check it out," Jacob said, grabbing Cara's gun, as he headed to the back of the house, with the rest of them following close behind. "Looks like someone took a shot at us," he concluded, after spotting a small hole in the wall.

"I didn't hear a gun go off," Savannah said, finally finding her voice.

"Maybe it was a silencer," Jacob said, digging out the slug.

"It was probably a warnin' shot, because he or she could've easily hit one of us," Brandon reasoned, still staring at the bullet in Jacob's hand.

"Maybe," Jacob admitted. Then, seeing movement, his instincts engaged. "They're still out there! I'm goin' after them."

"I've got your back. Let's go," Brandon said in support, although he feared more for whoever was out there than he did for Jacob.

Savannah watched as they ran out of the back door, her body paralyzed by fear. How could she allow the man she loved to put his life on the line for her business? Brandon was right. She could do what she did anywhere.

"Whoa, where are you goin'?" Marcus asked, reaching out to hold her back.

"Restoration is not worth risking anyone's life. I've got to tell them."

"Woman, you goin' out there will only get the man killed. If he's lookin' out for you, then he can't look out for himself. And what exactly will you do once you get out there, huh? Do you have any police training? At least Jacob's dad was a cop."

His words hit her hard but probably not the way he had intended. For the first time, Savannah realized that this whole relationship had been about her. She didn't even know that Jacob's father was a cop. So, he couldn't die—not like this. Not when there was still so much to learn. To throw Marcus off, she stopped fighting. As hoped, he released her. This time, she was able to get outside before he tackled her to the ground.

"You know you're strong," he told her, struggling to control her. "Perhaps I should let you face these crazy people because you're just as crazy."

"I'm just trying to help!"

"But this ain't the way." Having learned his lesson, he held on to her as he spoke. "Jacob would never forgive me if I let somethin' happen to you."

"Look, they're over there!" she said, pointing at Jacob, who was fighting with an intruder. "You've got to help him!" she pleaded with Marcus.

"Seems to me Jacob's handlin' his business."

Seeing he was distracted, she tried once again to run. "Oh no, you don't!" he said, tackling her again. "There might be other accomplices out there. You need to wait here."

"You wait here!" she retorted, biting his hand and then running like the wind. She didn't stop until she reached Jacob, although Marcus was right behind her.

"Goodness, girl," he stated when he caught up to her. "You definitely had your Wheaties this morning. Next time, you look after Savannah. I'll go after the criminals," he told Jacob, still trying to catch his breath.

"What're you doin' out here?" Jacob snapped. "Why didn't you keep her in the house?" he said, turning to Marcus.

"Let's just say that your girl is not the kind to be kept. But she's your problem now. I need to nurse my wounds."

"Wounds? Did I break the skin? Let me see?" Savannah asked, hoping to call a truce. "I didn't mean to hurt you. C'mon, let me see it."

Reluctantly, Marcus extended his hand. "What happened out here anyway?" he asked, as Savannah examined his hand. "And where's Brandon?"

"Brandon!" Jacob moaned. "Ah, man, I forgot. I got distracted by this dude. Brandon went down over there," he said, looking behind him. "I think he took a bullet."

"Bullet!" Savannah screamed, dropping Marcus's hand to look for Brandon.

"I'm okay, even though my arm feels like it's on fire. I think the bullet just grazed me," he said, sitting propped up against a tree. His shirt was bloody as he held his arm.

Savannah swallowed and stared. "It's bleeding badly," she said once she got the courage to actually examine the wound. "It does look like it's just a gash. We should get you back to the house." Tearing a piece off the bottom of her white, cotton dress, she tied it around his arm to stop the bleeding.

"When did you turn into Florence Nightingale?" Brandon asked.

"I was wonderin' the same thing myself," Jacob noted. She'd done it again—transformed.

"I'm not always a self-absorbed female. I can help others."

"Then how about helpin' me?" Marcus groaned, now nursing his own wound. "I'm sure I'll need a tetanus shot."

"Oh, man up. I didn't bite you that hard."

"You bit him?" Brandon asked, surprised.

"Well, I was trying to help you guys, and he kept getting in the way."

"Yeah and remind me to stay out of your way in the future," Marcus sulked.

"I said I was sorry. But isn't it weird that I'm able to get my target? But each time this guy shoots, he can't."

"No accomplices?" Marcus asked, focusing back on the unconscious man on the ground that Jacob was relentlessly guarding, even though it was clear that the man wasn't going anywhere.

"Nah, it seems like it was just him. I think this was about property damage," Brandon noted. "This guy may even have been told that no one should get hurt."

"Dag, Jacob, this guy's out cold," Marcus stated, now standing over the man. "Now how are you supposed to find out what he was up to?"

"Wake him up," Brandon suggested.

"There's smelling salt in the first aid kit behind the front desk," Savannah offered. "I'll get it," she said, getting up to leave.

"Oh no, you don't," Jacob said, grabbing her arm. "Marcus'll get it. Just in case there's a problem. You stay with us unless Brandon wants to head back."

"Next trip, the pain's killin' me. I must've pulled something when I tackled the guy. Maybe you could bring me some pain medication from that first aid kit?"

"You got it, bro," Marcus stated before taking off at a much slower pace than he had used to run after Savannah.

"So, you're some kind of female Rambo, huh?" Jacob asked.

"No. I just had a revelation. For the first time, it was real to me that the Carapones could take away the people that I love."

"Finally, you get it, and all it took was me gettin' shot up," Brandon stated sarcastically. "And we still don't know what this guy was up to. We should go before someone really gets hurt."

"Let's wake him up first," Jacob suggested. "Brandon, you got your phone on you?"

"Yeah."

"Then call the police to come pick up this piece of garbage." Looking up, he saw Marcus heading back. "Maybe now we can get some answers." Once Marcus joined them, Jacob administered the smelling salt. When the guy came to, Jacob was ready. "Who hired you?" he asked, showing the gun.

"I don't know," the man stated, disoriented.

"Wrong answer, dude. Try again." Jacob cocked the gun directly in the man's ear. When he failed to answer, Jacob fired the gun at the man's knee.

Both Savannah and the man screamed. Then a string of obscenities flew out of the man's mouth as the blood gushed out of his knee. Catching his breath, he was about to start another obscenity string when Jacob stopped him.

"Enough with the cursin'. Don't you see there's a lady present? And stop cryin'. I did warn you. Not my fault you didn't listen. That bullet was for sneakin' round my lady's house and for shootin' Brandon. But you've got another knee and some other nonvital parts. Do you really want to stick with that answer?

"I was contacted over the phone," the man quickly replied. "I didn't meet with nobody. I swear."

"No need to swear. Just tell us what you were sent to do," Brandon said.

"Set explosives and send a warning shot. That's it."

"And did you?" Jacob asked.

"Yeah, but no one was supposed to get hurt."

"How'd you do that?" Savannah asked. "We were all watching so closely."

Looking at her with annoyance, the man didn't answer.

"You want that other knee shot out?" Jacob threatened him again. "Then you better answer the lady."

"I put it in the kitchen—the one place that wasn't guarded," the man grumbled.

"How do you stop it?" Marcus asked.

"You can't!"

"Don't play with me!" Moving the gun to the man's head, Jacob snarled, "You've got two seconds to convince me why I shouldn't put a bullet in your skull!"

"You have to disarm it," the man hurriedly answered. "It's set to go off at midnight."

"Then you'll disarm it," Jacob reasoned. "Get up on your good knee."

"Jacob! It's a minute to midnight!" Savannah panicked. "Trinity and Cara, they're still in the kitchen!"

"Brandon, call Trinity!" Jacob yelled out. Brandon called, but there was no answer. It was the same for Cara.

Chapter Thirty-Two

"Trinity!" Brandon screamed, running full-speed toward the house, his injuries now forgotten. Then he saw her, and his body was flooded with relief. She had come out of the kitchen but was heading back in. Seeing her about to reenter, he yelled her name again. With everything in him, he screamed to get her attention, but he was too late. His screams were drowned out by a thunderous boom, followed by the sound of breaking glass as the kitchen windows blew out. He watched in horror as the blast sent her and the kitchen door flying several feet, her body slamming to the ground. He saw it all in slow motion—each bone of her body hitting the ground, absorbing the shock of the fall—her head being the last to hit. And then, there was no motion at all—only a still, lifeless Trinity.

Marcus too felt as though his insides had been ripped out. Watching the kitchen kindling, the smoke billowing out of the windows, he could feel the tears slowly rolling down his cheek. Only Trinity had stepped out of the kitchen. Cara was still inside. Collapsing to the ground, he watched in silence as Savannah and Brandon ran toward Trinity. But his thoughts were only of Cara. "God, why?" he screamed, looking up at the sky. "Cara was the most faithful one of all of us," he cried unashamedly. "Cara!" he screamed again as the knots formed in his stomach, his mind now picturing the flames engulfing her.

"Marcus?" Cara came around the corner hesitantly. "You were callin' me?"

Looking up, he saw her dressed in a long, white, flowing, Cara original maxi-dress. The moon provided the perfect stage lighting, making her appear larger than life. And although he didn't believe in ghosts, still he wanted to ensure that she was real, feel her beating heart against his.

"Marcus, what is it?" she said, loosening his grip, staring at his grim expression. "I went to tell you guys that the hot chocolate was ready, but everyone was gone. Then I heard a boom and came outside and heard you yelling."

"The Carapones blew up the kitchen. I thought you were inside. I thought … I'd …" but his words were lost as his feelings consumed him. All he could think about was kissing her, which he did. And for a moment, time stood still as he wondered how she'd been able to get under his skin, for no other woman had been able to do that.

"You say they blew up the kitchen … Trinity!"

"She'd come out of the kitchen," he explained, his thoughts now refocused. "But she got caught by the blast. Come on," he said, grabbing her hand and running toward where Trinity had been thrown.

When they reached the rest of the gang, they found Trinity lying on the ground, motionless. Brandon was still trying to wake her.

"Is she okay?" Cara asked.

"Trinity's breathing, and she's got a pulse, but we can't wake her up," Savannah sobbed.

"Where's Jacob?" Cara asked, panicking.

"He's with the guy who set the explosives. They're waiting for the police to arrive." Looking up, she saw Jacob and an officer approaching. "They're coming now." When the officer arrived, he took charge. Minutes later, the sounds of fire trucks and emergency vehicles were speeding toward them.

Instinctively, Jacob found Savannah. He held her as she explained about Trinity. Then Savannah remembered. "The diaries!" she blurted out, breaking away from Jacob's embrace.

"You can't go in there," Jacob said, pulling her back. "It's too late. The diaries are gone." As he spoke, the flames leaped out at her, almost in a taunting fashion.

"No!" she screamed uncontrollably while pushing hard against Jacob's hold. When her strength finally gave out, she collapsed into his arms crying. "So where's your God now?"

Chapter Thirty-Three

Breaking the yellow police tape, Savannah stepped into her beloved kitchen. The only positive was that the explosion had been contained and had not spread to the rest of the house. Looking around the kitchen, she saw only blackness. The tears stung at her eyes, remembering the bright colors that used to clothe the walls. The blue granite counters that had been so vivid and the cobalt-blue floors that had reminded her of the ocean. Now it was nothing but black ashes.

"You're just tormentin' yourself," Cara told her, coming in. "Jacob went to get some boards to close this room up. Come back into the lobby with me?"

"Can't," Savannah said, determined to face this tragedy head-on. Walking over the rubble, she shook her head. "How could someone have smuggled in enough explosives to do this much damage? You think Brandon's responsible?"

"Nah," Cara replied. "He could've stabbed us in the back, but he would've never risked Trinity's life. And her suggestion of hot chocolate came out of the blue. If Brandon had been involved, he would've never let her go back in that kitchen."

"Yeah, I guess." Savannah then kicked a scorched pot across the floor. "Trinity's wavering between life and death, just like Grandma Nene. And just like God didn't save Grandma Nene, He's not saving Trinity." Dropping to the floor, Savannah folded her arms across her chest and rocked herself. It was happening again. Everyone that she loved was dying.

"C'mon, Savannah, we have to keep the faith," Cara said, sitting down beside her. "I remember tryin' to control everythin' with the fashion show. Then Peggy drove up and told me about the Carapones. At that point, I just gave up. Poor Peggy probably thought that I was mad at her. Then Peggy must've gone to tell you guys. Still, despite everything, I knew that God would come through somehow. I'm tellin' you He's not done with this situation yet."

Cara's religious Energizer Bunny attitude was annoying. Needing to get away, she began pacing. Passing the hidden tunnel, she pushed the button out of curiosity. Surprisingly, it still worked. Then something that Cara said struck a nerve. "Peggy didn't tell us about the Carapones. Brandon did. So how did she tell you when she first drove up … unless … she was working for the Carapones. She probably helped the guy. But how?" Savannah sighed, frustrated by her own theory. "No one came in or out who wasn't escorted through the front door and through the pat downs. Unless she used the tunnel, but she didn't know about that."

"Uh … yeah … she did," Cara sheepishly admitted.

"Cara! How could you! How could you tell Peggy something that sensitive?"

"I didn't know she was a mole for the Carapones. In fact, we still don't know that!"

"Don't we?" Savannah shot back, her mind now racing to indict Peggy. "Remember how Peggy blamed Vanessa for the leak about the skeleton? Didn't you find it funny that Peggy only mentioned it after she learned about our involvement in Vanessa's firing? And it was also Peggy who told us that our business dreams were over. If it hadn't been for Jamie, the PR guy, she would've had us throwing in the towel. Then she tells you about the Carapones' plans before we tell her? And I heard her telling Brandon to get us out of the house. Why would she do all that unless she knew what the Carapones were planning?" It was even Peggy who suggested putting the diaries in my car, and then she distracted me. Peggy wanted the diaries destroyed."

"Aren't you just jumpin' to unsubstantiated conclusions?"

"You have another explanation? Someone sets up major explosives in the kitchen where Peggy is, but she sees nothing."

"Still, we can't prove it was her."

"Yeah we can. If someone came from the outside, we should know. The secret cabinet door works, which means the tunnel is probably intact too. Let's check it out." Savannah pushed the button and watched the cabinet door slide over again. It took only moments to confirm that the latch had been released from the inside.

"No!" Cara cried, the tears now streaming down her face. "What have I done?"

"Tied this bombing to the Carapones. That's what you've done. The explosives guy couldn't finger the Carapones, but if we're right about Peggy, she probably had all kinds of contact with them."

"But how will you get Peggy to confess?"

"Haven't figured that part out yet, but we should start by telling the police."

Chapter Thirty-Four

Savannah and Cara waited with the police for Peggy's arrival. They were hidden from the road but had a full view of the tunnel opening. Hopefully, Peggy had taken the bait that the police were coming to get fingerprints off the tunnel. If she was guilty, then she should be worried about them finding her prints. The truth was that the police had already tried to collect fingerprints but were unsuccessful. If Peggy didn't show up, then they were back to square one.

Peggy's heart was racing, driving along the bumpy road. How did she get into this mess? It was supposed to be so simple. Blow up a kitchen—not people. And she was pretty sure if things went wrong that the Carapones would not back her up. It wasn't like she started out double-crossing Savannah. But after Jacob rejected her, she had wanted to get even. She only hoped that "getting even" didn't mean going to jail. She had been in tight spots before and got out. Why should this time be any different?

Thankfully, the place was deserted. She had thought about calling ahead to make sure that everyone was at the hospital, but the fact that there were no cars eased her mind. Getting out of the car, Peggy popped the trunk and looked for the rag that she used to wax her car. Spotting the orange and white square piece of material, she took one more cautious look before running over to the tunnel door to wipe away any possible prints.

"Ms. Peggy Styles, you're under arrest for arson and attempted murder," the lieutenant said, coming out from hiding.

Peggy turned around in fear, her mind racing. "It's not what it looks like."

"Save it for the station. I've seen enough to take you in," the lieutenant responded as he told his men to cuff her and radioed for the police cars to come.

The sound of sirens soon filled the air, filling Peggy with terror. "Wait, you don't know the full story."

"I know you're responsible for Trinity lying in a hospital bed," Savannah said, coming out from hiding as well. "She dies, you're going down for murder. I hope you know that!"

"Savannah," Peggy gasped, now seeing the trap that had been set for her. "I'm not saying anything until I speak with a lawyer!" she snapped, refusing to give Savannah the satisfaction of seeing her fear.

"You're definitely going to need one. Do you think it'll be Brandon? Because I can just imagine the work that he'll put into your defense once he discovers that you're the one responsible for hurting his fiancée. Jacob truly showed good judgment in passing you up."

You little hussy, Peggy thought, her fear now turning to rage. "He didn't pass me up," she said with satisfaction. "A couple of weeks ago, you guys had a little fight, right?" She saw the look of surprise on Savannah's face. "He told me when he invited me over, and he put this little seduction scene on for me. He had that fake wine that he drinks and the champagne glasses nicely displayed. I slept with him out of curiosity, but then I dumped him. He wasn't that good, and honestly, I didn't like getting your leftovers. Jacob may've come back to you, but it was only because I wasn't impressed."

Without thinking, Savannah reared back and punched Peggy, hitting her so hard that she fell down, even though two police officers were holding onto her.

"That's enough," the lieutenant said, jumping between the two women.

"I'm pressing charges," Peggy said, touching her swelling lip while struggling to get back up on her feet. "I have witnesses!"

"I didn't see anything," the lieutenant said. "Now get her out of here." Turning to Savannah, he added, "Good work, and I wouldn't put too much stock into anything that she says."

"Jacob will never be happy with you," Peggy yelled over her shoulder as she struggled with the police officers to get loose. "He needs to be with a real woman. Not some pessimistic piece of trash like you! He had the best with Kimberly. Remember that," she said, as she was pushed into the police car.

"Peggy's right," Savannah sighed.

"She's not right! Peggy must've been at Restoration the night you and Jacob had your fight. I saw her car, but I dismissed it when no one else saw it. She must've followed him home and saw him setting things up for you. C'mon, you look way better than Peggy. If he turned you down for religious reasons, then he absolutely would've turned her down!"

"I know," Savannah said convincingly.

"You know! Then how's she right?"

"She's right about Jacob never being happy with me. He needs a woman who loves God, and I'm not that woman."

Chapter Thirty-Five

Stepping outside of his room, Jacob looked around Restoration. He'd boarded up the kitchen, but the damage had already been done. And Peggy's role in all of this was still mind-boggling. His blood had boiled just listening to how Savannah and Cara helped the police to capture Peggy. What had the Carapones promised her—money, power, position? Whatever the lure, they must now be elated. They had delivered a decisive blow. Trinity was in the hospital. The kitchen was destroyed. And most importantly, Restoration would never be free of danger.

"Savannah, honey, we've gotta go," he yelled, knocking on her bedroom door. They'd all agreed that church was the best place to pray for Trinity, who was still in a coma. Her thirty-six-hour clock, which the doctor had given before brain damage set in, was running out. "You're not ready," he responded, when she came out in faded jeans and a gray sweatshirt.

"What's the point? God doesn't care! And that's why Trinity is lingering between life and death! Let's face it. I'm never going to be the little model Christian wife," she said, falling to the ground, sobbing uncontrollably.

"Savannah!" he said, reaching out to her.

"Don't touch me!" she screamed. "I don't want your pity. Just leave me alone." Pulling off her engagement ring, she thrust it at him. "Take it! I can't marry you."

"You're just upset. Give it time." He knew he had to be patient. She was new at trusting God, and a blown-up kitchen and Trinity in a coma were hard even for him — a veteran Christian. He could only imagine how she must be feeling.

"Time," she repeated. "I've been this way for thirty-three years! I don't need more time! I need a miracle, and that's not what I've been given," she said in a softer tone. "Take the ring," she replied, her hand still extended. "You're the most beautiful man I know. You won't have any problems replacing me." Reluctantly, he took the ring. "Now leave!" she ordered. "You can come back for your things, but I want you out of my house ... and out of my life!"

"Savannah, this is crazy, I ..."

"If you love me, then let me go," she said, with a tone of finality.

"Fine," he said, going to the door. Looking back, he realized that for the first time he didn't like what his chameleon woman had become.

Once Jacob was out of the door, Cara and Marcus came out from hiding in the back alcove. "Did you just throw out the one person who was perfect for you?" Cara asked.

"He wasn't perfect for me—he was just perfect. And somewhere out there is the perfect woman. Peggy was right! I'm not the right woman for him."

"Peggy's a screwed up, homicidal maniac! You can't believe anything she says. I saw the difference God made in your life."

"Stop it!" Savannah yelled, covering her ears with her hands. "I'm as screwed up as always. I never should have come to Jamaica. I told you that I had a bad omen about this place, and I was right."

"You weren't right! Since you've been here, you've been stronger. And Jacob will never be happy with someone else. He loves you. Nahum 1:7 says, 'The Lord is good. When trouble comes, he is the place to go!'"

"Cara, you get out too. I can't help you start a business anymore. So why hang around?"

"You don't mean that!"

"Yeah, I do. Trinity's already in the hospital because of me. I won't be responsible for you too. Go back to the States where you have family."

"You're my family! And Trinity's in the hospital because of the Carapones, not you. And we know it was the Carapones, even though their hit man won't admit it, and apparently neither will Peggy. The night of the blast, Trinity told me that she stayed for herself, not for you. Cookin' is her dream, and she was willin' to fight for her dream. Why can't you fight?"

"We're done here," Savannah said, slamming her bedroom door behind her.

"Savannah!" Cara yelled through the door. "You stubborn mule, you'll regret this!" she said, banging loudly on the door.

"Babe," Marcus stated, pulling her off the door. "Give it a rest."

"You're siding with Savannah?" she said, looking dumbfounded. "Forget it," she sighed. "I'm goin' to church." Grabbing her purse, she headed for the door. "Aren't you comin'?" she asked, looking back at Marcus.

"I guess."

"I still don't understand why you're not supportin' me," she rambled on as they walked to the car. "You think Savannah's right to kick Jacob to the curb, to blame herself for Trinity's accident, or to push away those who love her?"

"No, but what she doesn't need is the Christian Energizer Bunny bombardin' her. Have you never been in a place where you found it hard to trust God?"

"No! Just this mornin', I was readin' Romans 12:12, 'Rejoice in our confident hope. Be patient in—'"

"Enough, Cara!"

"So you're mad at me for having faith?"

"No, I'm just sayin' that everyone's not in the same place as you. Maybe you should take it down a notch. And I'm not sure I'm feelin' church today," he said, stopping and looking down.

"It's not about feelin'. You've got to just trust Him—like a kid."

"Yeah ... well, right now, I'm feelin' like a kid who needs some space."

"From whom—me or God?"

"Both!" Then he turned and walked toward his car.

"Forget you, Marcus!" Heading toward her car, the tears began to fall. "I get you, God, but You need to do somethin'—'cause You're losin' the rest of 'em."

Chapter Thirty-Six

The sound of silence was deafening. What had Savannah done? Sent away the best man she'd ever known, gone off on one of her closest friends. But what was the point of dwelling on that now? Instead, she focused on cleaning the attic. And there was so much stuff up there it took twenty minutes just to clear a path. After her hard work, she was looking forward to sifting through an old desk, which is why she was doubly disappointed when she tripped over a floorboard and landed on her butt.

Angrily, she pounded the board back down, but it wouldn't stay down. Something was underneath it. Using a rod, she lifted one of the boards and saw something metal. Encouraged, she pried up a few more boards before discovering a box. Pulling it out, she set it down before her. She gasped when she lifted the lid. Inside was a beautiful diamond and sapphire necklace. After making a mental note to have it appraised, she set the necklace aside to see what was lying underneath. They were pages from Ruby's diary.

January 15, 1833
Dearest Charles,

If you are reading this, then I must have passed on. I'm writing down what I could not bear to say in person. I have spent my last days searching the Bible, looking for why I was born into a world where I did not belong. I found comfort in John 15: 18–19, "If the world hates you, ye know that it hated me before it hated you. If ye were of the world, the world would love his own: but because ye are not of the world, but I have chosen you out of the world, therefore the world hateth you."

Reading this, I knew that God understood me. I also read about how God's Son came to save man, but they killed Him. Yet, it wasn't mere men that killed God's Son, but men under the influence of Satan. That is why he was able to say, "Father forgive them, for they know not what they do."

Please know that I forgive you and the men who robbed me of my soul. I now know that it was not really them but Satan. God showed me in 1 John, *that if I cannot love those who I can see, how can I love God whom I have never seen?* You must forgive too. Forgive Ernestine because I have.

If you truly love me, then live a life that God approves of, and we will be together again, in a world where love is cherished and not forbidden. Protect Billy—body and soul. Don't let him or his children forget me. Take care of Bell too. Remember me always.

Love,
Ruby Lee

Overcome with emotion, Savannah sat silently as the pieces of her past came together. Grandma Nene's dying proclamation of wealth wasn't the house. Picking up the necklace again, her heart raced realizing its value. According to her grandmother, it was worth millions, which meant Savannah could pay off her debts and still have money to start over.

Grandma Nene's story had been a constant reminder that she was not alone. Before she had a need, God had prepared a way. Second Corinthians 4:9 came to mind, "We are troubled on every side, yet not distressed; we are perplexed, but not in despair; Persecuted, but not forsaken; cast down, but not destroyed." Finally, she understood. Trials would come, but they would never overcome her. Her first thought was to tell Jacob. And to get back the man that God had truly given to her.

Chapter Thirty-Seven

Finding Ruby's old letter was nothing short of a miracle, Cara thought as she drove to the villa to see Marcus after leaving church. She was still in shock from Savannah telling the entire church about her feelings for Jacob and what had happened to her. She'd responded to the minister's appeal, and then once she got down the aisle she'd grabbed the mic and shared her testimony. Who knew that Savannah had been through something so tragic, and how romantic to have Jacob come to her side for support and then to propose again in front of the whole congregation. Obviously, the family stories would continue, and now Savannah had stories that rivaled and maybe even exceeded Grandma Nene's.

Pulling up to the villa, Cara saw Marcus's car next to a green Honda. "Dag, he must be workin'." But that did not deter her from wanting to share her news about Savannah. It only made Cara more conscious of guests while looking for him. First, she checked his living quarters, but there was no answer. Then she tried his cell, but again no answer. Taking a chance, she went inside. She looked for Alice but didn't see her either. *Maybe they're outside*, she thought. Cautiously, she crossed the living room, and in doing so, she passed her old bedroom. Looking through the cracked door, she saw Marcus lying next to a young woman. "Marcus," instinctively slipped out of her mouth before she could catch herself. Her next instinct was to run.

"Cara!" Marcus yelled, jumping up from the bed. "Cara!" he called again. This time she stopped. "It's not what it looks like," he explained, pointing back toward the room. "She means nothin' to me."

"Why do guys always say that? Did I mean nothin' to you the first time you slept with me?" she asked him. "Newsflash, it always means somethin' to us women. If it means nothin' to you guys, then keep it to yourselves!"

"That's not what I meant," he said, running his hand nervously through his hair. "You're getting the wrong idea."

"Oh, I got the right idea. You're gettin' back at the Christian Energizer Bunny, right?"

"No, but you make a good point. Because you're so religious, I'm thinkin' that I may not be the right guy for you."

"Why?" she snapped. "Nonreligious women allow their boyfriends to sleep around?"

"I'm not sleepin' around," he snapped back in frustration. "That's Karen and ..."

But Karen interrupted them by stepping out of the bedroom. She was dressed in a green, thigh-high, back-out spandex dress, which she kept adjusting. "What's goin' on?"

"What's goin' on out here isn't the issue," Cara said in a superior tone. Dressed in a more conservative blouse and skirt, having just come from church, she felt a class above the trampy woman. Even though Cara probably had a similar outfit in her own closet, although it'd been awhile since she'd worn such an outfit. Without even realizing it, her wardrobe had changed. She was now covering up the assets more. "The better question is what was going on in there?" she asked, pointing to the bedroom door that was still slightly ajar. "You do know that fornication is a sin. And put some more clothes on—'cause your body ain't all that!"

"Excuse you! I don't know who you are, but I don't think I like you," Karen said, sucking her teeth.

"It's not your job to like me. That's my job. Your job is likin' yourself, and based on that outfit, you're not doin' a good job."

"I know you're not talkin' in that nonmatchin' nun outfit you've got on? Maybe if you stop dressin' like a nun, you wouldn't have to act like a woman who ain't gitten none. But I'm happy to show you what this body can do," Karen said, taking off her earrings.

"Whoa, Karen," Marcus jumped in. "It probably is best if you just go."

"Are you sure?" she asked, scowling at Cara.

"Yeah, he's sure," Cara answered for him. "Take your trampy, fornicating self home!"

"Why, you little—"

"Ladies," Marcus stated, standing between them. "Karen, really I'm with Cara."

"Fine," Karen snapped. "But call me if you get tired of religious psycho girl," she spat out before leaving.

"How come no one appreciates my commitment to God?" Cara asked once Karen left. "When I was a wild woman sleepin' around gettin' drunk, I was great, huh?"

"No, it's just that your commitment level is off the charts. Who even uses the word 'fornicate' anymore? And is it Christian to call people out like you just did?"

"Oh, forgive me for not wantin' to turn the other cheek. What did you want me to say? 'Go forth and sleepeth with my boyfriend?' Anyway, you're the one who stopped me from leavin'."

"'Cause you were leavin' with the wrong impression." Shaking his head, he added, "It doesn't matter. Bottom line—it's not workin'. You deserve better. You deserve a Jacob kind of guy."

"Don't go there!" she stated, her hands automatically moving to her hips. "If you want to leave—then leave!" she said with a swiveling neck. "Just don't bring Jacob into this! Be man enough to say you don't want me instead of usin' a disagreement to sleep with the first woman that drops by."

"You want manly? You got it! It's over, Cara. I've moved on!"

There was a moment of silence between them, and then her phone rang. When she saw the number, she had no choice but to answer. "Hello," she replied robotically, moving over to the couch to sit. "No, no, I'm good … Really? That's great … Okay, I'll see you back at the house."

"What?" Marcus asked, in a much more demure tone.

"Trinity woke up. She's going to be fine," Cara explained before bursting into tears. Her tears were partly for Trinity and partly for herself. For while she should've been ecstatic about Trinity's news, she was more concerned with what was happening between her and Marcus.

"Trinity came out of the coma. That's a relief," he said, taking her in his arms. "You know I didn't mean what I just said. I haven't moved on, but I need to," he said, looking down at her. "Sometimes I feel like Jacob when Kimberly was alive. Only when she was out of the picture did Jacob develop his own relationship with God. I feel like that around you. I feel … smothered. I keep thinkin' that I'm gonna disappoint you. You're havin' a positive impact bein' the Christian Energizer Bunny," he said, teasingly. "And I don't want to be the one who takes that away. The Bible says not to be unequally yoked. Translation—when you're a couple goin' in different directions, it can only end badly. I say we break up now while we're still friends."

"But I love you!" The words slipped out before her pride could stop them. She'd never been in this predicament—in love with a guy who wasn't in love with her.

"You just think you're in love with me. Actually, you're in love with God, and that's how it should be," he said, kissing her lightly on the forehead. "Give a brother some space. Let me figure out God on my own. Don't be like Adam, choosing Eve over God 'cause you see where that got us." He laughed. "You'll have to trust me on this one." This time he kissed her hand. "You're one of a kind, Cara, but I've got to find God for myself."

"Fine," she said, caving.

"Friends?" he said, hugging her tighter.

"Friends," she replied, wondering how she would settle for being a friend after being a lover.

Chapter Thirty-Eight

Sitting in the lobby, Savannah was filled with regret. Restoration had been her baby. It had come with structure, but she had given it heart and style. When she'd learned about Ruby, she had taken even more care to make it perfect. So how could she give it up? Why couldn't God just get rid of the Carapones? It's not like they needed to die. Just weaken them enough to leave Restoration alone. But the words of Isaiah ran through her mind. "For my thoughts are not your thoughts, neither are your ways my ways." Besides, the same God who gave them Restoration could give them another place. And the necklace, worth 3.2 million, provided the needed funds to start over.

"Why so serious?" Cara asked, plopping down beside Savannah on the couch.

"I'm not. I'm just waiting for Brandon to bring Trinity. She's being released today. And Jacob's hosting a dinner in her honor."

"Really." Cara had been out of the loop since her break up with Marcus.

"Yeah, can you and Marcus bring drinks?"

"Uh, not sure I can make it. I already made plans."

"Bummer. What're you doing?"

"Client consultation," Cara quickly lied and then changed the subject. "But it'll be so good having Trinity back. It hasn't been the same without her." Cara sighed, looking around Restoration. "So much has happened in such a short period of time. Makes you wonder what's next?"

"About that ... I mean the what's next part—"

"She's here!" Cara interrupted, seeing Brandon's car approaching. With that announcement, both women rushed to be by Trinity's side, completely pushing Brandon out of the way to help Trinity into the house.

"It's good to be home," Trinity told them once situated. "I'm tellin' you, hospital food is terrible, and the décor is even worse. If I hadn't gotten out of there soon, I'd have killed myself."

"But you're good now?" Cara asked, concerned.

"I'm a little sore, but I feel like me. I heard we're gonna have to start from scratch with the kitchen. I'm bummed 'bout that. Although in the hospital, I was reminded that everythin' happens for a reason. At least now I know why the appliances were delayed."

"Speaking of appliances," Savannah interjected, "I'm glad that we're all here." Taking a deep breath, she blurted out, "I'm selling Restoration to the Carapones."

"No!" Cara and Trinity cried out together.

"She's making the right decision," Brandon affirmed.

"Shut up, Brandon!" Cara and Trinity shouted simultaneously.

"Cockroach nuh business inna fowl fight," Trinity scowled.

"I agree," Cara said. "Although I have no idea what you just said. But, Savannah, you can't let the Carapones win. This morning I was readin' James 4:1–3." Pulling the text up on her phone, she read, "'You want what you don't have, so you scheme and kill to get it. You are jealous for what others have, and you can't possess it, so you fight and quarrel to take it away from them. And yet the reason you don't have what you want is that you don't ask God for it. And even when you do ask, you don't get it because your whole motive is wrong—you want only what will give you pleasure.' Now, doesn't that sound like the Carapones? And that proves that they don't deserve Restoration."

"People are getting hurt," Savannah reminded Cara. "Trinity's okay now, but if I'd sold the house, then she never would've been injured in the first place. And what about the people at Wednesday's fashion show? What if something had happened to them?"

"But nothing did. Our God is bigger than the Carapones," Cara said, standing, making her point like a preacher. "Remember, 'Greater is he that is in us than he that is in the world?' God didn't bring us this far to leave us. We just have to hold onto Romans 12:12, 'Be patient in trouble, and keep on praying.'"

"I have prayed about this," Savannah said, now also standing. "I don't believe that God's leaving us. I think He wanted us to come here, learn about Ruby Lee, become friends, and find the necklace. But Brandon's right. What we do, we can do anywhere. The necklace gives us the ability to start over somewhere else."

"Maybe you're right," Trinity reasoned. "Also, you shouldn't be the only one investing in our business. Brandon said he'd help," she stated, looking over at Brandon for confirmation.

"Absolutely. You guys are a good investment."

"No!" Cara blasted them again. "I see us right here changin' peoples' lives—the way our lives were changed."

"But should we knowingly put ourselves and others in danger? We take two steps forward, and the Carapones take us back four," Savannah said, frustrated.

"God said that if we just have the faith of a mustard seed that we could move mountains. The Carapones aren't mountains. We just have to wait and see how God's gonna work this out."

"Cara, stop it!" Trinity jumped in. "God's not Santa Claus."

"I get that, but if God wants you to sell, then He'll put the sell papers in your hands."

"We don't have time for this," Savannah said dismissively. "People are making plans to come here. We have a responsibility to limit their damages."

"She's right," Trinity joined in. "Can't you see that everyone's saying it's time to go—the Carapones, the bank, Brandon, Jacob."

"Don't confuse the will of the majority with God's will," Cara stated defiantly.

"You just don't get it!" Savannah said, dropping back down to the couch. "I don't *want* to leave. I *have* to!" she said, emphasizing the distinction. "The Carapones have done everything to us, including blowing up our kitchen. Based on Fredrick Haggerty, the next step is killing one of us." Looking over at Trinity, Savannah noted, "They almost went there this time." Sighing, she ran the back of her hand across the rich fabrics. "This was home for me. I don't have the strength, desire, or passion to put into another place what I put into Restoration. Perhaps that's what God wants to ensure, that we hate this life and long for heaven."

"That's nonsense," Cara said, sitting down beside Savannah. "God told us in Luke 19 to occupy until He comes, and in 3 John 1 it says to be prosperous and be in good health. He wants us to be happy on this earth. I truly believe that God wants us to have this house and not the Carapones!"

"Really? Because everything I've seen says otherwise. Basically, all hell has broken loose. Is there a text for that?"

"Psalm 27," Cara said without missing a beat. "From the Message Bible, and I quote, 'Light, space, zest—that's God! So, with Him on my side, I'm fearless, afraid of no one and nothing ... When all hell breaks loose, I'm collected and cool.'"

Clearly, Cara had a slew of texts about the need to keep Restoration. But were there any on how they were actually supposed to do that? "Then tell me how we do it," Savannah said, putting Cara on the spot.

"Don't look at me—look up. Psalm 121:1, 'I will lift up mine eyes unto the hills, from whence cometh my help. My help cometh from the Lord.' We just have to look up and be patient. Psalm 27:14 says, 'Wait for the Lord, and he will come and save you. Be brave, stouthearted and courageous. Yes, wait and he will help you.'"

The room again went silent as they waited for God to speak.

"Excuse me. Hopefully, I'm not interrupting. I'm looking for Savannah Hartford."

They were all startled by the good-looking, dark Italian man in his late thirties who entered the house. Dressed in a designer black suit, shiny shoes, and a very interesting purple, red, and yellow bow tie, he made a statement. Drying her eyes, Savannah quickly rose to her feet. "I'm Savannah, but we're not open."

"And my family may be the reason for that." Seeing her confusion, he explained, "I'm Antonio Carapone." His introduction made everyone gasp, except for Brandon, who'd instantly recognized him.

"Bully!" Cara exploded. "The police can't prove that you were involved in blowin' up our kitchen, but I know that you were. I don't know what you did to Peggy and that hit man of yours to get them to take the fall for you, but the wicked never prosper!" When her words weren't having the desired effect, she started in with her fists. Savannah and Brandon came to Antonio's rescue.

"I don't believe that I've ever been greeted quite like that," Antonio admitted, although he was more amused than mad.

"I'm happy to welcome you again!" Cara hollered, still being held at bay by Brandon. "I'm not scared of you or your psychotic clan. In fact, I'm scared for you! You have no idea what God does to those who mess with His children. And how do you have the gall to show your face here?"

"Let me explain," Antonio said calmly, although Cara wasn't ready to listen and again tried to pummel him.

"Cara, let him talk," Savannah replied, intervening.

"I'm the new CEO at Carapone Industries. I've been taking the company in a different direction, and my uncle disagrees. He likes the old ways. And unfortunately, he's got quite a network in Jamaica. Several months ago, I stopped the resort that was proposed for this property. Imagine my surprise when I found that things were still moving forward. When I heard about your explosion, I started digging. Let's just say I didn't like what I found. I can't prove that my family was involved in your misfortune, and I won't testify against them, but I can assure you that the Carapones or anyone associated with the Carapones' name will never bother you again. I also found out that there may have been some underhanded dealings with your bank. I've put a stop to that as well. Your funding should be flowing freely again. And finally, as a Good Samaritan," he said, smiling, "I'm willing to pay for the damage to your property."

His proposal was met with stunned silence, giving Antonio a moment to enjoy his surroundings. "It's lovely here," he said, admiring the unusual chandelier. "You've done an incredible job restoring this place. I'm sure that you're going to be quite successful. Please forward me the bill when you have it, and I do understand that it may be extensive. You'll probably have crews working around the clock to get you back on schedule. I've used my connections to make sure that this little event is downplayed by the newspapers and TV. Again, I apologize for the inconvenience."

"If what you say is true, then you're not to blame," Savannah finally said.

"That's kind of you." Antonio thought Savannah was breathtaking. She was tall, about five eight, and slender. When he first entered, she'd seemed broken, but now she was a tower of strength. He wasn't quite sure what had brought about the transformation, but something told him it went beyond his little gesture. Taking her hand, he kissed it. "I hope that this can be the start of a beautiful friendship."

"You're sayin' that the Carapones now want to be friends," Cara said skeptically.

"That's exactly what I'm saying."

"Unbelievable," Trinity gasped. "I wouldn't have believed it if I hadn't seen it with my own eyes. God saved Restoration." A moment of silence filled the room, but then it was replaced by screams of joy.

"I had no idea that my words would have this kind of an effect," Antonio commented, watching the women scream and hug.

"Don't let it go to your head," Brandon cautioned. "This is not about you. They were just talkin' about sellin' this property. You comin' here seems like a direct answer to prayer."

"I'm not religious, but I must admit that I was drawn to do this. There must really be something to this thing called faith." Then he looked directly at Brandon. "Don't I know you?"

"Brandon Anderson," he said, extending his hand. "I'm an attorney at Jenkins and Williams. I was the lead attorney on the Carapone project before I was reassigned because I couldn't get Savannah to sell. My girl has been after me to leave the firm, and after this, I think I'm gonna do it. I no longer want your world. I want that," he stated, pointing to the women.

"I'm not my uncle. Perhaps you should give me a call."

"Not interested. I'm goin' out on my own. It'll be hard, but again, when you know that God's got your back, it changes things." Then Brandon laughed at his own words. "I've never talked about God outside of church before, and now look at me."

"I am looking at you, Mr. Anderson, and I'm impressed. I'd love the opportunity to work with a lawyer with scruples. It'd be refreshing." Reaching into his pocket, he pulled out a card. "Call me. I may be able to make that move a little less daunting. My organization is legit. Think about it. Tell the women I said good-bye."

Brandon smiled as Antonio walked out the door. Obviously, the women weren't the only ones God was blessing.

Chapter Thirty-Nine

A double wedding. Who does that? Cara thought, now exhausted from running around all morning as the wedding coordinator for her two best friends. Savannah and Trinity had decided to combine their weddings, and Brandon and Jacob had smartly agreed, meaning the morning had been hectic trying to incorporate the views of two brides and ensuring that Restoration was ready for its first wedding.

Driving the six minutes to Jacob and Savannah's new home, Cara remembered how upset she'd been at them for buying it. After the wedding, she figured that Trinity would be moving in with Brandon, but she'd secretly hoped that Savannah and Jacob would stay at Restoration. But that dream shattered when they found their little jewel of a house—a small, three-bedroom cottage that Savannah would likely have a ball decorating.

Given its close proximity, the brides had opted to dress there. Carrying in the bouquets, Cara looked down at her watch. "You guys ready to get hitched?" she asked, bursting through the door. "I'd like for this weddin' to be on—" but then she stopped to stare at Trinity and Savannah. They were perfect brides but in completely different ways.

Trinity looked like she belonged on a couture bridal magazine. Her makeup was impeccable, and her hair was in a French roll with tiny ringlet curls spewing out of the top of a diamond tiara. Her dress was made of white organza in a mermaid style that suited her curvaceous figure. It had a sweetheart neckline, with bold fabric flowers on the bottom of the dress. It definitely was a statement piece, with a large, layered train. She was without a doubt a vision in white, perfectly resembling Brandon's dream bride.

Savannah was the complete opposite, choosing to wear her off-the-shoulder, yellow gown that she'd gotten from Petals. At first, against everyone's wishes. But then she explained that this was the first dress that she had put on that had made her feel beautiful. It had brought Jacob to tears, making her his Rachael, and it would honor Ruby's yellow dress that had been destroyed. Everyone then agreed that it was truly the perfect wedding dress for Savannah. Savannah's makeup was minimal, and her hair was loose and long with just a slight wave. And Cara loved the yellow, floor-length veil that she had made to complete the look. Cara knew that Jacob would find Trinity to be lovely, but Savannah would represent pure perfection.

"These guys don't stand a chance," Cara finally said.

"Really, you think we look okay?" Trinity asked.

"Okay? Are you kiddin'? You guys are beautiful and definitely making me cry," Cara stated, dabbing her eyes with a tissue that she picked up off the table.

"It's a good cry though, right?"

"A very good cry," Cara agreed, nodding her head affirmatively.

"I feel amazing," Savannah interjected. "And I'm glad we waited." When she got confused looks, she clarified, "The whole sexual moratorium thing. At first, I didn't see the point. I kept thinking that's so old-fashioned. But now I get it. When I wanted to sleep with Jacob, I still harbored ill will toward those men who hurt me. Sleeping with him back then would have only made things worse. Now, thanks to God, I've been able to forgive those men. So now sleeping with Jacob won't be in the shadow of that night. And Jacob was right about sex concealing faults. It's in marriage that you want a person's faults hidden, not when you're deciding who to marry."

"I certainly learned that the hard way," Trinity admitted. "Brandon got away with murder because he was a good lover. It was only when we stopped makin' love that I understood what I really wanted and made him live up to that."

"It's like that old sayin'," Cara added. "God's way may seem harder, but doin' your own thing is often harder on you. God told us in Luke 11:13, 'If you being evil know how to give good gifts to your children, how much more will your heavenly father give good gifts to you.' Through the Bible, He's gifted us an instruction manual to get us through this life with the least amount of pain. Good for you, Savannah, for finally understanding that. I'm happy for both of you guys," Cara stated before breaking down uncontrollably.

Grabbing a tissue off the table, Savannah handed it to Cara. "You saw Marcus, didn't you?"

Cara nodded her head as she wiped her eyes.

"Well, the good thing is that you look exquisite," Trinity observed. "Green is definitely your color. Your dress fits like a glove, and I love your makeup. So at least you made him sweat."

"Nope, I didn't even do that," Cara sobbed. "When he first saw me, my hair was all over my head, and I had on sweats and an oversized T-shirt." Shaking off the tears, she added, "But it's for the best. He shouldn't just want me because I look good. He needs to embrace all of me, the religious parts too." She was resigned to the fact that Marcus was gone, along with everything that she'd loved about him—his laugh, his amazing body, his blue-black color, his smell of cedar and maple, that dashingly handsome smile. The list seemed to be endless. "He wants us to be friends," Cara shared. "And as a Christian, I owe him that."

"As a woman, you owe yourself time," Trinity threw in.

"Have you ever considered that when God closes a door he opens a window—and maybe your window is Antonio?" Savannah asked.

"Maybe," Cara replied, considering the option. "At first, I was totally against the idea. But after that day when he came by and asked me to study the Bible with him, I started seeing him in a new light. He said he liked my passion for God and wanted that in his life. That's gotta be the best compliment I've ever had. But first, I have to get over Marcus. Maybe if I'd followed God's plan and I hadn't slept with Marcus, it wouldn't be this hard to walk away."

"Can you make it through today?" Trinity asked, turning practical.

"Oh yeah, I've now had my one good cry. It's out of my system. Besides, Marcus has been great. He was usherin' when I left. I didn't even ask him to do it; he just knew." And that's what she would miss most—the way he completed her. She had never met a guy who was so in sync. "But enough about Marcus. My weddings are rarely late. Are you ready?"

"It's time?" Trinity asked nervously.

"Okay, Ms. Why-Aren't-I-Married-Already, I know you're not gettin' cold feet."

"No, it's just that I've waited so long. I have to keep pinchin' myself to see if it's real. Brandon's waitin' for me, right?"

"Oh yeah, he is, and this is happenin'," Cara assured her.

"Then let's do this!" Trinity said, releasing a huge grin.

Chapter Forty

"What's going on?" Savannah asked after the ceremony, when they were ushered into Cara's sewing room.

"A private toast," Cara answered, pouring cider into champagne glasses. "For starters, let's hear it for your wedding coordinator," she said, taking a bow. "Was that a wedding or what?"

"Girl, you rock!" Trinity responded, giving her a hug, and then everyone joined in, except for Marcus, who looked on from the sidelines amused.

"Okay, seriously, here's to"—she raised her glass—"two incredible couples, Ruby Lee bringing us all together, and ... seeing Ruby Lee's restored portrait." She then pulled the sheet off the boxed-up portrait.

"Ruby's portrait came in, and you didn't tell me?" Savannah snapped.

"Don't be mad. It was a split-second decision. I was thinkin' Ruby's unveilin' called for a big event. I know that she's your relative, but we all love her. It just seemed right that we should see it together."

"You're right," Savannah concurred in a softer tone. It didn't take long to get the portrait out of the box, but it took forever to get it out of the bubble wrap. When the packaging was finally removed, Jacob lifted the picture and placed it on the easel.

"Savannah, you are Ruby Lee!" Cara gasped. There was no denying that the woman in the picture looked like Savannah. "And she's wearin' the necklace that you found in the attic," she said, gently touching the painting.

"Wonder why Ruby didn't write about it?" Savannah asked.

"Maybe Haggerty had the necklace painted on after she died as a clue of the treasure."

"Wow, Cara! Looks like you picked up a thing or two from Grandma Nene," Savannah said, impressed.

"Where will you hang it?"

"Not sure. It's far too special for the library like I'd originally planned. I'm thinking the lobby." Still mesmerized, Savannah noted, "I could stare at it forever."

"Forever will have to wait because, as your weddin' coordinator, I'm bringin' this party to an end. Your guests are waitin'," Cara said, pushing everyone out. Once the reception started, she maneuvered, massaged, and fixed things until everyone was seated, eating, and having a great time. But when no one was watching, she escaped. She needed to think about what was next for her. The world that she had come to know was changing. Savannah and Jacob would be moving out of Restoration tonight, and Trinity and Brandon, who were staying in the honeymoon suite, would probably be gone by the week's end. "While I'll still be here," Cara grumbled out loud. "God, I know that Your ways are better, but this hurts."

"Want some company?"

Turning around, she was surprised to find Marcus. "Not in the mood," she said crossly.

Undeterred by her tone, he pushed on. "You used to like my company."

"Marcus, I'm one step away from a nervous breakdown. If you don't want to push me over, then go back to the reception." Looking up at him, she was captivated by that five o'clock shadow that made him so sexy, his jacket that was open, revealing his dangling untied bow tie, and his muscled body that naturally stirred up her feelings. All of these things, she now forced herself to dismiss.

"I'll leave," he said in a soft, sexy drawl. "If that's what you truly want."

"That's exactly what I want!" Then, turning away, she headed toward the ocean. Glancing back, she saw him heading toward the house, and part of her was disappointed that he'd given up so easily. Continuing to walk, she figured someday she'd laugh at this heartbreak. But right now, it hurt too much. Looking up in the sky, she knew God was there. She just had to have faith that He would get her through this. "I trust You, God," she again voiced out loud.

"Is He the only one you trust?"

Turning around, she once again found Marcus standing behind her. "I thought I told you to go away," she said, although not with much conviction. Her heart was now racing because he'd come back for her, although she wasn't sure if that was a good or a bad thing.

"I'm not leavin' until you've heard what I've got to say. I never slept with Karen. She made all the moves, but I rejected every one of them. In fact, I haven't slept with anyone since you. I went out a couple of times, but every date brought me to the same conclusion—that I was in love with you."

"Stop it, Marcus! I can't do this right now! I don't want to be with a man who doesn't share my religious beliefs. You said it yourself—it would never work!"

"I was wrong. You are the one, Cara Williams, but I was jealous of your relationship with God. I kept wondering why I couldn't stay committed. Like Ruby, I studied nonstop. But I got nothin'. Then I went outside to take a walk, and a car drove by blastin' the song 'Don't Give Up on God, Because He Won't Give Up on You.' Then I remembered the text 'Ye have not chosen me, but I have chosen you, and ordained you, that ye should go and bring forth fruit.' After that, I realized that I hadn't been runnin' from you or God. I'd been runnin' from my purpose. Right there, in the middle of the street, I stopped runnin'. I know this may seem like a line and …"

Touching his lips, Cara quieted him. "You had me at 'I stopped runnin'.'" Taking a deep breath, she suddenly realized that she wasn't going to be alone. "Why don't we get married too?"

"You're askin' me to marry you?"

"It's a bit unconventional." She laughed. "But I know what I want. And it sounds like you now want the same things." She paused before adding, "That was your cue … why aren't you answerin'?"

"It's … complicated."

"Complicated?" Cara spat out. "Actually it's quite simple, and apparently, so am I. If you would excuse me, I'm going for a walk—alone!"

"Cara," he replied, catching her by the waist. "Goodness, woman, you're always jumpin' to the wrong conclusions."

"What conclusion should I come to? Either you love me enough to marry me or you don't," she said, remembering Trinity's words that a man shows love by being able to commit.

Still holding on to her, he said, "If this was just about me being in love, then my answer would be an automatic yes. But there's more to it than that."

"Like what?"

"Like my callin'. What if it was to be a minister and not an architect? I've enrolled in the seminary in the States. I start in January. I didn't want you to think that you're marryin' an architect that could give you dates at Orion. When I ask you to marry me, I need to know that you're willing to marry a poor minister. And I get that you're a modern woman, but I'm an old-fashioned kind of guy." Getting down on one knee, he pulled out a ring from the inside pocket of his tuxedo. "So, if you're okay with spending your life with a minister, I was wonderin' if you'd make me—"

"Yes!" she exclaimed, dropping down to her knees. "I've waited so long for this, and our breakup just makes me appreciate it that much more." She was going to say more, but she looked up and saw the gang approaching with champagne glasses. "You knew I'd say yes?" she asked, turning suspiciously to Marcus.

"Uh-uh, I told them they'd either be providin' congratulations or condolences. I said read the body language and act accordingly."

"You guys know everythin'. That he's goin' to school and all that?" Cara just shook her head in disbelief as everyone nodded yes.

"When's the big day?" Trinity asked. "Don't be like Brandon and take forever."

"We could do it tonight," Marcus piped up.

"Don't even think about it," Cara scolded. "I want a weddin'. I say we wait until the end of summer. It'll be a slower time for Restoration, and you'll be on break from school."

"Look at you, the shrewd businesswoman," Marcus said, smiling, taking her in his arms.

"I'll drink to that." Savannah laughed. "We've all come such a long way. When I first came here, I didn't even believe in God, and Jacob told me to look up. And now every night I read Psalm 8:3–4: 'When I look at the night sky and see the work of your fingers, the moon and the stars that you set in place, what are mere mortals that you should think about them, human beings that you should care for them?' Our story is a testament of that. Here we are—all friends, two couples married and one about to be, the promise of a booming business, and partnering with the Carapones. It doesn't get any better than this, except … maybe … if Grandma Nene were here."

"Don't worry," Cara said, refusing to let Savannah sabotage the moment. "When God comes back, you'll have an eternity to fill your grandmother in—her, Kimberly, and Ruby Lee."

"You're right. God does give the ultimate happy ending."

"You guys remember the weddin'?" Cara asked. "You need to get back in there."

"I vote for goin' straight to the honeymoon," Jacob suggested, hugging his new bride.

"And I veto those plans. The honeymoon will come. Now it's time to party with your friends, and as your weddin' coordinator, I have the final say."

"But we didn't finish our cider," Brandon said, holding up the unfinished bottle.

"Don't worry—we'll use it to announce our engagement," Marcus suggested as they headed back to the house.

"Good idea," Brandon said, slapping Marcus on the back.

"Yeah, bro, you really had us worried," Jacob said, slapping Marcus as well. "We thought you'd lost your mind. Walkin' out on Cara—who does that?"

"A fool, but thank God I saw the light."

"Oh, I forgot the tray," Trinity replied, looking back toward the beach.

"I'll grab it," Cara offered, pushing them on to the reception. When she headed back to the house, she saw the two couples walking hand-in-hand and Marcus waiting for her. Staring down at the sparkling oval-shaped diamond on her finger, she remembered Jeremiah 29:11: "For I know the plans I have for you, declares the LORD, plans to prosper you and not to harm you, plans to give you hope and a future." *Oh yeah, God, I'm lovin' Your plans!*

Author's Note

If this book struck you as just another novel, then read it again. It's more than just a good story. It's a reminder of God's amazing power to transform lives. Although the characters are fictitious, the principles are true. Keep yourself pure, internalize His word, and spread His love, and you will triumph over all obstacles. "In everything you do, put God first, and he will direct you and crown your efforts with success." Proverbs 3:6.

Printed in the United States
By Bookmasters